THE B-SIDE
OF DANIEL
GARNEAU

Essential Prose Series 210

 Canada Council   Conseil des Arts
for the Arts   du Canada

 ONTARIO ARTS COUNCIL
CONSEIL DES ARTS DE L'ONTARIO
an Ontario government agency
un organisme du gouvernement de l'Ontario

Canadä

Guernica Editions Inc. acknowledges the support of the Canada Council
for the Arts and the Ontario Arts Council. The Ontario Arts Council
is an agency of the Government of Ontario.

We acknowledge the financial support of the Government of Canada.

THE B-SIDE OF DANIEL GARNEAU

DAVID KINGSTON YEH

GUERNICA EDITIONS
TORONTO • BUFFALO • LANCASTER (U.K.)
2023

Guernica Founder: Antonio D'Alfonso

Michael Mirolla, general editor
Lindsay Brown, editor
David Moratto, interior and cover design
Guernica Editions Inc.
287 Templemead Drive, Hamilton, ON L8W 2W4
2250 Military Road, Tonawanda, N.Y. 14150-6000 U.S.A.
www.guernicaeditions.com

Distributors:
Independent Publishers Group (IPG)
600 North Pulaski Road, Chicago IL 60624
University of Toronto Press Distribution (UTP)
5201 Dufferin Street, Toronto (ON), Canada M3H 5T8

First edition.
Printed in Canada.

Legal Deposit—Third Quarter
Library of Congress Catalog Card Number: 2023938669
Library and Archives Canada Cataloguing in Publication
Title: The B-side of Daniel Garneau / David Kingston Yeh.
Names: Yeh, David Kingston, author.
Series: Essential prose series ; 210.
Description: Series statement: Essential prose series ; 210
Identifiers: Canadiana (print) 2023044542X | Canadiana (ebook)
20230445470 | ISBN 9781771838221 (softcover) |
ISBN 9781771838238 (EPUB)
Classification: LCC PS8647.E47 B25 2023 | DDC C813/.6—dc23

*For Toronto, Canada—my mentor,
my muse, my home.*

We live in a rainbow of chaos.
—Paul Cézanne

CONTENTS

THE B-SIDE
OF DANIEL
GARNEAU

CHAPTER ONE

Baby Have Some Faith

"**G**ay love is so punk rock."

"What do you mean?" I asked.

"I mean," Pat said, "when you guys love each other, it's like you're giving the finger to the Man. It's like you're going up against corporate mass culture and all the bourgeois hypocrisy that's made the rest of us blue-pill-popping automatons. When you hold hands in public it's direct action; it's fucking protest! It's beautiful, Dan. I've got so much respect."

We were walking along Queen Street West on our way to Steve's Music Store. I had absolutely no idea what Pat was talking about. "It's like I'm 'giving the finger to the Man'?"

Pat doubled over with laughter. "You got me there. No pun intended." He whipped out a roll of packing tape and posted a flyer. It was the first sunny break of the new year and pillows of snow sparkled on rooftops and store signs. Outside the Rivoli, aproned staff wiped down cocktail tables and set up patio heaters. A red-and-white streetcar trundled past.

"Look," said Pat, buckling his shoulder bag, "I've been working on learning clawhammer banjo in the old mountain style. It's not what people expect, but it's what they need. The scene needs a shake-up, man. It's what keeps music alive. Shakin' it up."

Mouth wide open, he grinned at me, raised his elbows and began jerking his hips side-to-side.

Pat was my brother. But he was also a freak.

A toddler ran up and started dancing with him. Pat pirouetted the kid over to a woman with a stroller. "You've got a little Chubby Checker here!" he declared. The woman and her friend stared at Pat's moose-antlered toque and the battered guitar case slung over his back. When he winked at her, the woman actually blushed. Pat asked the kid: "Does Mommy want to dance?" The kid squealed with laughter and Pat held out his hand.

What kind of mom dances with a total stranger in public? Apparently, this one did. Now the three of them were doing the twist. I looked to Mommy's friend, but she was cheerfully recording everything with her BlackBerry while sipping her Triple Venti Half Sweet Non-Fat Caramel Macchiato.

Patrick Garneau might be a freak but he was no blue-pill-popping automaton either.

Pat high-fived the toddler and thrust out two flyers. Both women waved goodbye, rosy-cheeked.

So," Pat said, "you and David coming to our show Saturday?"

I hefted my gym bag and shook my head. "Sorry, not this time. I really have to study."

"It's Nadia's opening night, we've got a couple duets lined up."

"I didn't know Nadia could sing."

"Neither did I!" Pat threw an arm up. "It's like she's totally channelling Nelly Furtado or something."

Since the fall, Pat and my friend Nadia had started hanging out. But every time I asked, Pat would only shrug and mumble: "We're just like, y'know, casual dating for now." Except I happened to know he wasn't seeing anyone else. Pat never exclusively dated one person. Ever. I also knew Nadia had turned down his invitation last month to come up to Sudbury for Christmas.

"So where's this gig of yours?" I asked.

"Grossman's Tavern." Pat slapped a flyer into my hand. "Did you know, back in the day women weren't allowed to patronize these establishments, so they had to sneak them in through a back door?"

"I did not know that."

"Change, Dan, is the one universal constant. Only question is: what kind of change do you want to see in your life? It's never too late to shake things up. Just look at Grandpa and Betty."

After Christmas, Grandpa and his lady friend Betty had gotten married at Sudbury City Hall. Technically we'd known Betty Lalonde for years as the manager at Grandma's nursing home. Even after Grandma passed away, we'd still come by every Thanksgiving and Christmas to drop-off Grandpa's famous sugar pies and tourtières.

When I asked about the rest of Betty's family, Grandpa just shook his head. "Oh no, she don't talk to them, not for a long time. No, she's a part of our family now. You just call her Betty."

We were glad to. Betty loved to laugh and she gave the best hugs in the world. You can always tell when

someone meant it when they hugged you and Betty was
the real deal. According to Grandpa she could also fillet
a pike in under three minutes, and make the perfect dirty
gin martini. At their wedding, she demonstrated spot-on
imitations of all four distinct loon calls (the tremolo, the
wail, the yodel and hoot). Grandpa called her a class act.
Mr. and Mrs. Milton had called her a good woman. That
meant a lot to Grandpa since the Miltons were practically
family themselves.

Now the two were honeymooning in Varadero, soaking up the tropical sunshine and all the piña coladas they
could drink. Grandpa deserved it; he'd worked hard his
whole life. His company had helped build half the homes
in Valley East. Both of them were also nudists (what
Nadia called "naturalists") who summered weekends up
at the Good Medicine Cabin. I just hoped Grandpa and
Betty remembered to keep their clothes on in Cuba.

Outside Steve's Music Store, Pat turned to me. "Hey,
so you'll come out and see Nadia, right? We're also trying
out a lot of new material."

"Okay. Let me see what I can do."

"You'll ask David, okay?"

"Sure."

"Big brother, you're the best." Pat punched me in the
shoulder. "How are you two lovebirds doing?"

"We," I said, "are doing just fine." I stepped aside as a
dreadlocked guy exited the store hauling a keyboard and
amp. "So what are you picking up here anyway?"

Pat took off his toque and shook out his shaggy hair.
"It's a Deering Goodtime open back 5-string. It's my super
sweet Christmas present to moi. You're off to meet Parker?"

"Yeah. He said he had some important news to share with me."

"Right on. Well, thanks again for the squash lesson. Bing bam boom!" He snapped his fingers. "Saturday then?"

I waved the flyer. "Saturday."

Ten minutes later, I walked into the Java House at Queen and Augusta, a dive bar with busted tables, cheap drinks and surprisingly decent pad thai. Parker was waiting for me in one of the booths, nursing a gigantic orange mug of tea and studying a *NOW* magazine. Although he didn't actually drink, Parker Kapoor was the quintessential barfly. He also looked ten years younger than his actual age and was constantly asked to show his ID. Today, Freddie Mercury, in a jewel-encrusted crown, beamed from the front of his T-shirt. Parker's large and perfectly straight nose followed me as I stamped the snow from my boots and slid into the booth across from him.

"Hey Parker," I said, "how're you doing?"

He gripped the table edge and leaned forward, round eyes protruding from his head.

"Parker, you okay?"

"Daniel. You will never guess."

"Okay. What is it?"

"You," he said, "are looking at the newest participant in an internationally produced literary salon."

"A what?"

"Naked Boys Reading! Next month, hosted by Glad Day Bookshop. It's their Valentine-themed event. Love, romance, heartbreak. The repertoire is immense. Of course, for the life of me, I can't decide what to read. You have to help. I've narrowed it down to two choices and now I'm at an impasse: 19th century literary realism, or shunga tentacle erotica."

All I could offer was a shrug.

"I know!" Parker exclaimed. "How can one decide? Public reading is terrifying enough, without having to second guess one's material. Will it be *Sense and Sensibility* or *Kinoe no Komatsu*? I definitely want to draw from the classics. Did you know both were published at exactly the same time? I'm leaning toward Jane Austen's irony and feminist critique. But there's something so compelling about Hokusai's sensuality and playfulness. Happy New Year, by the way. How's your family? How are you and David doing?"

"David and I are doing just fine. Parker, what did you say this event was called?"

"Naked Boys Reading."

"Is that what it sounds like it is?"

"Aah, you mean the 'naked' part." Parker slurped from his tea mug. "Of course, yes, that's right. The readers are completely unclothed."

"What? Why?"

"It's a celebration of body-positivity, a blissful union of nudity and the love of literature. The salon started in England, but now there are readings all over the world. Kyle and I attended one in Ottawa last year. It was thrilling. We promised we'd do this the next chance we had."

"Kyle's reading too?"

"He's chosen an excerpt from Marian Engel's *Bear*. It's the quintessential Canadian novel and it won the Governor General's Award. It's such a spiritual work— loneliness in the northern wilderness, existential desire. I suspect your brother Liam would appreciate it, and your grandpa too. Come to think of it, this whole event might be right up their alley."

"And what's this book about?"

"It's a love affair between a librarian and a bear." Parker carefully extracted his tea bag, squeezed it between his fingertips and set it aside. "It's what actually inspired me to consider Hokusai. Did you know a bear's tongue is capable of lengthening itself like an eel? That's in chapter fifteen. There's something so intimate about reading to someone or having someone read to you. Do you remember bedtime stories growing up?"

"Um. Sure."

"There you have it! Tell me, Daniel, what was it like?"

As if on cue the waitress arrived, cracking her gum, with a pencil poised over a notepad. I imagined her reciting the specials of the day: "Curious George, Babar the Elephant, and half-priced Wild Things with any pitcher of beer." I wondered if Winnie-the-Pooh had a tongue that was capable of lengthening itself like an eel.

While Parker fussed over the menu, I ordered the burger special and a pint of Moosehead. Bedtime stories had always been Grandpa's purview. Grandma, of course, had been an English teacher and could recite dozens of poems by heart, long after she could remember any of our names. The truth was, my brothers and I had grown up on poetry and music more than we had with books or even TV.

I remembered Dad puttering in the garage playing his beloved artists: Leonard Cohen, Joni Mitchell, Neil Young. Sometimes he'd crank the volume on "Summer of '69" and blast it on repeat until Mom finally stuck her head out the kitchen window and told him to knock it off.

After dinner, the family would play board games or cards. Pat liked to suggest Monopoly just to see if Dad might chuck the whole game box down the basement stairs like he had once, shouting: "Too fucking capitalistic!" But Dad never had a problem with Miss Scarlett bashing in someone's head with a lead pipe in the billiards room.

Later in the evenings, our parents might dance in the kitchen to Oscar Peterson, sharing a cigarette and a rye and Coke. He'd whisper in her ear and she'd slap his ass. Then he'd pretend to be a vampire and drink her blood while she shrieked with laughter.

At the end of the day, I was the one who made sure my brothers and I finished our homework and brushed our teeth. At bedtime, it was always Grandpa who'd tuck us in.

"*Le Petit Prince*," I said. "Grandpa would read us that."

"Antoine de Saint-Exupéry. That," Parker said, "is a classic."

"And what about you?"

"Me? I grew up on Ruskin Bond and Robert Munsch. Ooh, and Roald Dahl." Parker hunched his thin shoulders and shivered. "His stories would give me nightmares. But they were so delicious! I'd beg my sisters to read them to me, which they did in secret since Mother strictly forbade it. When I had nightmares I'd wet the bed. I used to call the neighbourhood bullies Boggis, Bunce and Bean. I'd pretend I was Fantastic Mr. Fox and Karenjit would be Mrs. Fox. We were the original saboteur anarchists. Karenjit sends her regards by the way."

I'd never actually met Parker's childhood best-friend Karenjit. Those two had grown up together in the rural Ontario town of Sarnia. But when Parker was thirteen, she moved away. Years later, she'd make it onto the cover of *Penthouse* magazine.

"Well." I cleared my throat. "Tell her I say hello."

"Karenjit's very grateful, Daniel, you're in my life. She used to play street hockey with the boys. She was always protective of me. She's working in Mumbai now for MTV. I'm so proud of her. Her plan is to take over Bollywood. She is such an international career woman."

Lunch was cut short just as our food arrived. One of Parker's group homes called. Bill had wandered off again and had been spotted getting onto the 312 bus. Parker apologized, throwing on his pea coat and Burberry scarf. I told Parker to give Bill my regards when they found him. "He misses you," Parker exclaimed. "You introduced him to *The Golden Girls*."

"He's probably in the frozen desserts section," I said, "at the Sobeys by Balfour Park."

"It's the first place I always look," Parker said. "Wish me luck!" He dashed out the door, doggy bag in hand.

Years ago, Parker and I had met working in a group home. Now he was a full-time housing manager, while I was still in school chalking up a gazillion dollars in debt.

I should've been a hockey player.

I looked down at my plate. I'd asked for a side salad, but had gotten a pile of fries instead. I loosened my belt which had inexplicably shrunk over the holidays. Living with an Italian boyfriend who loved to cook didn't help. During high school, I'd played midget AA at least twice a week. Now I wasn't even sure where I'd stored my skates.

When I bit into my burger, mustard and grease dribbled down my chin. The waitress slid into the booth and sat down across from me.

Her freckled face was round and inquisitive, her bleached blonde hair done up in a dozen baby-blue barrettes. I stared at her.

"You don't remember me," she said, "do you?"

I shook my head.

"You were Julia's roommate's best friend's boyfriend. You wore my Tigger onesie."

Of course, then, I did remember.

"We all met and hung out earlier that night at Vazaleen?"

That night had been my very first date with Marcus Wittenbrink Jr.

"At Lee's Palace?" she said.

I swallowed the food in my mouth. "You're Claire."

"Oh wow!" Claire let out a sigh of relief. "I can't believe you remember. I mean I'm just awful with names myself, but I never forget a face. It's like my super power, you know. When you walked in today I was like: Hey, shazam, I know that face! I mean you were such a sweetie. What's your name again?"

"I'm Daniel."

"Daniel, of course. So listen look, Daniel, I just wanted to say hi, you know I mean, I know it's been a while, but people like us we're family. It's important we stick together." She helped herself to a fry. "So, like, are you still with that Marcus guy?"

"Um, no. We broke up years ago."

"Oh that's too bad. For a while there, he kinda swept

all of us off our feet, didn't he? Well, good times, eh?" She squeezed my arm and stood up. "How's your burger?"

I regarded the fries on my plate. "Could I get some spicy mayonnaise?"

"Sure thing. A side of spicy mayo for Daniel-Boyfriend-of-Marcus coming right up!"

The truth was, Marcus and I had only lasted five months. Now, five years later, I didn't think about him every day any more. Last fall, Pat announced Marcus had taken over management of Three Dog Run. I wondered if he was going to be at Grossman's next Saturday.

It'd been three years since I moved in with David. We mixed up our socks and underwear and looked after our neighbour Liz's cats when she was away. Friday nights I'd take a study break and we'd order pizza and play video games on his PlayStation. David would smoke a bowl. I'd polish off a bottle of wine. Sometimes we'd fall asleep together on the couch. It didn't feel punk rock. It felt, well, normal.

So why did I hesitate every time people asked how we were doing? When two people love each other as much as we did, it should be easy to say so. But constant worry was my normal.

It was, unfortunately, my super power.

I studied Pat's flyer. David had designed the band logo: three puppies inside a spiral circle. It was my brother Pat, in fact, who had introduced me to David. I owed him for that, even if he had let me down in a hundred other ways. Nadia was a good friend of mine and I tried not to worry how he might let her down too.

Just when everything seemed balanced and right,

something always came along to shake things up. Pat might argue change was the one universal constant. But sometimes, life just felt to me more like one inevitable game of Jenga.

∿ When I climbed the stairs to our Kensington Market loft, I had a hunch David was watching porn.

I could smell it.

Opening the door, I spotted a fresh-baked loaf of bread cooling on the counter. "You're back!" David closed his laptop lid, tossed aside a box of Kleenex and jumped up from the couch. "I hope you're hungry. I'm making an eggplant parmigiana, Nonna's recipe. Did you get the wine?"

"A merlot and a chardonnay, like you asked." I set two magnums on the kitchen island. Any time spent cooking or baking always made David horny and when David was horny his go-to was porn.

I put the flyer on the table as he buckled his belt. "Pat's got a gig next Saturday. Can you make it?"

"Yeah, sure." He examined the flyer. "They're playing Grossman's? That place is legendary."

"Nadia's singing back-up."

"Sweet. I didn't know Nadia could sing."

"Neither did Pat. So, were you jacking off just now?"

David stared at me wide-eyed. "Maybe."

"I told you to wait for me."

"I know but sometimes it's just easier to, you know, take care of things yourself." He examined the two bottles. "Very nice. I also just want to make sure everything's in working order."

"David, I don't think you ever have to worry about that."

"Never hurts."

"Did you come already?"

"Not yet."

"Okay then. We'll take care of it tonight."

"How was squash with Pat?"

"Useless. He kept beat-boxing and pretending he was inside a giant pinball machine. I mean, I don't even know why he asks to play in the first place."

"Pat wants to spend time with you. You're lucky you got a brother who actually wants to do that."

"Yeah. All your brother wants," I said, "is your sperm." I hung up my jacket and straightened out the boot tray.

David stood with one hand in his pocket and the other behind his neck. His hair was dishevelled and his Deadpool T-shirt half-tucked. Growing up, he'd idolized his brother Luke. But then Luke Moretti left home and was gone twelve years, slumming it in Vancouver's Downtown Eastside. Even after he moved back to Toronto two years ago the guy was like a ghost, vanishing for weeks at a time.

"So," David said, "can we discuss this? Luke and Ai Chang are coming over in an hour. We should talk about this."

In the kitchen I soaked a rag in hot water and wrung it out. "What's there to talk about?"

"Look. They want to be parents. They need my sperm to get pregnant." David raised and dropped his arms. "I'm doing them a favour. It doesn't have to be that complicated."

"Who said it was complicated? You've already agreed to it. What more is there to talk about? It's your sperm."

"I don't think," David said, "you realize how angry you sound when you talk like that."

"Angry?" I got down on my knees and started scrubbing the salt stains out of the floor. "What possible reason could I have for being angry?"

"Daniel." David drew a breath. "I love you very much. You know that, right?"

"Yes." I got up and tossed the rag aside. "I know that."

"You know I want to spend the rest of my life with you. And we're making a home together, right?"

"Sure." I brushed past him and collapsed on the couch.

"Well, Luke and Ai Chang are doing the same. They've moved back to Toronto; they've got great jobs; they're saving up money. Now they want to start a family. A family, Daniel. And I have a chance to help them. He's my brother. You'd do the same for Pat or Liam, wouldn't you?"

Pat, Liam and I were triplets but we couldn't have been more different. Pat gallivanted through the world like it was a three-ring circus. Liam was a Thoreauvian recluse who lived alone in the forest. Would I donate my sperm to help either Pat or Liam start a family? I wasn't so sure.

"Families," I said, "are complicated."

"Yeah." David sat down next to me. "It's a big deal."

"You'd be a father."

"No. Luke would be the father. I'd just be the donor. Daniel, we've gone over this."

"You and Ai Chang don't even like each other."

"That's not true. I mean, we don't dislike each other. I respect her, a lot. She's like my sister-in-law."

"Are they getting married?"

"No, you know they're not. All I'm saying is that Ai Chang is Luke's partner and that makes her family. We don't need to be best friends."

"But your sperm," I said, "is going to go inside her body, and she's going to have your baby. Your baby, David. However you spin this, you're going to be a dad. And if you're a dad, then that makes me a dad."

I scraped my fingers through my hair. I needed a haircut. I hadn't shaved in days. I could feel another headache coming on.

"Listen, Daniel." David knelt on the couch. "Listen to me. We are not going to be dads. I'm not claiming any paternal rights or joint custody. We'll just be Uncle David and Uncle Dan. I can't wait for us to be uncles. It'll be so much fun. Don't you want to babysit?"

"You've always told me you wanted kids of your own."

"I know. And I do. And we will. But this is different. Luke and Ai Chang are going to be the parents. They came to me about this, remember? This was their idea. It's going to work."

"And this get-together tonight?"

"Tonight we're just hanging out, the four of us. We'll have dinner, a few drinks. Afterward, we can step out to Graffiti's or Cold Tea if we want. When was the last time the four of just hung out on a Saturday night?"

"Never?"

"That's right. Never. Trust me. Everything's going to be okay. We're going to have a good time."

"You promise?"

"I promise."

⌒ An hour later, Luke and Ai Chang called to cancel dinner plans. David paced in the kitchen for five minutes, before handing his phone over to me. "Luke wants to talk to you."

"What does he want to talk to me for?"

"I don't know. Just take it."

Although I'd never said it out loud, the truth was Luke Moretti intimidated me. Not because he was five years older, or because he was David's big brother, or because he was loud and in-your-face, or even because he was a fitness instructor and part-time model. But it was because (although I could barely admit it to myself) I harbored secret fantasies about him.

Luke Moretti was the only guy I knew who always smelled great. Stepping out of a shower, his towel slung low over his hips, he'd give off this subtle, musky, animal scent. At first I thought it was his body wash, but he insisted he never used soap. In my fantasies, he'd raise his arm and point at me and wink in cinematic slow motion.

Of course, I'd never told anyone (except maybe Nadia). If David ever found out, I'd be mortified. Speaking purely academically, my post-doc friend Charles assured me sexual fantasies about family members were more than common, and I took his words to heart.

"Luke." I cleared my throat. "How's it going?"

"Yo, Daniel." The voice on the other end was brusque. "I need a favour. Sorry for cancelling, by the way. Ai Chang's dad fell off the roof. She's at the hospital. I'm on my way to meet her."

"Oh my god. Is he alright?"

"They're just waiting on some x-rays. They'll probably

discharge him tonight. So here's the thing: David's birth-day is next month, and I want to plan a surprise party for him. I need your help."

"Oh." I blinked. "Sure."

"The kiddo's right there, isn't he?"

David was bent over, peering into the oven. "Um, yeah, he is."

"So look, I just wanted to give you a heads up. I'll catch you later about this, alright?"

"Sure. No problem."

"Sei il massimo! Ciao."

He hung up.

"Ciao," I said.

David straightened, hefting the baking dish. "My egg-plant parmigiana," he said, "is perfect. Just look at it."

It did look fabulous and smelled even better. Hell, I'd jack off to something like that.

"Nonna would be proud. This is so going on her Facebook page. Hey, what did Luke want to talk to you about?"

"Um, nothing. He just wanted to apologize for can-celling. Your nonna's on social media?"

"No but my cousin Carina is." Carefully, David set the dish down on the island counter. "She's the one who posted all of Ma's wedding photos last year."

"So, is Ai Chang's dad going to be okay?"

"It sounds like it. Luke just wanted to make sure I was still on board with being the donor and everything." He tossed aside his oven mitts.

We observed the four table settings, the long-stemmed wine glasses and new cloth napkins. We'd never owned cloth napkins before. David leaned back against the counter. "Shit."

"You," I said, "were really looking forward to tonight."

He hung his head. "Yeah."

"We'll reschedule. It's no big deal. What's important is that Ai Chang's dad is okay."

"She doesn't get along with them."

"Who?"

"Ai Chang and her parents. They don't approve of her career. They don't approve of her piercings or her tattoos. They definitely don't approve of her relationship."

"Have they even met Luke?"

"Not yet. I guess they will tonight."

"And now," I said, "their daughter's going to have her Catholic-Italian boyfriend's gay brother's baby."

"Yeah." David's face tightened. "About that."

"What?"

"Just for now, it's on a need-to-know basis."

"What's that supposed to mean?"

"It means, Daniel, we're not announcing this to the whole world. Not just yet."

"Ai Chang's not telling her parents?"

"Are you kidding me? Absolutely not! You haven't told anyone, have you?"

"No. So is this a secret, then?"

"It's not like a secret secret. We can tell some people. But, you know. All I'm saying is not everybody needs to know."

"Okay. I get it."

"Do you?"

"I do." I understood discretion. People judged, all the time. "What clinic are they going to use?"

"Clinic? We can't afford a clinic." David opened a bottle of wine. "Ai Chang said an IUI is basically a doctor-assisted turkey baster, anyway. No, we're going to do this ourselves, the old-fashioned away."

"Does your mom know?"

"Not yet. When Ai Chang's pregnant, then we'll tell her."

"What'll she think?"

"Ma? She'll be thrilled. She met Ai Chang already, last summer in Sicily. They have a lot in common. And Ma's always wanted a grandkid."

"You sound pretty confident about this."

"Hey, we're Italian. Little Buddy here's never let me down."

"But you were still practicing."

"Okay, Daniel. Listen. I was horny." David threw the oven mitts at me. "You know that when I'm in the kitchen I get horny."

David was almost twenty-six but the guy jacked off every day like he was still sixteen. "Yeah. I know. Maybe you should start up your own cooking show. It could launch a whole new food porn channel."

"Maybe."

"So, if you had to," I asked, "would you rather have sex with Martha Stewart or Gordon Ramsey?

"What sort of a stupid question is that? Julia Child, hands down." David showed his teeth. "It eez 'er verrry spéciale French sauces."

"I've got special French sauce."

"French-Canadian sauce." David bit his lower lip.

"Okay, now I'm hungry. Let's eat. And then we can have dessert."

"Or maybe," I said, "we can have dessert, and then eat."

"Or ..." David leaned over the baking dish and wiggled his eyebrows. "We could pull an *American Pie*."

"A threesome, with the parmigiana? David Gallucci, what would your nonna say?"

David's nostrils flared. The golden mozzarella had bubbled and browned over the thick tomato sauce and moist, fried eggplant, crusted around the edges. He braced himself and arched his hips.

"This," he said, "would only be on a need-to-know basis."

CHAPTER TWO

Born to be Wild

"If there's a nuclear war," Pat said, "the three things left standing will be Keith Richards, cockroaches and Grossman's Tavern."

"It's all that devil music they've been playing the last sixty years," David said.

Pat and David laughed and high-fived.

I had no idea what they were talking about. Pat grabbed the back of my neck, the contents of his pint sloshing onto my boots. "The blues, man! You, big brother, are standing in the New Orleans of the North."

This Saturday night, four bands were lined-up to play and the grotty venue was packed. A Dixieland quartet had just finished its set. Three Dog Run had opened to an enthusiastic crowd. The venue was packed with college students, jazz aficionados and grizzled regulars. Faded photos of past performers papered the nicotine-stained walls.

"Did you know," Pat said, "Dan Aykroyd got his inspiration for the Blues Brothers right here?"

David raised his eyebrows. "No shit."

Pat poked me in the chest. "Did you know Dad and Mom partied with Rough Trade at Grossman's?"

"Yeah. Right."

"Dan, really. They won this radio contest along with three hundred others. The prize was a private concert: April Wine at the El Mocambo. So after that show, same night they end up right here at Grossman's. This was before anyone ever heard of Rough Trade. I think," Pat whispered, "they might've had a threesome with you-know-who."

"Pat, fuck off. You're making this up."

"Why would I make up something like that?"

"Because, Pat, you make things up all the time. Why would you even think I wouldn't think you're making this up?"

"Okay." Pat burped. "So maybe I'm conjecturing the threesome bit. But listen to me, I want to show you something." He searched his phone, mumbling: "Hold yer wild horses. Hold onto yer hat ..." Musicians on stage completed a sound check, oblivious to the crack of pool balls and the din of the crowd. He thrust his phone into my face. "Check this out. Ride on baby!"

I squinted at a photo of a faded Polaroid of a young Mom and Dad draped over a woman in leather pants and bondage gear. BDSM Lady was running her nails through Dad's dishevelled hair. His wide-collared shirt was unbuttoned and he was giving the finger to the camera. Mom was in platform sandals wearing some weird floral poncho, doubled-over with laughter, one hand on her outthrust hip. In her other hand, she held aloft a bottle of vodka. A banner in the background announced: GOOD TIMES GUARANTEED.

"Is that," David said, "who I think it is?"

"March fifth, Saturday night." Pat grinned like the Cheshire Cat. "Looks to me they were standing right about over there."

"How come I've never seen this before?"

"It's not exactly the kind of photo you put in the family album, Dan."

"So how do you have it?"

"Dad gave it to me. He told me to keep it secret. He thought I would appreciate it."

"We were kids!"

"I," Pat said, straightening, "was nine years old."

I wondered what else those two might've kept secret all those years. At the same time, a part of me didn't want to know. Our parents had died fifteen years ago.

"This," David said, "has got to go on your website."

Pat cracked his neck. "You think?"

"Dude, it's your legacy. That's your dad with Carole Pope! And now you've just played Grossman's? How sick is that? Egster," David shouted, "where's Bobby and Rod? Photo-op time!"

On the band's website, there was already an image of a four-year-old Pat sitting on top of Dad's jukebox, a vintage Wurlitzer 1015, grinning from ear to ear. Story went Dad had picked it up at a barn sale the same day my brothers and I were born and spent the next three years fixing it up. It was his pride and joy. No one was allowed near that jukebox without his permission. I swear, he could spot a fingerprint on it at ten paces.

Pat and Dad always had shared a special bond.

While Pat inherited Dad's passion for music, our brother Liam preferred the solitude of nature. On a night like tonight, I imagined Liam ice fishing in a shack on Lake Nunya, a thermos of tea and his dog Jackson at his side. Four hundred klicks separated Sudbury from Toronto, but the real distance between us was harder to measure, and harder to cross. David was right. At least these days, Pat made an effort to reach out.

As David set out to corral the band, I volunteered to fetch Nadia who had stepped outside. I paused to text my best friend Karen Fobister, promising to send her photos of the show. Karen would appreciate a venue like Grossman's. If she still lived in Toronto, she'd be throwing back shots and cleaning the table with the best of them.

Outside, streetlamps and neon signs illuminated the falling snow. Nadia stood on the corner wearing a white cashmere turtleneck, her camel coat draped over her shoulders. "Daniel." She waved. "I want to introduce you to Amy."

Her companion, one of the bartenders, shook my hand. "Nice to meet you." She gave Nadia a hug. "And congratulations again. Think about it, will you?" She flashed a smile before hurrying back inside.

"I didn't know you smoked."

"I don't, normally." Nadia appraised the cigarette in her kid-gloved hand as if it were an antique book. "It's an occasional indulgence."

Snowflakes glinted in her dark lashes and perfectly coiffed hair. Under the streetlamp, with the beauty mark on her cheek, Nadia looked like a Hollywood starlet from the 1950s.

"The band," I said, gesturing over my shoulder, "they're getting together for a photo-shoot."

But Nadia only stepped out to the edge of the curb. "This city," she murmured, "is beautiful, don't you think?"

Across the wide, tree-lined avenue, signage buzzed over glowing restaurants, tchotchke emporiums, and shuttered fish and grocery stores. Chinatown was a strange conflation of tackiness and glamour in equal parts. To the southeast, skyscrapers towered. I'd lived in Toronto close to eight years, but there were still always moments that surprised or made me pause. "Yeah, it is."

"How was it for you," Nadia asked, "moving here for the first time?"

I could hear the faint roar of a passenger jet, invisible above the night clouds. In high school, Karen and I had made a pact. The first chance we got, we'd escape Sudbury together. When we both got accepted into U of T, we'd celebrated with a bottle of Prosecco and built ourselves a vision board. "It changed my life," I said.

For three years, Karen and I had shared an apartment in Little Italy, cycling around town with coffees in hand, talking to strangers, discovering new locales: Philosopher's Walk, Graffiti Alley, secret paths through High Park. The city was an endless patchwork of storied neighbourhoods.

"When we were kids," I said, "Grandpa would take us to games at Maple Leaf Gardens. We loved those road trips. When the Air Canada Centre opened, he got us all tickets."

"That," Nadia said, "was when the Leafs beat the Habs in overtime."

"The Hip also played the ACC that weekend. I remember Pat lost his voice from screaming so much."

"You have a lot of good memories of this city."

I stamped my feet. "Still working on it." I wondered if the band was waiting for us, but Nadia seemed unconcerned.

"And how are you and David doing?"

"You know," I said, "people keep asking me that."

"And?"

"It's all good. I mean, I just never thought we'd last this long."

Nadia regarded me. "Does that bother you?"

"No! I mean, we're happy together. All I'm saying is, it wasn't anything I'd imagined for myself."

On our vision board, Karen and I had cut-and-pasted pictures from brochures and magazines: a Blue Jays logo, the CN Tower, the Hockey Hall of Fame. After I came out to Karen on our prom night, she made a point of gluing on pics of cute guys and a rainbow flag. "The first time we hit up the Gay Village," I said, "that was something."

"Except," Nadia said, "you told me you never felt like you fit in."

"True. I didn't, not really. The clubs and bars, not really me. But at least it was some place I could start."

"You had a place to play and discover who you are." Nadia exhaled a nimbus of smoke. "That's what living well is all about."

"Is it?"

"Living artfully? I think so."

"Marcus always said life is art."

Nadia laughed. "I did get that impression."

"What do you mean?"

"When Pat suggested I join Three Dog Run, it was Marcus who auditioned me."

"What?" I stepped back. "What the hell does Marcus have to do with whether you join the band or not?"

"I didn't mind. I was actually looking forward to meeting him. I enjoyed the time we spent together."

"Of course you would. He's like a game show host. Everyone loves Marcus Wittenbrink Jr."

"We both know," Nadia said, "he's much more than that. You didn't fall in love, Daniel, with a game show host."

I glared at Nadia. But of course, she was right. Last year, Marcus' one-man show *Face* had swept the Dora Awards. This winter, he was artist-in-residence at Montreal's Station 16.

"That was a long time ago," I said. "I was just a kid. Marcus introduced me to Toronto. I fell in love with my tour guide."

"You fell in love," Nadia said, "with your impresario."

"What's that?"

"Someone who believes life is art."

If I'd ever thought my ex had become my brother's band manager just so he could still be a part of my life, I never said it out loud. I kicked at a dented newspaper box. "So," I asked, "what was the audition like?"

Delicately, Nadia put out her cigarette. "Pat thought I might contribute some backup vocals. It was meant to be just an afternoon in Rod's garage. The session went on twelve hours. In the end, it was Marcus who insisted I sing the duet, and the solo."

I knew Nadia as a PhD student in English, a yoga instructor and a book store clerk. She'd never told me she was a singer. "You," I said, "really were amazing tonight. You know that, right?"

"Thank you."

"So are you like a permanent member of the band now?"

"Pat wants me to be. The boys like me and I like them. But, no, I haven't made that kind of commitment."

"What did Marcus say?"

Nadia shrugged. "He told us to have fun."

"Did you?"

"Tonight?" Nadia bowed her head. "Yes." She smiled. "Yes, I did. Growing up, I used to pretend I was Dorothy Dandridge. When we were little, my sister and I would choreograph our own song-and-dance routines. Amy thinks I should perform my own work."

"Your own songs?"

"Sometimes my poetry takes on a life of its own."

"You're friends with the bartender?"

"Amy Louie's parents own Grossman's. I've been coming here on my own since high school."

"This place?" I couldn't imagine a more dilapidated venue.

"I like jazz," Nadia said. "And I like R&B."

"I thought you liked rock bands."

"I like a lot of things. Don't let appearances fool you. Grossman's is an institution. Is this your first time?"

"Yeah."

"I see." She hooked her arm through mine. "Well, welcome to the Home of the Blues."

"It's the devil's music, you know."

"So I've heard. One must be careful. In this house of sin, many temptations await."

"All sorts of debauchery."

"It was once a haven for hippies and draft dodgers."

"A veritable Sodom and Gomorrah."

"Time," Nadia said, "has a way of standing still at Grossman's."

I imagined Mom and Dad gamboling down Spadina Avenue, an irreverent and joyful couple in the heyday of punk and glam rock. The Village People, Bowie and Queen would've been at the top of the charts.

"Hey, buddy!" Pat stuck his head out the front door. "You trying to steal my girlfriend?"

"Patrick Garneau." Nadia cocked her head. "I didn't know I was your girlfriend."

"Whoa, dude. Nadia, I was just joking." Pat raised his hands. "Except, I mean, hey. What I'm trying to say is, I'm not saying I wouldn't want you to be my girlfriend." He winced. "Okay, so like, do you want to be my girlfriend?"

Nadia folded her arms, leaning back. "Is that a proposition?"

Before Pat could answer, David and the other band members appeared, spilling out onto the sidewalk. "What's going on?" the Egster asked.

"Pat," I said, "is proposing to Nadia."

Rod's unibrow rose. "Right on."

The Egster beamed. "No ways!"

Bobby chewed on a toothpick. "Awesome."

"Shouldn't you get down on one knee?" David said.

Rod elbowed David. "That's old school."

"Old school rocks," the Egster said.

"Agreed." Bobby pointed with his toothpick. "Except he needs a ring."

"He doesn't have a ring?"

"Dude, not cool."

"Hold on, I have a ring!" The Egster pulled a foil package out of his fanny pack and ripped it open. "Here take this." He thrust out a Ring Pop, strawberry or cherry-flavoured by the looks of it.

Pat took the ring, and got down on one knee.

A herd of seniors shuffled past, bowed like musk ox beneath enormous fur caps. They glanced back at Pat, their expressions inscrutable. When Bobby shouted out something in Cantonese, they nodded in approval, flashing big gold-toothed smiles, and shook their clasped hands at us.

"Nadia …" Pat said, holding up the ring.

Nadia brushed the bangs from his forehead. "No."

"What?"

"No," she said. "I won't be your girlfriend." She rested her hand against his cheek. "But I will be your friend."

"What? But we're already friends."

"No, Pat. We're lovers. There's a difference."

"We're not friends?"

"I just said I'd be your friend. Will you be mine?"

"I guess so?"

"A true and good friendship is rare and treasured thing."

"But." Pat bit his lip. "Do we still get to, you know?"

"Yes, Pat, we can still be lovers."

"But if we're lovers and if we're friends, then doesn't that make you my girlfriend?" Nadia shook her head. "I'm confused."

"That's alright." She took the Ring Pop and slipped it onto Pat's finger. "There. Now you're my lover-friend."

"Suck on that," Rod said.

Bobby trumpetted "La Marseillaise" on a kazoo. With-out missing a beat, the Egster whipped out his drumsticks and started to sing: "Love, love, love …" Gripping my shoulder, Rod clambered onto the newspaper box, flung open his arms and serenaded the new couple.

The snow fell like confetti.

Nadia and Pat kissed.

After that, everyone joined in on the chorus. I thought of Grandpa and Betty honeymooning in Cuba, and Luke and Ai Chang planning a baby. Just last spring, David's mom had moved back home to Sicily and gotten married for the fourth time. Maybe love really was all you needed. I staggered as David bear-hugged me from behind. Swaying arm-in-arm, the fur-capped bystanders joined in on the titular refrain: "All you need is love!"

Inside Grossman's, the audience burst into applause. As snowflakes filled the universe, David planted a kiss on my cheek. Everyone's faces were radiant and for one brief moment in our lives, time did seem to stand still, and everything in the world felt right.

↷ At the start of Pride Month, we kissed in the grimy stairwell of a cinderblock club. His nails were painted black and he smelled of Jägermeister, cigarettes and cinnamon gum. Alexisonfire headlined the Kathedral, their heavy bass beat a military march. We were brothers-in-arms, in-surrectionists shooting off bottle rockets, pirates swash-buckling on a stormy sea. Just blocks away, within the iron-gated chambers of Osgood Hall, Toronto's Court of Appeal prepared to confirm Ontario as the first jurisdiction in all of North America to recognize same-sex marriage. But with his hard-on beneath his jeans pressed against my thigh, I was oblivious to history or justice or the monumental advance of civil society. I only knew the heat of his body and his arms around me. His front tooth was chipped, his eyes searching and bright. It was my twenty-first birthday and I held his face between my hands and kissed him with all the lust and desire of a grown man.

That night, we fucked so hard we broke his futon. Afterwards, we lay in the dark, ankles crossed in the tangled sheets, and shared a cigarette. I observed the smoke curling from his parted lips. Then he told me how, at the age of twenty-one, the Italian violinist Giuseppe Tartini had a dream in which he sold his soul, and upon waking wrote the Devil's Sonata, his greatest work; and how at the age of twenty-one, the Macedonian prince Alexander marched his armies against Thessaly, Athens and Thebes, defeating every rival and unifying ancient Greece; and how at the age of twenty-one, the French poet Arthur Rimbaud parted ways forever with his lover Paul Verlaine, and never wrote another verse the rest of his life. Then this man, David Gallucci son of Isabella de Luca, drew a record from its sleeve and played for me the song "Twenty-One" from the Eagle's album *Desperado*. After that, he put on a cowboy hat, smiling and swaying his hips. As he danced, he touched himself unselfconsciously. Then he knelt and whispered in my ear how the two of us were as strong as we could be, that we had just begun, that there was no stopping us because we both knew what freedom meant, and that there was no reason why we should ever want to die.

By the end of that summer, David would ask me to move in with him. He would tell me that he loved me. And he would confide in me his desire to spend the rest of his life at the side of Daniel Garneau.

Marcus Wittenbrink Jr.

My ex-impresario.

He was naked, tarred and feathered, and standing in a pool of bloody viscera the first time I saw him. That performance art piece won him accolades from the Dalai Lama Foundation itself.

At an age when most young men were still playing Nintendo and road hockey, Marcus was studying and touring under Robert Lepage. In a CBC interview with Shelagh Rogers, Michel Tremblay had named Wittenbrink one of the nation's brightest young rising stars.

It was true, Marcus was Toronto's *enfant terrible*, an award-winning poet, performer and multi-disciplinary artist. I also knew he professed to be vegan when Swiss Chalet was actually his favourite meal, and that he claimed to be Two Spirit when his parents were white bread lawyers from Burlington. I also knew how he considered all his friends, and past and present lovers, to be his true and chosen family.

David once joked how Marcus reminded him of an elf from Middle-Earth: seven feet tall and of a far more beautiful race than men. He'd often cultivate the image of a young David Bowie, heedless and otherworldly. Of course, I secretly hoped he might fall in love with me. Later I realized Marcus evoked this longing in everyone he met, igniting the vainglorious beneath our breastbones so that it smoldered and sparked. Whatever he might have felt for me, he never said out loud. He only smiled like a magician and drew me down his rabbit hole. Long after midnight, at underground events, we drank cheap wine out of plastic cups, consorting with saintly motorcyclists and human seraphim. He introduced me to alternaqueer dance parties and avant-garde art shows. Gels and filters, greasepaints and flash pots littered his life. He had me watch *The Man Who Fell to Earth* and the original *Frankenstein* by James Whale. He delighted in quoting Oscar Wilde and Quentin Crisp. Near the end, when our relationship began to unravel, he called me his Jed Johnson, in a tone that was both sad and bittersweet.

We'd been seeing each other a month when Marcus asked if he could take a plaster casting of my face. He removed my clothes in preparation, in his studio loft. He scrubbed my hair with peppermint shampoo and a cilantro conditioner, then used a bergamot body wash on my torso and limbs. His own body was proportioned like Greek statuary; narrow hips, trimmed pubic hair, the broad head of his penis pierced with a thick and heavy, stainless steel ring. Afterwards we wore Turkish cotton bathrobes and sipped on peach schnapps out of gilt glasses.

He cleared a work area, boiled water and cut strips from a dusty plaster roll. Binding back my hair, he studied my face. He asked if he could shave me first, and I said that he could.

He sat me in an enormous leather recliner that was stained and scarred. It had once belonged to his grandfather from Strausberg, the son of three generations of furniture makers. That man had died before Marcus was born, in the death throes of a war that was already lost. In the Battle of Berlin, the invading Red Army had advanced street by street through the city. The fighting was close quarters, bloody and hopeless for the depleted German infantry. Twenty thousand civilians died in that single assault. He recounted this while applying pre-shave oil and a hot towel, massaging the lather into my cheeks, jaw and throat with his bare hands. I had the impression this was a monologue Marcus had crafted years ago.

Marcus removed his bathrobe and tied it around his waist like a bustle skirt. The gleaming Solingen razor he produced was monogrammed, a gift from his father when he turned thirteen. I'd never seen such an object up close before. It looked cinematic, like a prop. I tried not to flinch at the steel scraping against my stubble. Marcus used slow, even strokes, tilting my chin back, drawing the skin taut beneath my jaw. When my brothers and I were children, Grandpa regularly cut our hair. But I'd never been shaved by another man before. Marcus' brow knitted in concentration. My Adam's apple rose and fell. I observed the frame of his ribcage, the musculature of his arms. His skin was pale and blue-veined, his hands overlarge, his fingers long and precise. When he was finally done, he filled a porcelain basin with ice water and had me immerse my entire face.

His father had salvaged few items from the bombed ruins of the family home; this chair had come with him all the way from Germany. His mother, raised in York Mills, hated the thing. The hideous relic had no place in their suburban Georgian Revival mansion and so was banished to the attic. This was a secret retreat where Marcus played as a child, elevated and hidden from the rest of the world. Rummaging through dusty trunks of leather-bound books, he once discovered a tin cigar box containing Wehrmacht postcards, Reichsmark coins and his grandfather's Iron Cross. Over the years, surrounded by Nazi memorabilia, he read the works of Ibsen, Chekhov and Strindberg. When he was sixteen, bent over this very chair, he lost his virginity to the principal's son and the school's star quarterback (neither of whom spoke to him again after that day). Then Marcus read Camus, Nietzsche, Kafka and Brecht. When the time came to move to Toronto, the chair was the one thing he asked if he could bring with him (where it became the single set piece in his first one-man-show).

Marcus offered this extraordinary confession in a casual and matter-of-fact tone. I sat speechless beneath a print of Warhol and the Factory, as Marcus applied a thin layer of Vaseline over my face. He didn't seem to expect any reply and I did not offer any. Afterwards, he lay me down on a mat, placing a pillow beneath my head. He dimmed the lights and lit thin tapers. Once he began, it was imperative I remain perfectly still. He put on a CD by a band called Delirium. Then, kneeling by my side, with his hands on his knees, he asked if he could blow me while we waited for the cast to dry, and I said that he could.

He began soaking white strips of plaster in hot water and layering them on my face. His fingertips lingered over the crevasses of my eye sockets, nose and lips. The heavy plaster eventually covered all my features expect for my nostrils. By the time the cast was complete, I felt drowsy and cocooned. Marcus told me people often fell asleep during this stage.

Slipping a hand beneath my robe, he stroked my chest. He lay his ear over my heart, resting the full weight of his head upon me. After that, he opened my robe. I'd never felt more protected or more exposed. He kissed my stomach. He pressed his lips against the tip of my shaft. I was a captive, in every way. He knew this and took his time with me. He spread my legs and gently tugged on my balls. His mouth was warm and his tongue muscular. Honey bees buzzed and swarmed inside of me. When I finally came, I breathed harshly through my nose, gripping the sides of the mat. Afterwards, he cleaned me with a hot towel and covered me in a quilt. I felt empty, weightless and for a moment, may have actually fallen asleep. As the plaster began to grow cold and hard, he instructed me to begin moving my face: tiny motions of my mouth and brow. I felt the cast split away. Carefully, Marcus lifted it off, starting from the chin. Its edges were brittle, snagging in my hairline.

But then I was free.

When he presented it to me, I was amazed by the details in its concave surface: the tiny lines of my lips, the individual lashes of my eyes. Marcus' expression was one of expectant delight. He lay next to me, like a Renaissance figure gilt in candlelight. He would reinforce it later, he said and use it to make a proper mask. I could tell he was aroused but he did not expose himself. Instead, he asked if he could include me in his next theatre project, a celebration of the winter solstice, and I said that he could.

I think that moment, perhaps, was the closest Marcus ever came to saying he loved me.

On New Year's Eve, he introduced me to his best friend, Marwa, a drug dealer who baked the most fabulous confections and cakes. That same night we took a lover named Fang, a DJ and part-time go-go boy. I felt Marcus drifting away from me. We were not growing in the direction I'd hoped. I no longer felt vainglorious, but overshadowed and unbalanced. I felt I was losing my way. Our final weeks together were a kaleidoscope of elixirs and drugs, smoke and mirrors, his words a maze. (What the hell was a "polycule"?) Our skins felt like glowing Technicolor screens on which we projected our pleasure and desire. When I lay alongside their bodies, I felt an impenetrable film of stained-glass separating us.

In the end, I was the one who walked away.

Marcus insisted we remain friends. He wouldn't take no for an answer. It was never clear to me whether I'd been his boyfriend or lover or sidekick or protégé. I suppose I let him believe we could still be close. To be honest, I said whatever it took to get as far away from him as I could.

But by then I was already changed. I'd grown up in the nickel-smelting, northern Ontario town of Sudbury. But gone now was that sheltered kid with a mullet who rode to school in the back of his grandpa's pick-up. Gone now was the teenager who hid behind sunglasses lusting after shirtless lacrosse players, who got drunk and belligerent too often at tailgate parties, and who jerked off to a cum-stained photo of his assistant hockey coach. In the dark labyrinth of the city, my encounter with Marcus

Wittenbrink Jr. had been primordial and operatic. It was as if I'd met a unicorn, or a Fairie King. Now a glittering, rainbow sliver of him had broken off and lodged inside of me. And it remained there still, a stiff, aching brightness, pricking me forever.

CHAPTER THREE

The Kid is Hot Tonight

"Creamy." Karen licked her lips.

I wiped my mouth. "Rich but not overpowering."

"Mmm. It's divine."

"It is."

Karen's face was flushed, her hair just a little bit dishevelled. "Honestly, Daniel, I'm going to have to give this a five."

"I might have to agree with you. A perfect score, then?"

"It's perfection." Karen's face loomed on my laptop screen. "I'm getting myself another bowl."

"Me too."

It was Sunday evening and our monthly ice-cream-Skype-date. I jumped up from the couch and came back with the tub. Our selection for January: President's Choice Black Label Madagascar Bourbon Vanilla. I rearranged my pillows and adjusted my laptop on David's battered steamer trunk.

Tonight, Karen and I wore our matching sweat pants and Habs jerseys. Ice cream was just one thing we had in common. There was also road hockey, Fireball and whiskey shots, zombies and sweet potato fries. And my brother Liam. Those two must've broken up half-a-dozen times before she finally moved on. If I wasn't a six on the Kinsey Scale, Karen and I might've ended up a couple ourselves. We'd joked about it often enough.

"So," Karen said, "this is the big night, eh?"

"Yep." David had already left for Luke and Ai Chang's. They needed to time this just right. "It was either do it now or next month. They didn't think there was any reason to wait."

Sitting cross-legged in a bean bag chair, Karen tucked her hair behind her ears. I knew she was at her aunt's farmhouse from the broad, oak ceiling beams behind her. Her wide cheekbones and brown eyes reflected the warmth of the fireplace. "So explain to me how this works again? Like, do they actually use a real turkey baster?"

"What? No, you just use a plastic syringe. You can buy home insemination kits, but they're way overpriced."

"And David, he masturbates into a cup, right?"

"Yes," I said. "And you use the syringe to suck it up. Then you inject it into the woman when she's ovulating."

"Wow. Okay."

"You want to make the deposit as close as you can to the cervix. It's called intracervical insemination. She should also stay prone for about twenty minutes afterwards. Also, during this time, she should try to have an orgasm."

"Really?"

"It allows the cervix to dip into the vaginal pool and draw up the sperm. If the woman's aroused and if she can have an orgasm, it can, well, help speed things along."

"I see." Karen nodded. "And they teach you this in medical school?"

"Not exactly. I looked it up on YouTube."

"But you could," Karen said, "just use a turkey baster."

"I suppose, if you really wanted to."

"To inject David's spunk."

"His seminal fluid. That's correct."

"His splooge."

"If you say so."

"His protein shake."

"Seriously?"

Somehow, ice cream was now dribbling down Karen's chin. "His love mayonnaise."

I leaned into the camera. "My boyfriend's baby batter."

"David's man yoghurt."

"His jizz jambalaya." After that, Karen cracked up and couldn't stop laughing for a whole minute.

On this night, a snow squall in Toronto had whited out our skylights. Reindeer antlers adorned the stone lions flanking the TV, and Christmas lights lit up my giant palm. As a gift to ourselves, David and I had finally replaced two dozen milk cartons with actual book cases. I was just glad the hot water tank hadn't broken down yet. It was about as cantankerous as our building manager Rick.

"So what's the chance of success?" Karen asked.

"The same as regular sex. They'll know in about two weeks if it worked. Usually it takes four or five tries."

"So, realistically, Ai Chang's getting pregnant this summer then?"

"If things go as planned."

"Well, that's exciting." Karen poked at her bowl. "And are you feeling any better about all of this?"

"David's super excited. He's looking forward to baby-sitting and changing diapers. He was ready to be a dad the first day we met."

Karen's gaze narrowed. "But he wouldn't be the dad."

"That's what he keeps telling me."

"You're still afraid, Daniel, he's going to be too involved."

"David says he's talked things through with Luke and Ai Chang. He keeps telling me it's not going to be a problem."

"But you don't trust him?"

"I want to trust him." I sighed. "I have absolute trust that he trusts himself. He's convinced everything's going to turn out great. Except, raising a family, it's a big respon-sibility."

"It takes a village."

"Yeah, it does." My phone buzzed. "Hold on." It was a text from David: *Thinking of you—needing to come.*

"It's David. I think he's doing it right now."

"Is he? Ooh awesome. Let me text him!" Karen dis-appeared from the screen.

"Karen, let the guy concentrate!"

Another text: this time it was David asking to FaceTime. The phone rang, his image appeared, blurry and shaky.

"David, what's going on?"

His face was flushed and he had no shirt on. "I just occurred to me," he said. "I need you to be part of this."

"What?"

"So, Daniel, I'm doing it right now, or I'm trying to. I'm in their washroom. Luke gave me this jar. I think it used to be for baby gherkins. Anyway, so I'm like watching porn on my phone, right? But it's not helping. So I start pulling up pics of Turkish oil wrestlers, but that's not doing the trick. So I go through my collection of Wincest art, and even that's not working. Then I realized this is special, this is big! This isn't just any jack-off session. We're making a real baby right now. Like, a real human being! This is for real. Then all of a sudden I just realized I need you to be part of this. It's important you're a part of this, Daniel. I need you to help me out here me."

"Help you out?"

David made a face. "You know."

"You're joking, right? David, you're masturbating into a pickle jar. How hard can it be?"

"I know! That's what I thought too. This has never happened to me before. But my big brother Luke, he's like waiting right outside. His girlfriend Ai Chang's in their bedroom lighting beeswax candles and doing Pilates." He lowered his voice. "This is a lot of pressure. Look, Daniel, I just need you to talk dirty to me."

The shaky image settled into place. David had set his phone down and leaned back against the bathroom vanity.

"David, are you naked? Why are you naked?"

"It's more comfortable. I'm still wearing my socks. So like can you do the pirate thing, the one where you kidnap me? No wait. Do the other one."

"What other one?"

"The one where we're lumberjacks."

"You mean voyageurs."

"Yeah, that one."

My brow knit. "Alright. I guess so." I cleared my throat. "Right now?"

"Yes, now. That would help. Now's the time."

"Eh, Jean-François!" I shouted.

"Guillaume!"

"What is the matter?"

"There is a splinter in my thumb." His Québécois accent was terrible and I tried not to laugh. He sounded like Celine Dion.

"Well." I scratched my head. "Come on over, mon gars, and let me take a look at that. Ah-yoy! That is a big piece of wood là. But I can help you with that. I place my hand on your chest and push you up against a tree. I unsheathe my hunting knife, and I straddle your leg. Are you ready for this? My manly hips press up against yours. I grip your hand in mine. Ah, câlisse! My weight pins you down. Hold still, I say. Finally, it comes out. Tabarnak! There is blood. I put your thumb in my mouth and I suck on it. My eyes hungrily search your face. My mouth is warm and wet. I stab my knife into the tree. Bacon sizzles over the campfire. I lean in closer. My swollen manhood grinds against yours. We are young bucks, companions lost alone out in the wilderness. We smell like cretons and sweat, wood smoke and tobacco. I reach down with one hand and unbuckle your belt. I have never done this before, but you do not stop me. I spit into my palm and slide my hand into your pants. I grip your stiff, aching cock and start to stroke you. Then, all of a sudden, we are kissing. I am biting your lip, my stubble is scraping against yours, my tongue is hot and thrusting in your mouth." I hesitated. "Um. I forget what comes next."

David had started to jack off again. "You rip open my plaid shirt, and you throw me onto a pile of beaver pelts. You take a shot of maple whiskey and you spit it into my mouth."

"Right."

"And after that we have a threesome with our guide, the one you said looks just like Justin Trudeau."

"Okay." I drew a breath. "David, I'm not sure I can do this."

"Daniel, c'mon. I'm really close. Just jump to the part where the two of you do the spit-roast thing."

"Alright." I gathered my resolve. "Jean-François! I straddle you and pin you down on the beaver pelts. My loins are on fire. I devour your neck. I bury my face in your armpits. C'est putain de sexy! I kneel like I am at Mass, and take all of you into my mouth. Suddenly, our tall, dark and handsome guide Justin, dressed in buckskin and furs, returns to camp. He sees us—"

"Oh shit," David exclaimed, red-faced. He groped behind him. "I'm coming."

All the muscles in David's torso tensed. He hunched over, trying his best to catch everything in the jar. When his head hit the wall with an audible thud, the image abruptly went dark.

After a moment, David picked up his phone. "Hey," he said. "Thanks."

"You're welcome. Are you okay?"

"I'm great. You're the best, I love you. Gotta go."

He ended the call.

I put down my phone. I realized I'd spilled vanilla ice cream all over my lap.

"Well." Karen said, licking her spoon. "That was special."

I stared at her on my laptop screen. I'd forgotten we were still Skyping. "Sorry about that."

"Never apologize," Karen said. "Not for spitting maple syrup into your lover's mouth. Own your fiery loins."

I wiped at myself with a handful of napkins. "It was maple whiskey."

"Tomato tomahto."

"You weren't supposed to hear that."

"Excusez-moi?" Karen arched one eyebrow. "Hello. This is, like, me you're talking to."

"David kinda likes to fantasize about these kinds of things."

"Don't tell me," Karen said, "you've never spat in his mouth before."

"In real life? No."

"Why not?"

"It's gross."

"Well, it sounds like it's a turn-on for David."

"Just because we talk about it, Karen, doesn't mean we actually do it. Sometimes a fantasy works because it's just a fantasy."

"Fair enough. But have you and David ever acted out a fantasy?"

"Well. Once he dressed up like a giant kangaroo."

"And you guys had sex?"

"Um, yeah, we did."

"I'm impressed. So, are you two boys into the furry thing?"

"What's the furry thing?"

"It doesn't matter."

"He also wore a jock strap. He knew that was a turn-on for me. And, just a few weeks ago, I went down on him while he ate eggplant parmigiana and drank merlot."

"I see."

"He said it was best blowjob he'd ever had."

"Food sex, mmm." Karen nodded. "Kinky, definitely. So, explain to me, what exactly is this 'spit-roast thing'?"

"Look." I cringed. "Can we not talk about this?"

"Alright." Karen sat back. "You know, you and David are really good for each other."

"You think?" I set my crumpled napkins aside in a sticky pile. "Sometimes I wonder. I mean, I've been wondering if we could be doing better."

"What do you mean?"

"David wants to have sex, like, all the time."

"That's a bad thing?"

"School's really exhausting, Karen. We hardly ever have regular meals together. I've gained weight. He keeps masturbating to porn. I dunno. It's hard to keep up. I keep thinking I'm disappointing him."

"Listen, Daniel." Karen crossed her arms. "You have a boyfriend who tells you he loves you all the time. Who keeps saying he's going to marry you some day. Do you ever think about that?"

"I suppose."

"Are you kidding me? Daniel, you and David have got a really good thing going. Trust me."

"It's hard to be confident in a relationship when you haven't been in that many."

"How many have there been?"

"Well, there was Sean. That lasted a whole four weeks. Then I was with Charles three months. After that, it was Marcus."

"You forgot Stephan Tondeur."

"Stephan?" I exclaimed. "Karen, that wasn't a real relationship. He was married, with a wife and a kid."

"It still counts, Daniel. It was real for you."

"What's your point?"

"All I'm saying is that you have a lot more experience than you think. You and David have been together almost five years. That's a long time. You're doing something right. You should be proud of that."

"Karen, you know he cheated on me two summers ago."

"In Italy, with a girl. I know."

"I know he didn't plan it. I know he'd never do anything on purpose to hurt me. But that just makes you wonder what else might happen."

"Yeah and? When does life ever go just the way we plan?" Karen straightened her laptop. "You told me he was sorry. You talked about it, and you forgave him. Maybe one day David will be the one forgiving you. We never think these things will happen. But when they do, and when we work them through, it can bring us closer. It can make us stronger. You two boys loving each other is what matters most. What you did there was really loving."

"What?"

"Talking dirty to him like that."

"Oh jeez."

"I'm serious."

"I'm not very good at it."

"Yeah, well. No kidding. But you did it anyway. And you didn't hesitate, even when you're not convinced he's making the best decision. You," Karen said, "are a good boyfriend."

"I try."

"And that's the best anyone can do. We make mistakes, Daniel, we fall down, we learn. We get up, we do better, and we keep on going."

"There's an Alanis Morissette song in there somewhere."

"Hey. Life isn't all about the big hits. But it's the little things too, the everyday moments. The B-side also counts for something."

"You make it sound easy."

"Did I say it was easy?" Karen shook her head. "Life's never easy. It can be awful and ugly, and painful as hell. And sometimes. Sometimes it can also be so beautiful and wise and stupid wonderful, it takes your breath away."

I wiped at my eyes with the heels of my hands. "There are these moments, you know, when I think everything's good, when I think everything's going to be okay."

Karen sat back. "Just moments?"

"Like now."

"Sweetheart."

I pulled my computer closer into my lap. "You're still moving back to Toronto, right?"

"That's the plan."

"You promise?"

"Yes, Daniel, I promise. Except you have gone and built yourself a life already. You've made new friends. You've moved in with David. You two boys are going to be uncles. You're going to be a doctor. You got any room left for little ol' me?"

"Karen Fobister, you know I do."

"Well." Karen's dimples showed. "Then, Daniel Garneau, I'm looking forward to it."

 That February, Glad Day Bookshop in Toronto's Gay Village hosted its Valentine-themed event, Naked Boys Reading.

Just before the show, David and I grabbed a bite to eat at a Vietnamese restaurant across the street. Over a steaming bowl of pho, I read the Facebook description out loud: "An intimate nude literary salon featuring in-the-buff readings by local beefcakes, bears, twinks, otters, butch femmes, sissy sluts, boys-next-door with an exhibitionist streak and lovers of naturism with a well-endowed library."

David munched on a spring roll. "I've never been to a literary salon before."

"Well," I said, "there's a first time for everything."

"Don't knock it until you try it, right?"

"This isn't a peep show, David. Parker says it's not sexual at all."

"It's not sexual." David raised his eyebrows and thrust out his chin. "It's a salon."

"Yes." I rolled my eyes. "It's a salon."

"A literary salon. With naked boys." David's mouth formed a round O. "Nope, this isn't at all about objectifying the male body."

"I'm not sure how to respond to that."

"You don't have to, mister. Look, I'm excited to go. This peanut sauce is awesome, by the way. And I'm excited to go with you. It'll be fun. So what are we?"

"What do you mean?"

"Twinks, otters, sissy sluts?"

"I am not a bear. Don't even go there."

"What, are you kidding me? Look, first of all, bears can be hot. But I wasn't even thinking that." David sat back. "You're more, I think, boy-next-door. Definitely. I was this emo skater and might've turned out a brootal kid, except Luke groomed me into the fixed gear anarchist I am today. Mind you, I got into the queercore on my own. Before he transitioned, Luke went through this mosh warrior phase, but he was always a rockabilly punk at heart."

I picked a soggy wedge of lime out of my rice noodles. "Why would you say I'm boy-next-door?"

"You've just got that look. You know, that wholesome, corn-fed, varsity thing going there. Like a porn star from the Eighties."

"What?"

"Daniel, I'm just saying."

"I am not a porn star."

"Hey," David exclaimed, "isn't that Parker and his boyfriend?"

Across Church Street, Parker and Kyle were peering into the glass front of Glad Day. Even bundled up in their parkas, I recognized them from their matching toques with fuzzy fox and wolf ears. They were also wearing matching furry tails. As we watched, Kyle opened the door for Parker and the two disappeared inside holding hands.

"I wonder," David said, "what's going through their minds right now."

I'd been friends with Parker close to six years. We'd been through a lot together but I'd never seen him naked before. I was both terrified and fascinated by what the next few hours might hold. "If I was performing tonight," I said, "I'd just be afraid of getting a boner in front of everyone."

"Attaboy," David said. "That's my porn star."

After our meal, we hurried across the street. A broad pink awning sheltered the Glad Day entranceway. It was pay-what-you-can at the door. A mic stand was set up against a wall brimming with hundreds of colourful titles and covers. As the longest-running LGBT bookstore in the world, Glad Day had a notorious history of run-ins with Canada Customs over obscenity laws. In recent years, it had evolved into a coffee shop, bar and community space hosting literary events, dance parties and Sunday Drag Brunches. It was Parker's favourite home away from home, and the indisputable heart of Toronto's Queer Village.

Tonight, bookcases on castors had been rolled aside to make room for audience seating. Every folding chair was filled and it was standing room only for latecomers. David and I arrived just in time to find stools at the bar. Parker and Kyle waved to us from the front row. The handsome bartender Terence was friendly and efficient as ever. The event was to be hosted by Igby Lizzard, Toronto's adored Queen of Filth. The packed house buzzed with anticipation. As we waited for the event to begin, two older women seated in front of us carried on a lively conversation.

"Men are so much more attractive when they're reading," one declared.

"Smart is sexy."

"Nothing is more arousing than intelligence. A book lets us know he's got more to offer than just his looks."

"And when the men are naked?"

"Why, that just adds an artistic dimension. Then reading becomes performance art. I believe there's a voyeur in every literary enthusiast. The male nude simply offers a compelling new interpretation of the text."

"Or," said David, leaning forward, "the text adds a new interpretation of the male nude."

"Exactly my point," the first woman exclaimed, turning. Her face lit up when she saw us. "Why, David and Daniel! What a delightful surprise. I haven't seen you since M's closing night party."

This was Rebecca, the wife of professor Frederic, Marcus' former mentor and lover. Marcus prided himself on remaining close with all his ex-lovers (and their partners and second cousins and baristas). Over the years, we'd often crossed paths with Rebecca and Frederic. The couple had even entertained us in their Tudor-styled home in the Junction once. Tonight, Rebecca looked radiant, draped in a champagne shawl with her silver hair braided and pinned in a Grecian bun.

"At Buddies in Bad Times," David said.

"That's right." Rebecca clasped her companion's hand. "This is Amanda, my dearest friend. David and Daniel here are friends of M."

Amanda looked us up and down. "Of course they are." She was a busty blonde, sporting bold red lipstick and a strapless cocktail dress. "Will you two boys be reading tonight?"

I cleared my throat. "Um, no." I was conscious of how both women were exactly eye-level with our crotches. "Not tonight."

"Maybe next time." David smiled.

"That is a pity." Amanda touched Rebecca's knee. "It is unfortunate your M is away, I would've loved to have seen him read again."

"Marcus," I said, "has read at this thing?"

"You've attended before?" David asked.

"M," Rebecca said, "performed at Toronto's inaugural Naked Boys Reading some years ago. And yes, you could say we are repeat customers." Both women glanced at each other and burst into laughter.

"Let me tell you what I love about this salon," Amanda said, plucking an olive from her drink. "Tonight we're here in praise of storytelling, and bodies of all shapes and sizes. People in this community are so busy judging each other. It can get vicious, and it's never healthy. The last thing we need is people under our flag hating on each other. Tonight we celebrate diversity, and the freedom to be truly seen and heard."

"Hear-hear." Rebecca raised her glass.

"What was that wonderful quote by Josephine Baker?" Amanda struck a pose. "'I wasn't really naked. I simply didn't have any clothes on.'"

"Now that woman," Rebecca said, "was a beacon to the world. We are all her Rainbow Tribe. Did you know Freddy lectures about her in his semiotics of fashion course?"

"A cultural icon," Amanda said, pointing with her skewer.

"A subversive," David said.

Rebecca thrust out her chin. "Let us all take inspiration from our dear Josephine."

David raised his pint. "May her spirit shine on."

Amanda nodded. "We'll just need some bananas daiquiris."

"Let's not skirt the issue, dear," Rebecca said. "A bunch of them will suffice." Then all three burst into laughter.

The truth was I had no idea who Josephine Baker was, or what they were talking about, at all.

"Amanda," Rebecca said, squeezing my thigh, "hosts sex parties."

Rebecca's companion glanced at me over her shoulder, and then up at my face. "You should come to my club."

Before I could reply, Igby Lizzard leapt onto the podium in a sequined wig and leopard-print body suit, and all conversation halted as the evening's salon launched into full swing.

Two hours later, Naked Boys Reading was over. Six readers had taken the stage, the audience had cried, gasped and cheered, and true to her reputation, fierce queen Igby Lizzard had somehow managed during her MC duties to deepthroat a dildo. I'd also learned that William Shakespeare was, in fact, the foremost enthusiast of racy innuendos and dirty jokes.

However, my biggest discovery was just how short-lived the novelty of public nudity turned out to be. Each reader, upon stepping up to the mic, had disrobed completely. Of course my eyes instantly fixated on their private parts. (I tried my best not to crane my neck.) But within minutes, that became the least interesting part of the performance. If there was anything sexual about the evening at all, it was conveyed in the readings themselves. Most were romantic, others more sensual.

The highlight of the salon came when Parker read Katsushika Hokusai's *The Dream of the Fisherman's Wife*. (Shunga tentacle erotica had prevailed over Jane Austen in the end.) Not only did Parker take on all three distinct speaking parts (Large Octopus; Maiden; Small Octopus) in the English-language translation of the text, but during his reading he also contrived to consume, with chopsticks, a plate of spicy grilled calamari, and to share with the audience the flavourful recipe. (The trick, it seemed, was to first pound the muscular mollusk with a mallet to tenderize the meat.) The audience was in stiches. Parker was at heart a raconteur, and tonight he was in his element. Maybe he'd broken the rules of the salon by parting from the text, but nobody seemed to care. I'd never been more proud of him.

The only real shock for me had come when the first reader took the stage. It was Rebecca's husband, professor Frederic himself. The man was tall and strikingly handsome, with a thick head of snowy white hair. As it turned out, he was in better shape than most men half his age. He also had the second largest penis I'd ever seen in my entire life. It's prodigious girth and length raised more than a few eyebrows.

In a stentorian tone, wearing only his reading glasses, he shared an excerpt from James Joyce's private letters to his beloved wife Nora Barnacle. The strangeness of the whole affair was off-set by the gravitas he commanded. I could see why he'd been selected to kick off the evening (and also what Marcus might have seen in him, both as a mentor and lover). Rebecca beamed and applauded warmly when he was done, remarking how the selection of Joyce had been her idea.

Last to read was Parker's boyfriend Kyle. I'd always thought of Kyle as a nerdy hippie, with his scruffy beard and khaki messenger bag decorated with Greenpeace pins and Magic The Gathering buttons. As I watched him shyly take off his clothes, David elbowed me in the side. The guy was uncut with low-hanging balls and the physique of a hockey player, his broad thighs dusted in glinting hair. Now I imagined him climbing trees barefoot and swinging into lakes like a young Lord Greystoke. The excerpt he read from Marian Engel's *Bear* was poignant, his voice a gentle baritone. It evoked memories of cottaging near Wanapitei and camping in Killarney. Parker had suggested my brother Liam might enjoy this book. Nature's solitude had always been his retreat. Karen knew, more than anyone, how far into the darkness Liam sometimes fell. The northern wilderness had saved his life. As it turned out, Engel had dedicated the novel to her therapist. I had to agree with Igby Lizzard, that this was truly a work that made you proud to be Canadian.

Afterwards, people milled and thronged, drinks in hand, while Glad Day staff cleared the chairs. Parker thanked me for coming, clutching Kyle's gift of a single long-stemmed rose. When I congratulated him, he told me that reading tonight had been the single most terrifying thing he'd ever done, and that he and Kyle couldn't wait to do it again.

David and I stayed until closing time. By now I was pleasantly drunk and happy to hug everyone goodnight. David and I helped Terence stack the remaining chairs and tables. Michael the manager saw us out, locking the door behind us.

A crystalline glow bathed the city, the streetlamps and condo towers shining like moons and stars. I hooked my arm through David's to keep from stumbling. Leaving the Village, we crossed Yonge Street and entered Queen's Park behind the Ontario Legislative Building. Red tail lights winked and faded as cars traversed the roundabout.

We approached the imposing, bronze equestrian statue of King Edward VII. Every year, university students ritually painted the horse's testicles, and sure enough tonight they were bright orange.

"C'mon," David said. "Let's make a wish." Climbing the icy plinth, he gripped the horse's balls, and insisted I do the same. I climbed up next to him, grasping his shoulder to steady myself. From this precarious vantage point, we surveyed the vast expanse of snow-laden trees. Queen's Park was a known cruising ground but in the heart of winter we were the only people in sight. "I wish," David said, "nothing ever comes between us. I wish we could be together forever."

Before I could reply, in the distance I saw Mom and Dad. They were walking beneath the naked boughs, a beautiful couple holding hands, their cheeks and noses rosy from the cold. When they saw me, they raised their arms and waved.

"Daniel?" David glanced across the park.

"I wish," I whispered, "I wish I knew my parents better. I wish I had more time with them."

David peered into my face. "Oh, sweetheart."

My eyes welled with tears. In that moment, David might've said all sorts of things, to comfort or to encourage me. But he remained quiet, holding my arm. Our breath formed frosty clouds in the air. After a minute, I wiped my nose against his shoulder. We clambered down and jumped back to earth.

David straightened, clapping the snow from his gloves. His blue-grey eyes shone. "I had a good time with you tonight."

"Me too."

He leaned in and kissed my wet cheek.

"Happy Valentine's, mister."

"Happy Valentine's."

CHAPTER FOUR

Fight the Good Fight

Ai Chang Cho's face was immaculate.

It was elaborately painted, with at least two dozen piercings. The look suited her. If she wasn't a fashion designer, she might've been a make-up artist. When we first met, she had a full set of braces and a habit of mumbling. David once described her as having a resting-bitch-face. Now when she laughed, she displayed a perfect smile and a warmth that was both surprising and welcome. Five years ago, Ai Chang had quit her job as a dental hygienist after winning a top fashion scholarship. Last fall, she landed a coveted spot on Toronto's design team for Club Monaco. Unlike Luke Moretti who was loud and in-your-face, Ai Chang Cho was quiet and diffident. At least until she wasn't. Those two were each other's yin and yang. She was most relaxed in ripped jeans and a metal band shirt. It was Ai Chang who had walked up to Luke, a total stranger, and asked if he would model for her graduate year fashion shoot. Now she worked for an international lifestyle brand that promised "affordable luxury with modern sensibility." And she was three weeks pregnant with my boyfriend's baby.

"So, how do you feel?" I asked.

Ai Chang made a face. "Bloated. And I keep having to pee."

"She feels pregnant," Luke said.

"And I threw up into my cereal bowl this morning."

"And she threw up," Luke said, "into her cereal bowl this morning."

We sat in a corner at Sneaky Dee's, a Tex-Mex bar and restaurant. Its student menu with gigantic portions was a no-brainer. The upstairs concert venue offered up some of Toronto's best indie rock and punk. Dense layers of band stickers and colourful graffiti splattered the walls and booths.

When Luke and Ai Chang invited us out, I wondered if they had something to tell us. When David ordered a pitcher of Amsterdam Blonde and Luke said three glasses only, my suspicions were confirmed. Tonight Ai Chang sipped on a virgin margarita, sporting purple Docs, a tasselled scarf, and an I Mother Earth concert tee. She didn't look like someone who wanted to be a mom. But who says an expectant mother couldn't also turn a badass look, with full-on snake bites and eyebrow rings?

I glanced at David. "How're you doing?"

David sat straight-backed and slack-jawed. "Unh." He let out a breath. "I don't know what to say."

"Hey." Luke winked. "We couldn't have done it without you."

"I didn't think," David said, "this would actually happen so soon."

"Yeah, well, neither did we," Ai Chang said. "First try."

"Way to go." Luke reached across the table and punched David in the arm. "Sharpshooter."

"Well. Technically," I said, "Luke, you were the one who gave the injection."

"I heard, Daniel," Ai Chang said, "that you also helped out."

"Who told you that?"

"Justin Trudeau," she said, "is pretty hot."

Luke nodded. "Definitely."

I stared at David. "What?" he exclaimed, raising his shoulders. "I thought they oughtta know." He refilled our glasses. "Daniel here has this thing for Justin. Personally, I would've gone for Keanu Reeves."

I blinked. "Really?"

"Or Scott Speedman." David smirked. "Lycan-vampires, mmm, so damn sexy."

"Personally," Ai Chang said, "I'd rather have Drake's baby."

Now Luke shot her a look. Ai Chang took a sip from her margarita, trying to keep a straight face. I'd never seen the two look so happy. Luke had just started working full-time as a trainer at GoodLife and already had a wait-ing-list of clients. Luke Moretti could be a good ol' boy one moment and a suave metrosexual the next. He and David shared the same tight build and the same broad smile. Anyone could tell that the two were brothers.

"Nine months," Luke said, "takes us to November."

"Ma's gonna want to fly out from Sicily. Oh my God, she'll be here for Christmas." David's face flushed. "Where's she going to stay? Do you think she'll want a Catholic baptism?"

"Whoa, slow down, kiddo," Luke said. "It's only been three weeks."

"Usually you wait until the end of the first trimester," I said.

"We're telling you now." Luke lowered his voice. "But we're not telling anyone else, okay?"

"Except …" Ai Chang's eyes turned to him.

"What is it?"

"My mom." She winced. "She asked me already."

"She asked you what?"

'Well." Ai Chang rested her hands on the tabletop. "You know how I stopped by there yesterday, to check in on my dad?"

"Yeah?"

"Here's the thing. I walk into the kitchen and my mom's making dumplings. She hates making dumplings but they're my dad's favourite. She's been feeling guilty about the accident ever since it happened. Anyway, so we're talking for a few minutes when she just stops and stares. Then she jumps up, pork and chives all over her hands, walks around the table and sniffs at me."

"She sniffs at you?"

"She smells me, yeah. She's always had this sixth sense. She could tell my uncle had cancer before he had any symptoms. She insisted he get these tests, and she was right. He got treated and he's healthy now. She saved my bobo's life. And that's not the only time. She knew days before my first period that it was going to happen. She also knew when my brother's turtle was dying, and a week later it was dead as a doorstop."

"Okay," Luke said. "And?"

"Well, she asked me. She like shouts: 'Dazui! Are you pregnant? Are you having baby?' Of course, I said I had no idea what she was talking about. But now she's insisting I get a pregnancy test. She's invited the two of us over for dinner. She wants to know what your favourite dish is."

Luke sat back. "You sure she said the two of us?"

"Listen. You know she wasn't happy when she found out you weren't Chinese. She was definitely not happy when she found out we were moving in together. But none of that matters anymore. First of all, she wants to thank you for visiting my dad in the hospital. You stayed with us all night. You made a big impression on them. And now." Ai Chang rested a palm over her stomach. "This is the only thing that matters. You're the father of her very first grandchild—that makes you family. I told her you like Chinese food. It's all she knows how to make anyway."

"What's 'da-zway'?" I asked.

"Oh." Ai Chang rolled her eyes. "Dazui means 'Big Mouth.' My little brother started calling me that when we were young. I was a brat back then. Then everyone in my family started using it."

"You don't mind?"

"It's a term of affection now. My brother's still a total doughhead. But, no, I don't mind."

"And your dad," I asked, "is going to be okay?"

"He'll be fine. A physiotherapist visits the house every week. My mom also has him seeing an acupuncturist and an herbalist. He was up on the roof because she had him checking the satellite dish. He slipped and fell into her vegetable bed. Now she feels awful about it. She's totally bossy and narrow-minded but her whole life's about taking care of family. The point is, Luke, my mom knows."

"So." David cleared his throat. "What are you going to tell her?"

I elbowed David in the side. "Ai Chang's going to tell her," I said, "that she's pregnant and Luke's the father."

"Right." David cracked his knuckles, then drummed his fingers on the tabletop. "And what about Ma?"

"Ma can wait," Luke said. "This spring, you and I can tell her together. She'll want to know you're the donor."

"This is really happening." David's eyes shone. "This is real. We're making a baby."

"We're making," Luke said, "a family."

Ai Chang squeezed his hand. "Hey, baba."

"Hey, mama."

Ai Chang gave me a sidelong glance. "Hey, shushu."

"What's 'shoo-shoo'?"

"Shushu means uncle. Although, specifically, it means your father's younger brother. Now, if David was older than Luke, then he'd be bobo. The thing is, normally, Daniel, you'd be shenshen, which would be your father's younger brother's wife. We can't call you that. We might call you gufu, which would be your father's sister's husband, except that would be weird since David's not Luke's sister. So as far as I can figure, you and David are both shushu."

"We figured David could be dashu and Daniel could be xiao-shushu," Luke said.

Ai Chang nodded. "Big uncle and little uncle."

"But Daniel has twelve kilos on me," David said.

I gave him a shove. "You're older by three months.

And given these circumstances, David, you are definitely big uncle."

"Alright." David grinned. "I'm dashu. And you're xiao-shushu."

"Okay, then."

"Thanks," Luke said, "for meeting us like this. We didn't want to wait to tell you."

"Are you kidding? I am so gobsmacked right now." David laughed out loud. "Holy bajesus." He wiped his eyes and grabbed my hand. "Congratulations. We did it." We all raised our drinks. "Here's to family."

The truth was, I was thrilled. I was still just getting to know Luke and Ai Chang but already felt the four of us made a good team. Those two were meant for each other. They were going to be great parents, and I was glad I'd been able to help out in whatever way I could.

Karen was right. Life wasn't just about the big hits. But the small stuff counted for something too. Sometimes, it was the quiet, everyday moments that held it all together. New cloth napkins, a long-stemmed rose, homemade dumplings.

Or spitting in my boyfriend's mouth.

We were three years into our relationship when David suggested we have sex without condoms.

He'd committed to spending that whole summer in Italy with his mom. Their flight wasn't for two months, but David wanted us to do something special before he left. So just before Easter, we got tested. When the night finally came, both of us douched. This would be a first for each of us. To be sure, there was a whole lot more to gay sex than anal. But David loved fucking, and he talked about it all the time. All the porn he ever watched was bareback porn. During high school, David had slept with girls, but he insisted he wasn't bi. He just called himself an opportunist. I knew there were straight guys who kept on the down-low their whole lives. But until I met David, I'd never known a gay guy who'd sometimes sleep with women.

Later that summer in Sicily, David had sex with a girl named Silvia Sabatini. It was a drunken, unplanned hook-up and he hadn't used a condom then. Karen had reminded me that learning to forgive each other was part of growing up. That was something I'd learned long ago. Otherwise, I doubted I'd be on speaking terms with any of my family, given all the stupid and hurtful things they had done. If I could forgive my parents for dying in a drunken car accident, then I could forgive David for what happened in Sicily.

David never did come out to his mom. But it was Luke who told her. No Catholic mother imagines her child might be gay, or that the daughter she raised might in fact be a transgender man. But if Isabella de Luca truly believed her family was cursed, she never loved her children any less.

Last December, David received a wooden crate from Sicily, packed with preserves, almonds, cured meats and cheeses. The Christmas card inside was addressed to both David and me, and contained a three-page letter in his mom's precise handwriting. Kneeling in a pile of straw, cradling a bottle of extra virgin olive oil from the De Luca family farm, David had burst into tears. If my own parents were alive today, I figured they'd be as accepting as Grandpa was. It was hard for me to imagine the kind of fear David had lived with his entire life.

A magnet on our fridge displayed a quote from Paul Cézanne: "We live in a rainbow of chaos." It was the epigraph from Isabella de Luca's best-selling book, *Painting Outside the Lines: Rebels, Radicals and Revolutionaries*. David told me it was also a daily reminder. One of his earliest memories was of crashing his tricycle and his ma picking him up. She'd brushed the gravel from his bloodied knee, held him tightly to her breast and whispered in his ear: "We live in a rainbow of chaos, cucciolo."

This meant leaning into everything the world had to offer: all of its triumphs and pain, its fear and desire. Life, according to that woman, was a chiaroscuro journey of the heart.

Once, my drag queen friend Pussy Pierogi (née my old school nemesis Gary Kadlubek) ordered two shots at last call, and told me a story. "Let me tell you, Garneau," she said, "about the time I came out to my family. All my miserable life, my parents kept me on the tight end of a short leash—Sunday Mass, weekly penance, Bible boot camp. I put up with it because I had no choice. I was a kid, right? So of course I dropped my mitts every chance I could. I had built up so much anger and resentment; it was enough to make you choke. I hated everyone and everything and most of all I hated myself. But then I found moi, Pussy Pierogi. And she was the opposite of everything I knew. She was fearless. She was powerful. She was beautiful. This was Joan of Arc hearing the angels, y'know what I'm saying? This was Moses and the burning bush. Pussy here was an acid trip cyclone to Oz.

"There finally came this moment when it was either nosedive off an overpass, or let it all out. So I let her take me, and I was lifted up and I was born again. And I showed them, literally. On a Sunday evening, when my parents had the District Marshall of the Knights of Columbus over for dinner and his oh so very lovely wife, I came down the stairs. Everyone was already seated. It was the entrance of a lifetime. My mother screamed and dropped the casserole. I sat down at the table. I draped my stole over the back of my seat. I told them I wanted to say grace. And I thanked them. You want to know why? Because Pussy Pierogi here is a diamond. She is a diamond cut and polished by a lifetime of concentrated toxic bullshit fuckery, and she wouldn't be here today if it weren't for them. So I thanked them. And then I said Amen. You should've seen their faces. After that, I downed my glass of wine. I picked up my suitcase and walked out the front door. I walked across Sudbury in my heels. I walked all the way to the bus station. I had on my face and hair. I was just jonesing for someone to try to stop me. But no one did. That night, Garneau, I bought my one-way ticket to Toronto and I have never looked back." She threw back her two shots, licked her top lip, raised her arm and snapped her fingers. "Taste the rainbow, bitch."

Later Kadlubek told me it took a lot longer to forgive himself for the hateful bully he'd been in high school, but that he'd never lost his faith. In Toronto, he still worshipped every Sunday at the Metropolitan Community Church. According to Reverend Dr. Brent Hawkes, creating meaning out of chaos was the universal, precarious truth of our lives. Some people found it in religion, others in art. Kadlubek had found it in both.

David told me Paul Cézanne wanted to do away with all barriers, to truly see and sense what he created. Painting for Cézanne was a visceral and spiritual communion with God. Everyone craved intimacy, whether emotional or intellectual or spiritual. It was as primal as any human need. It was what defined us as human.

For David and me, sex without condoms was a natural next step. The irony of doing it Easter weekend wasn't lost on us. I wondered if this was David's way of reclaiming that sacred part of himself, the way Kadlubek had come out at Sunday dinner. Because a non-practicing Catholic is still a Catholic. Or maybe this was coming full circle, since Easter was in fact far older than Christ, named after Ēostre. For this pagan goddess of rebirth and fertility, the ancients held festivals in the spring, honouring the deity with lavish sex rituals and orgies. What better occasion, then, could there be?

God's medieval gladiators were martyrs and saints, performing for the masses, converting audiences to His cause. The gay icons and drag queens were no different. Pussy Pierogi had been Kadlubek's champion, his protector and guide. David told me once about the Band of Thebes, the finest and most famous warriors of fourth century BC. What fiercer fighting force than one hundred and fifty pairs of male lovers? The Band was sacred because of vows each couple took at the shrine of Iolaus, beloved of Heracles. In addition to military skill at arms, their training including riding, wrestling and dance. These three hundred, between the ages of twenty and thirty, were the elite shock troops of their age, winning the independence and glory of Thebes, elevating the city-state to a power equal to its legendary adversaries, Sparta and Athens. Such an army of lovers, Plato declared, could not fail.

That Easter Weekend, on Holy Saturday, David had "rainbow of chaos" inscribed over his heart. He announced that it was his birthday gift to himself. After a quarter century on this earth, he was more than ready to live with Cezanne's words the rest of his life. As David sat in the tattoo chair, as I listened to the whine of the needle and observed his shaved and bloodied chest, I considered how all our tests had come back negative. The two of us were healthy and we were young, and our bodies belonged to no one but ourselves. The twenty-first century had just begun, and for this brief moment in our lives, together at the edge of the world, we were the beloved, the chosen ones. We were the first and the finest, among the invincible.

⌒ As epic rock blasted, the "Canadian Buzzsaw" Corey Stone picked up a metal chair and smacked it across the head of Chris Chambers the "Half-Baked Kid." Fans pumped their fists in the air, roaring in approval. It was David's birthday and we were celebrating front row ringside at a Superkick'd Pro Wrestling Rock Show at The Great Hall in downtown Toronto.

Beefy, hairy men stomped past, wild-eyed, nostrils flaring, drenched in sweat. The event was billed as a "rock 'n' roll Fight Club." This close, I saw nothing fake about their throws or falls. As they clambered back into the ring, no one doubted their athleticism or brute strength. This tag-team contest had quickly degenerated into a brawl involving half-a-dozen other wrestlers taking sides and joining in.

Back in January, when Luke asked for my help organizing a surprise party for David, he'd already bought a Superkick'd VIP groupon package. He just needed to put out the call to David's circle of friends. I hadn't planned to invite our neighbour across the hall. Liz McLaren was a hoarder who hot-boxed in her rusty Volkswagen and fostered kittens. Her idea of a good time was dumpster-diving in the Fashion District. During a chance meeting in the laundry room, she'd asked what our plans were the coming week. When I told her, she dropped her detergent and exclaimed: "Shut the front door!"

As it turned out, Liz was a self-proclaimed wrestling super fan. She'd grown up adoring the legends: Hulk Hogan, Jake "the Snake" Roberts, Randy "Macho Man" Savage. "Now those, Daniel, were real men." Of course, dearest to her heart was the incorrigible and incomparable "Rowdy" Roddy Piper. Did I know he hailed from Saskatoon? No, I did not. As far as Liz was concerned, Piper's career peaked with his Royal Rumble Intercontinental Championship victory against the corrupt and despicable Mountie. Even after all those years, Liz whispered, the sound of bagpipes never failed to bring her back. Her lower lip trembled, her chest heaving. After that, I had no choice but to invite her along.

Tonight, Liz was wearing a floral muumuu, clutching a red plastic cup of beer, and screaming louder than anyone: "Kill the bastard!" I'd never seen this side of her before. Half-a-dozen of David's friends had also shown up, including our building manager Rick. Rick was a big, surly metalhead who lived in the basement, and could typically be spotted roaming the premises with a monkey wrench in hand, snuffling and muttering under his breath. David and Rick were on friendly terms but I was convinced the guy was a former Hells Angel and gave him a wide berth. None of us had ever been to a wrestling event before, and David was having the time of his life.

The evening climaxed when "Psycho" Steve Havoc climbed the top turnbuckle, blood streaming from his face. He thrust his fist over his head, inciting the crowd: "Psycho! Psycho! Psycho!" He leapt spreadeagled across the ring, propelled by his partner, Kabuki "the Krusher," crashing into all three of his opponents. Everyone went down in a mass of flailing limbs. It was a spectacular finisher. Psycho Steve and his two allies, Shane Sabre and the masked Kabuki, wasted no time executing in unison a piledriver, a powerslam and a backbreaker on their stunned and bewildered rivals. It was game over. The crowd went utterly and completely wild. I'd never encountered so much raw testosterone in my life.

After the show, the crowd poured out onto Queen Street West where streetcars rumbled past trendy bars and hip resto-lounges. There were parting hugs, birthday well-wishes and claps on the back. It was Friday night but David's colleague Arthur had to take his son to swim lessons the next morning. Nadia and Pat had weekend plans at Niagara-on-the-Lake. David's high school buddies had a long drive back to Scarborough. All evening, Ai Chang and Nadia had cheered on the women wrestlers. I was glad the two of them had hit it off, but now Ai Chang was heading home to drink a glass of milk and rest. In the end, the only ones left were Luke, David and myself, Rick and Liz.

I could tell David was disappointed more people hadn't stuck around but was happy with the five of us. When Liz produced a medical grade joint (ostensibly for her arthritis), he and Rick joined her in a parkette nearby. They were an odd but companionable trio. For years, those three would smoke up on the rooftop of our loft building. As it turned out, Luke didn't do drugs or party in any way. Apparently he never had.

"But," I said, "you used to deal."

"I did." Luke shrugged. "But I never touched the stuff. A good Negroni or a truly perfect martini, now that's my Achilles' heel. For a few years I was an AA sponsor, back in Vancouver. But I realized it wasn't for me. If there's one thing I've learned in life, Daniel, it's that the world's not so black and white. I have no regrets, mind you. It's what I needed to do at the time." He lit a smoke and snapped his lighter shut.

"Now I stick to beer and wine." He examined his cigarette. "I'll be quitting these, before the kid's born. It's also bad optics for work. It won't be easy. But a man's got to do what a man's got to do."

I considered his words. I happened to know that for twelve years Luke and his mom had been estranged. While still in high school, he'd recruited David into dealing drugs. For that transgression, Isabella De Luca had been unforgiving. But Luke had since cleaned up his act.

Now he had a steady job and even volunteered with the LGBT Youth Line. Hell, he was planning to be a full-time dad.

In Sicily last spring, it was Luke who walked their mother down the aisle at her fourth wedding.

Tonight, he had on his bomber jacket over a black dress shirt. His thick, glossy hair had grown out and he'd styled it in a faux hawk that seemed the apex of cool. Although, I thought to myself, Luke Moretti could probably duct-tape a Twinkie to his head and he'd still look ready for a fashion shoot.

He gestured toward the others. "Thanks for connecting me with David's friends. I got a surprise for you boys." He draped an arm over my shoulder. "You're gonna like it." The corner of his lip curled up. He smelled great. If I didn't already have a hard-on from two hours of watching half-naked, sweaty men pounding each other into submission, I got one now. I was definitely not signing up for Naked Boys Reading anytime soon.

When the others strolled back, Liz insisted she take us to her favourite bar. She was wearing an ankle-length muskrat coat and a matching fur hat. For once, her eyelash extensions and make-up seemed more or less in place. I'd never imagined someone like Liz could look so glamorous. (Although a part of me was concerned someone might run up and spray-paint her.) She wouldn't take no for an answer. Even Luke, who was stubborn as they come, acquiesced. This woman was on a mission.

We followed Liz four blocks west. A three-storey brick building loomed at the corner. Golden light poured from arched windows and an attractive crowd gathered out front. A plaque indicated the Romanesque Revival-styled building had been constructed in 1889. This, Liz told us, was where she'd got married forty years earlier.

"Welcome," she said, "to the Gladstone Hotel."

Inside the polished lobby, a flock of winged watch-faces the size of dinner plates soared through opalescent clouds suspended from the ceiling. Liz led us to the adjoining Melody Bar. The entrance was cordoned off, and a sign indicated the space was booked for a private event. "Well," Liz said, peeling off her gloves. "This just won't do at all, will it." Gesturing to the concierge, she unhooked the red velvet rope.

The double doors swung open before us.

The Melody Bar was packed, and the people inside cheered. Three Dog Run struck up a rousing rendition of "Happy Birthday." Nadia and Ai Chang greeted us. Everybody was here: Arthur and all his work colleagues, David's Scarborough high school friends, neighbours from our building and others I didn't recognize. Parker and Kyle (fully clothed) waved to us from the 1940s vintage bar. By the marble pillars, I even spotted professor Frederic and his wife Rebecca in elegant evening wear.

As the room embraced David and pulled him in, I turned to Luke. "Wow," I said. "Holy shit. No ways. Holy fucking shit."

"Yeah. Well." Luke folded his arms in satisfaction. "I wanted to surprise the both of you." He winked at me and leaned in. "Between you and me, this ain't just about kiddo's birthday. I wanted to thank you guys. Ai Chang and I wouldn't be where we are without you. So, thanks." He gently slapped the side of my face. "Grazie dal più profondo del cuore—from the bottom of my heart." He clapped a hand over his chest. "I mean it."

We stepped aside as hotel staff passed through the lobby bearing a cake in the shape of a unicycle crowned with sparklers.

I didn't know what to say. There was still so much about this man Luke Moretti that I didn't know, that David himself was just beginning to learn. But what I knew already was what mattered most. David and I weren't married yet, not by a long shot. But for the first time in my life, I realized that I had a brother-in-law, and that David's family had become my own.

CHAPTER FIVE

The First Day of Spring

On the first day of spring, David and I met our old friends Charles and Megan at the Madison Avenue Pub. The place was, in fact, three Victorian mansions in one—forming a single labyrinthine warren of bars and billiard rooms, patios, a dance floor and even a piano lounge. We'd arrived early enough to avoid its notorious frat boy crowds. Years ago, Karen and I regularly got tanked at the Maddy. I recalled having one too many Jägerbombs and throwing up in a busted washroom stall while Karen guarded the door. Good times. Those days, I hoped, were long behind me.

Charles was a U of T postdoc who would sometimes meet his own students at the Maddy over poutine and pints. Karen had become friends with his fiancée our first year in Toronto. Back then, Megan was a mousy and nervous girl, perpetually distracted and disorganized. But the couple had undergone a lifestyle makeover and were now athletic and coiffed. Tonight, Megan wore a black-and-white polka-dot blouse with a scarlet choker. Charles looked dapper in his cardigan and Oxford shirt. "One day," Megan said, "Charles is going to be Professor Ondaatje. I'm so proud of him. Poopsie, you know I'm proud of you, don't you?"

"Thank you, sweetie," Charles said, sitting straight-backed in our booth, nursing his Guinness. "I'm very proud of you too."

Megan hiccoughed. "Last weekend," she explained, "my mentor helped me host my first munch. I had all these icebreakers and activities prepared. I think people enjoyed themselves."

"It was a grand success," Charles said.

I poked at my iceberg salad, observing a waiter walk by with a plate of thick-cut, golden fries and spicy aioli sauce. "What's a munch?"

"It's a social," Megan said, "a kind of meet-up."

"To discuss shared interests," Charles said, "for people who enjoy BDSM."

David blinked. "Awesome."

Charles and Megan let us know they'd recently attended an adult goods trade show called Sexapalooza. It took me a second to fully grasp what they meant. "It was highly educational," Charles said. "Megan and I met some lovely people. The ambiance was quite welcoming."

Megan squeezed his arm. "I bought myself two pairs of crotchless pegging panties. One in pink and another in black satin."

David coughed. "Wow."

Megan nodded vigorously, sipping from her cherry sour. "There was a two-for-one special."

Apparently, there had also been tutorials and demos on burlesque and pole dancing, body art, and kink for couples. All sorts of experts and vendors offered up advice on tools and toys to spice things up in the boudoir.

"Now," Megan said, 'Charles and I practice our Kegels every day. It's important I keep my vagina tight."

"And that I have greater control," Charles said, "over my ejaculations."

"Great sex," Megan said, "is what, poopsie?"

Charles kissed her on the nose. "A cooperative endeavour."

A "dungeon" on site required participants to sign a waiver before entering. There was even a museum showcasing the history of human sexuality: the origins of porn, vintage lingerie and some truly weird sex laws. "Did you know," Megan said, "it's illegal in Minnesota for a husband to make love to his wife if his breath smells like garlic or sardines?"

David and I both shook our heads.

'Which is why," Charles said, cutting into his bone-shaker BBQ ribs, "I always use breath mints."

"We even attended a workshop," Megan said. "It was on The Art of Kissing by a doctor from Singapore. She asked us to describe the best kiss we ever had. Honestly, I didn't know how complex a good kiss could be!

"Oh, we also got you boys a little something." Megan rummaged in her red crocodile purse and thrust out two tiny jars. "Nipple Nibblers! Tingle Strawberry Twist and Luscious Watermelon. You can order them off Amazon but we got them wholesale."

"Um, thanks ..." David said.

"It's like lip balm," Charles explained.

"But for nipples." Megan's nose scrunched up in delight. "They're tingly and they're tasty."

"It's the menthol." Charles set down his fork and drew circles with his index finger over one nipple through his cardigan. "It also acts as a weak kappa opioid receptor agonist."

"Why of course it does," David said. "It's just a tingly, tasty treat."

I kicked his foot under the table.

"Those two are my favourite flavours. You can also use them," Megan whispered, "on your naughty bits."

"She means," Charles said, "your erogenous zones."

I pushed my salad away. The croutons were soggy. "We know what naughty bits are, Charles."

"And," Megan said, "they're vegan and cruelty-free."

David squinted at the fine print on his jar. "If they're cruelty-free, can you still use them in BDSM?"

Megan stared at David blankly before Charles burst into laughter. When Charles laughed, it was like a Great Dane trying to cough up a hair ball. To think I used to date him. As far as Charles was concerned, I'd introduced him to Megan. Now they'd been engaged for two years and I'd agreed to be his best man when the time came.

"Well, thanks," I said. "It's nice of you to think of us."

"We bought ourselves some bondage bed sheets," Charles said. "They're quite well-fitted. We're looking forward to testing them." He turned to Megan. "Now may I go to the washroom?"

"Yes you may, sweetie."

Later, on the streetcar ride home, David asked: "So are those two still seeing other people?"

"If you mean are they still experimenting with other couples," I said, "then yeah. They've been going to play parties for a while now."

"You mean sex parties?"

"I'm not sure Charles and Megan would call them that. But sure. The BDSM community means a lot to them. It's really changed their lives."

"Rebecca's friend hosts sex parties."

"Who?"

"Amanda, from Naked Boys Reading. She owns a nightclub on Church Street. She hosts all sorts of themed events. Would you ever be interested in going?'"

I glanced around but there were only two teenagers making out in the back. "Um, I dunno."

David poked me. "It'd be fun to check out."

"I'd be afraid to bump into Rebecca and Professor Frederic."

"C'mon, I'm serious."

"I'm serious too. I like my privacy. I like to be discreet."

"Daniel, you've been to bathhouses, and you've been to some pretty wild parties from what I've heard. You've had all sorts of threesomes with Marcus. That's more than I've ever done."

"You and I," I said, 'had sex with Gee."

"That happened once. That's was hot though, wasn't it? Gee's a nice guy. We should invite him over again."

Gee was a nice guy. He was also stage manager for Marcus. Since we first met, David had spoken often about opening up our relationship. Hooking up with Gee last year had been a milestone. And yes, it had been hot. But I'd always imagined that our default was still monogamy.

"Maybe."

"And Goodhandy's?"

"What?"

"That's the name of Amanda's club."

Now the two teenagers were giggling and whispering in each other's ears. One of them glanced our way. "Can we talk about this later?"

"Sure."

I sank down in my seat, gazing out the window. The city lights flashed and faded, slipping past. The truth was I'd been to Goodhandy's, more than once. The first time had been with Parker for a fundraising event. The last time had been with Marcus and Fang. Over the years, my time spent in bars and clubs had become one blurry (and frankly messy) montage. Marcus was always experimenting like a kid with a chemistry set. Sometimes our role-plays got elaborate. Most of the time, I'd felt like a voyeur. Marcus and Fang liked to put on a show. None of it looked comfortable. Some of it looked downright painful. But I supposed that was the point.

"Hey, it's not like a sex party is on my bucket list," David said. "You're my porn star, and that's what counts." He gave me an affectionate squeeze. "You, Daniel Garneau, are my main event."

Crossing the roundabout of Spadina Crescent, we got off at the edge of Chinatown. Even at this late hour, we could spot diners enjoying dim sum and dumplings. The El Mocambo's giant neon palm tree flickered and buzzed.

David nudged my arm. "Hey, what did Megan mean when she said she had a 'mentor'?"

"I don't know. You'll have to ask her."

"They seem like a happy couple."

"They are. They're good for each other."

David turned to me. "And are we good for each other?"

"What sort of a question is that?"

"I know you're good for me," David said. "You keep me grounded. And I love just being with you. But. I dunno. Sometimes I think you put up with me, like I stress you out sometimes."

"What? No, David." I was completely taken aback. "Why would you think that? I mean, no relationship's perfect. Karen says we're good together."

"But Daniel, what do you think?"

We stopped in front of Free Times Cafe. Crusted, dirty snow banks edged the sidewalks and storefronts. Across the street, a sculpture on a pole featured a bright yellow kitchen chair bearing the blue planet Earth. Farther down the block, the Bellevue Fire Station clock tower rose like a beacon against an orange-pink twilight sky.

"I know I don't say 'I love you' as often as I could." I reached out and pulled David's jacket zipper up and adjusted his collar. "But I do. I love you, David. It took me a while to wrap my head around the whole sperm donor thing. But now I'm glad it's happening. You're doing something really important for Luke and Ai Chang. Their lives are going to change forever. And we're going to be uncles. That's exciting, right? Life just moves fast sometime, and it's hard to keep up. These last few years I feel like I've just been digging myself further and further into debt. But I finish school this summer, and after that I can actually start making some money. Things are going to change this year. Our friends and family are good. Grandpa's remarried. Your mom's opened her own art gallery. You love your job, right? Life is good. We're good."

"Daniel, I manage a bike store. You are going to be a doctor. That doesn't bother you?"

Now I was genuinely shocked. "Are you kidding me? Of course not! Look, I might be the first person in my family to get a university degree. But me and my brothers, we grew up working in a sawmill. Our grandpa spent his life as a contractor, building homes for other people. I have more respect for him than anyone in the world. David, I love that you love working with your hands. And you're one of the smartest people I know. You're fun to be around. You keep my chin up. You're a fantastic cook. And you're totally awesome in bed. You're the best thing that's ever happened to me."

David's face tightened. "I've never heard you say that before."

"Well, it's true."

"How awesome am I?"

"What?"

"In bed. I mean, is there anything more or different you want me to do? Or that, you know, you want us to do?"

"You mean when it comes to sex?"

"Yeah." David kicked a pop can out into the street. "Talking about sex is important. Charles and Megan talk about it all the time."

"We talk about sex."

"Yeah, and so I'm just like, checking in, because I think you're an amazing lover. I just want to make sure I am too."

"Okay. Listen. David." I planted my feet. "You are awesome. I think you're incredibly sexy. I love touching your naked body. I love the way you kiss. I love the smell of you. You've got the most perfect, beautiful ass. I love how your toes curl when you come. And just spooning you in bed, well, it's the best feeling in the world."

"Better than chocolate milk?"

I nodded.

"Better than lasagna?"

"Mm-hm."

"Better than Creamsicles?"

I looked skyward. "I'd say you're tied with Creamsicles."

"Wow."

I nodded. "Yeah."

"Okay." He opened his arms and I hugged him. I realized he was crying again. David was crying a lot these days.

"And one more thing," I said. "We are going to get married, okay? I guess I haven't talked about it, but I've been thinking about us a lot lately. We're going to do this, David Gallucci. We're going to spend the rest of our lives together, you and me. You're my somebody to love. You're the love of my life."

David's voice was muffled, his face buried in my shoulder.

"What did you say?" I asked.

"You just quoted two songs by Queen."

"I did?"

"You really are gay, aren't you?"

"I try."

David wiped away his tears, and kissed me. "It's good enough for me."

⌒ Marcus never liked kissing.

Not normally. And never when we were in public. On

some occasions, when we were together, he might lean over and press his lips against the top of my head like I was a beloved and cherished pet.

Maybe it was a Pretty Woman thing.

Who cared.

But David knew how to kiss. David loved to kiss. When he kissed me, he kissed with his whole body. Whether it was a peck on the cheek or a make-out session in the shower, David paid attention.

Over dinner at the Madison, Megan had asked us to describe the best kiss we ever had. Then David told the story of the first time we met. It was my twenty-first birthday at the Kathedral on Queen West. Pat had introduced us. David always said that first kiss sealed the deal for him and that he knew instantly I was the one. He loved to tell this story, and I let him do the talking. After that, the conversation moved on to other topics.

But the truth was, the very best kiss I'd ever had wasn't with David. He was in my arms at the time. It just so happened to take place the night we took Gee home with us.

Gee was short for Ghazwan Al Numan. He was a stage manager and theatre artist who had won a Dora Award for Outstanding Set Design for Marcus' show *Philophobia*. When he and Marcus were working, I barely registered even in their peripheral vision. Watching them together, one might even wonder if they'd been lovers themselves. But Gee told me they never were. They'd first met in one of Professor Frederic's classes, debating the difference between pornography and art. Gee had worked on all of Marcus' stage projects in Toronto. They were like Bernie Taupin and Elton John.

Gee was one of those tall people who stooped, not because he was ashamed of his height, but because he really paid attention. He had a habit of watching your mouth when he listened, and looking you straight in the eye when he spoke. His own eyes were thick-lashed, round and dark, and his own mouth seemed to be always slightly parted, like he was in permanent awe of the world. Gee spent most days working as a produce manager at Loblaws. Once he opened a crate of bananas and a tarantula (*Acanthoscurria geniculata*) crawled out. He scooped it up in a Tupperware box, named it Josephine, took it home and nursed it back to health. (In hindsight, I realized even he knew who Josephine Baker was.) His real passion was for the theatre.

I suppose I never noticed him because my eyes were always on Marcus. I know that was unfair and unkind of me. It was also my loss. Gee was a handsome man, just not in any conventional way. Inevitably, the moment came when I did look twice. Apparently, he'd noticed both David and me from the get go. It wasn't hard to convince him to come home with us.

It turned out that Gee was more than a competent lover. I wondered if all stage managers were so skilled, accustomed as they were to caretaking for everyone's needs. The first thing he asked was our HIV status. He let us know he was positive but undetectable, but that what he really wanted was to watch. So that night David stood with one leg up on the arm of our couch while I barebacked him from behind.

Charles once told me how the term "bareback" was first used by G.I.s during the Vietnam War. Most of them were even younger than we were, many of them conscripted. I tried to imagine what it must have been like in the jungles at night, so far from home, surrounded by the Viet Cong. I imagined these soldiers bruised and beaten, taken captive, stripped naked except for their dog tags and combat boots. I wondered what those boys used for lube.

David arched his torso and came first, red-faced and grimacing like he'd been shot. A moment later, Gee rose from the couch and French kissed me, filling my mouth with David's cum. After that, I felt the familiar, prickling heat flushing up the inside of my legs. My own climax was explosive as I gripped David's hip, one arm around his chest. It carried on and on, seemingly without end. As I crushed David to me, Gee kept his mouth locked to mine. Along the way, Gee's own ejaculate hit my thigh and he bruised my tongue without meaning to. Finally, it was over. For one long moment, the three of us clung to each other in a sweaty embrace, reining in our breath.

The strange thought overcame me, in that moment, that we were as strong as we could be. We were not lost. We knew what truth and freedom meant. And I knew, with a profound and deep-seated certainty, that there was no reason why, as long as we had each other, even in the darkest chaos of the world, we should ever want to die.

And that (until then) was the best kiss I ever had in my entire life.

〜 Sunday night Skype date with Karen.

We'd agreed on Screamin' Brothers Orange Pineapple. It was smooth and flavourful, scoring a respectable three out of five. I sat back with my bare feet propped up on our steamer trunk. Behind the couch, David unplugged his iron and waved. "Hi, Karen."

Karen waved back. "Hey David."

I fed him a spoonful of Screamin' Brothers. "Is that low fat?" he asked, licking his lips.

"It's actually zero fat. It's non-dairy."

"Yeah." He made a face. "I didn't think that was real ice cream."

"Look." I sighed. "It's me trying to lose some weight, alright?"

David peered into my laptop screen. "Karen, I'm surprised you're going along with this."

"Hey." Karen shrugged. "I'm a team player." She was sitting on her back deck in a hoodie and ski pants. Ice and snow still covered the branches of the tall pines behind her.

"You know," David said, sampling another bite, "it's actually not bad. Does this mean you're including gelatos and sherbets now?"

"Don't forget sorbets," Karen said.

David raised his chin. "A sorbet at the salon."

"Or frozen yogurts."

"I have absolutely no idea," I said, "what the difference is between any of those."

David straightened. "Well, an ice cream is an emulsion of dairy and at least ten percent butterfat, which is then whipped and frozen. A gelato, on the other hand—"

"And," I said, "I don't need to know. I'm just happy to be the doofus on the couch who eats this stuff."

"And are all Italians foodies?" Karen asked.

"Hey." David puffed out his chest. "We cook for more sex. What can I say? It's a prerequisite to master at least three recipes to lead a lover to your bed."

"So, you've been seducing Daniel with food all this time?"

"That," I said, "explains a lot."

"Everyone loves a foodie, Daniel." Karen pointed with her spoon. "A man who knows his way around a kitchen is sexy."

"Then what do you call a man who reads and also cooks?"

"My future husband."

"I read," David said, draping himself over me.

I laughed. "Comic books!"

David stuck his tongue in my ear. "If there was ever was a Naked Boys Cooking salon, I'd sign up for that."

"Cooking naked is fun," Karen said. "But wear an apron. Frying up bacon is a liability."

"Has anyone," I asked, "ever tried combining bacon and ice cream?"

"Oh my God." David clapped me on both shoulders. "I'm on it! Karen, this summer, when you move to Toronto, I'll whip you up some homemade bacon ice cream Gallucci-style."

"There's such a thing?" I looked back at him.

"There will be after I'm done."

Karen made a gang sign. "Whip it, Gallucci."

David crossed his arms. "I'll whip yo ass, K-Dawg." After that, he helped himself to another spoonful of Screamin' Brothers, kissed my laptop's camera and went to put away my shirts.

I pulled out a napkin and wiped down the lens.

"Speaking of the summer," Karen said, "I have a job interview next week. There's a teaching position coming up at the First Nations School of Toronto."

"Karen." I sat up. "That's amazing. Congratulations."

"I know, eh? But don't congratulate me yet. It's only an interview and it's just a summer contract. Can I stay at your place?"

"As long as you want."

"It might be a week. I've been talking with Anne. She's done living in a co-op. We're going to look for an apartment."

"You and Anne are moving in together?"

"Yeah, and …?"

"You two fight, like all the time."

"Anne and I bicker." Karen said. "There's a difference. Anyway, my little sis is all grown up. We're two adults now. We'll make it work."

Karen's sister was now two years into her studies at the Ontario College of Art and Design. She and David had become fast friends, sharing interests in graffiti and skate culture. Last year, the two hit up Comicon and David had even hired Anne to work part-time in his store.

"Did you know," Karen said, "I've moved five times in the last five years? I just want a place where I can finally settle."

"Karen, this summer, it's going to be a whole fresh start."

"You promise?"

"For the both of us."

"You've got what, one month of school left?"

"I'm taking my transition-to-residency course as we speak."

"And then you," Karen said, "will be Doctor Garneau."

"And then," I said, "it'll on to the real world, and doing real work."

"Four years of med school. That's a huge accomplishment."

"Thanks. David's been really patient and supportive."

Strolling past with a toothbrush in his mouth, David pulled down his sweatpants and underwear, and wagged his penis before moving on.

"I'm sorry I missed his birthday last month. Megan said it was really special."

"Yeah. Luke went all out. He got Three Dog Run and all of our friends in on the surprise. He's a good guy. I'm looking forward to you meeting him and Ai Chang."

"I've met Luke already," Karen said, "over the phone. He called to invite me down."

"Luke called you?"

"Yeah. We talked for a while."

"What did he have to say? What did you say?"

"Daniel, relax. I got your back. Mainly, he said he could see for himself how happy David is with you."

"He said that?"

"Yes, he did."

"Okay." Karen always knew just how to reassure me. "I'm sorry you couldn't make it." I hugged a pillow. "And how did the pow wow go this year?"

'It was great. It's a lot of work, but I love helping out. People come together from all over. It's where I feel I can belong. I get to see a lot of relatives and friends. I have four cousins from the Soo. They grew up sitting through Mass in three different languages: French, English and

Ojibway. This year, my mom also came up to volunteer. She says hi, by the way. She misses you boys."

"Liam's still in Sudbury."

"And that," Karen said, "is why I need to leave. I just don't think either one of us can move on while the other one's around, you know?"

Now I fell silent. Part of me wanted nothing more than to see Karen and Liam get back together again.

"So." Karen cocked her head. "Any updates on Ai Chang?"

I sat up cross-legged on the couch. "For a while, the morning sickness got pretty bad. Her parents took her to this Chinese herbalist. They got her drinking all this ginger tea. It seems to be helping. She was also told to sleep with a knife under her bed."

"Pardon me?"

"To keep away evil spirits. When you're pregnant, you're also not supposed to gossip, or lose your temper, or laugh too loud, or eat foods that are too hot or too cold. I forget all the rest. There's a lot."

"That is a lot."

"Luke and Ai Chang are handling it pretty well."

"And how are you handling it?"

"Me? I'm good. I mean, we're good. David and me, we're looking forward to being uncles."

"I'm dashu!" David shouted. He stuck his head out the washroom with a towel around his waist. "And Daniel's xiao-shushu!"

"What?"

"I'll explain later." I pulled the laptop closer. "So look, Karen. I know northern Ontario means a lot to you. But you've also got family and friends here in Toronto. You can belong here too. I've told everyone about you. Everyone's looking forward to meeting you."

"Megan says Three Dog Run has a new singer?"

"That would be Nadia."

"Is this the same Nadia who's also Pat's new girlfriend?"

"You'll like her."

"And Marcus, is he still their band manager?"

I crossed my arms. "Yeah."

"I thought Marcus was in Montreal."

"He is. It's a winter residency. He'll be back this spring. So look, Karen, when are you moving back?"

"It'll have to be the start of May. Anne needs to be out of her co-op by then."

"May? Karen." I sat up. "That's like in a month."

"I know, eh? Ready or not, here I come. If I don't get this job, I figure I can always bartend or wait on tables this summer."

"Look. I mean. Karen, should I come up and help you pack?"

"Liam will help. And so will Bob."

"Bob? Oh, okay. Are you sure?"

"Yes, Daniel. I'm sure."

Bob Panamick, father of two, tackle shop owner and fishing guide, was Karen's ex on Manitoulin. He was a giant of a man who'd lost an eye after being mauled by a bear, and who owned a dog the size of a full-grown wolf. Bob was a man who also read books about art and spirituality and nature. In the kitchen, banana chocolate chip pancakes were his specialty.

"Bob and Elsie," Karen said, "had me over for dinner

last weekend. It was really nice. The girls, they call me Auntie."

I wanted to ask; and what does Bob call you? I'd never known Karen happier than when she was with Bob. The man had been separated three years before they met. It'd got serious enough for Karen to move in with him and his two daughters. For one brief moment in their lives, she was packing lunches every day and dropping the girls off at school. Bob even had the two enrolled in Karen's after-school program.

Then Bob and his wife Elsie decided to get back together.

Karen didn't deserve that kind of heartbreak. But Karen Fobister was also one of the strongest and kindest people I knew. Apparently, she and Elsie were now friends. There also came a moment when Karen found out she was pregnant and wasn't sure if the father was Bob or Liam. Karen had left Toronto for Manitoulin for a simpler life. But real life, it seemed, always had a way of hunting you down and kicking you in the ass. At the abortion clinic in Sudbury, I'd held Karen's hand and pretended I was the father.

"Well," I said, "don't forget to pack your skates."

"I won't."

"We can rustle up a game of pick-up this winter."

"Daniel." Karen pulled her hood up over her head. "When I come down next week, I'm going to be super busy with my interview and apartment hunting and you'll be studying. But can we make room for some one-on-one time?"

"I think we can schedule that in."

Karen peered at me. "Maybe we can head out for some Jägerbombs and sweet potato fries?"

"With spicy mayo?"

"And Creamsicles."

"Now we're really going balls out. You buyin' there, Karen Fobister?"

Karen's dimples showed. "Yes, I'm buyin', Daniel Garneau."

"Alrighty then. I'm in."

CHAPTER SIX

As Makeshift as We Are

When Karen and Anne were seven and four years old, their father shot their mother dead.

The defense attorney claimed it was an accident. The crown prosecutor argued a different case. While their parents had shouted in the kitchen, the two girls hid upstairs. I knew this story because I overheard my own parents talking about it late one night. Our neighbour Mrs. Milton was a cousin to the deceased. In the end, the incident was ruled manslaughter. "Slaughter" was such an awful word. It was something a crazy person like Vlad the Impaler did with a two-handed sword in a lightning storm, or Rambo with an M60 machinegun. This was a single stray bullet in the quiet spring countryside. The apple trees were just beginning to blossom. Baby ducklings paddled on the lake.

It had been a horrific accident. Karen had also said her father was the kindest, most gentle person in the world. I'm pretty sure it was her testimony that got the second degree murder charge dropped. Still, kids should never have to testify about these kinds of things.

The day the Miltons adopted Karen and Anne, we were all at the court ceremony: Mom and Dad, Grandpa and Grandma. The judge reminded everyone how the two girls were chosen and beloved. That afternoon, sunshine flooded the cornfield as guests showed up with potato salads and casseroles. Dad brought over his banjo and Mr. Milton took out his saxophone. The world, it seemed, was just busting with life and not to be denied.

A moment came when us kids retreated across the street back to our pirate ship treehouse. I'd packed cheese and veggies; Karen had scored a whole six-pack of fruit juice boxes; Liam contributed a fistful of barbecued wieners in a greasy napkin. Anne insisted on climbing the rope ladder by herself, clutching her giraffe.

Pat had smuggled out a beer.

We all stared at it like he'd just produced Aladdin's lamp or the Ark of the Covenant.

Pat had forgotten a bottle opener but Liam snicked one out of his pocket knife. Pat knelt, tucking his hair behind his ears, his jaw set. When the cap popped off, we all jumped. But no big blue genie burst forth and nobody's face melted off.

Munching on a baby carrot, it was Anne who pointed out that the cap had fallen over the edge of the deck.

The five of us lay on our stomachs, staring down into the grass far below. The cap was silver with a red maple leaf, and shone bright in the clover as a fresh-minted dime.

Of course, one of us would have to retrieve it.

Before we could decide who would go, Grandpa appeared around the house and marched over to us. His steely chest hair poked out the top of his Hawaiian shirt.

He yanked on the rope that rang our pirate bell to announce his arrival. "Hey Musketeers," he said. "Ça va?"

We were five raccoons caught up in a tree.

"Yeah, everything's great, Grandpa!" Pat shouted.

Grandpa squinted hard.

He took a swig from his own beer bottle.

I held my breath, my knuckles white. Any second, he'd look down and spot the silver cap by his foot.

This was a man who'd served in the Battle of the Atlantic. His hands were scarred and his big forearms patched with tattoos. He was treasurer of the League of Merchant Mariner Veterans of Canada and of the Club Amical du Nouveau-Sudbury. Three centuries ago, a man like this would've been a pirate captain skewering sailors with his cutlass on the bloody high seas.

But we lived in a civil society. Here was when the adult would call us out. With whimsical wisdom and stern kindness, Grandpa would confiscate what we'd stolen and save us from the debacle of our alcoholic depravity. And, in a consummate act of conspiratorial generosity, he'd keep the whole incident secret from our parents.

Because that was what grandpas did.

"Well." He burped. "You forgot dessert." With the accuracy of a marksman, one after the other, he tossed up five Vachon cakes.

"Jos Louis!" Pat exclaimed. "Gee, thanks Grandpa!"

After that, he saluted us and sauntered away. We heard him rummaging in the garage, and then spotted him heading back to the party with a weed whacker over his shoulder.

We exhaled a collective sigh of relief.

The way to hell now was clear.

Karen climbed down the ladder and recovered the beer cap. Anne, to her credit, was content sipping on a juice box.

Pat took the first swig.

"Not bad," he said, smacking his lips.

Then it was my turn.

The beer was lukewarm and, frankly, disgusting. (Exactly how long had it been stuffed down Pat's pants?) If I had to imagine what piss tasted like, then here it was in a brown bottle to go. Karen also made a face, noting it didn't taste like root beer at all. Nor should it have, Liam pointed out.

We passed it around until the bottle was empty.

Karen made Anne promise not to tell a soul. In exchange, she'd have honourary membership (without voting rights) in our pirate ship clubhouse. We did agree to swear in her giraffe as our official mascot.

After that, we finished our snacks and returned to the party. Nothing awful happened that afternoon. Grandma regaled the guests with naughty limericks she'd make up on the spot. Mom and Dad slow-danced in the greenhouse when they didn't think anyone was looking. At one point, Mrs. Milton brought out a cake and trays of watermelon, Mr. Milton made a speech. There was bubbly for the adults and Canada Dry for the kids.

Memories are fluid, like the fractured images in a kaleidoscope, fragments fanning and fusing, revelatory flashes of clarity and meaning.

A moment came that day when a dragonfly landed on Liam. We were all still up in our tree house, basking in the success of adventure and mischief managed. The canopy of leaves protected us; the sky beyond sang a pure electric blue. The dragonfly, when it landed, looked like it was made from pure gold. "Make a wish," Liam said. "Make a wish."

We all knew Liam was our animal whisperer. Songbirds would perch on his head and frogs hop into his hand. As we crowded close, the dragonfly clung to his scraped knee, iridescent and quivering.

We each made a silent wish.

And as if on cue, the dragonfly rose, hovered for a second, then spun away.

That same summer, my wish came true.

In the last, balmy days of August, Mom and Dad got married. The ceremony took place in our own backyard. Our parents rented a red-and-white striped party tent. Mrs. Milton repurposed an old pair of oven mitts so I could be Lobster Boy. Liam dressed up as The Strong Man and Pat was a hobo clown. Anne insisted on being The Dog-Faced Girl. Karen wrapped a towel around her head and gave Tarot-readings to anyone who asked. Mr. Milton officiated as a ringmaster. Mom wore wildflowers in her hair and Dad a peacock feather in his hat. They exchanged gold rings beneath our two-hundred-year-old maple tree, while Liam scattered rose petals down from above.

It was the most beautiful, magical moment of my life.

Over time, we might forget what people say, or even what they do. But long after they're gone, we'll always remember how they made us feel. Our first great love, our first great grief. Of course Mom and Dad would have wanted a carnival-themed wedding. Life was a Big Top for them. It was a never-ending party.

At least until it ended.

When Grandpa was twenty-one, he built a cottage deep in the forest. He built it for Grandma, the love of his life. He built it with his best, most trusted friend in the world. They christened it the Good Medicine Cabin. Years later, he built for his grandkids our pirate ship treehouse. At bedtime he'd read to us about the Fox and the Little Prince. He taught us boys how to bait a hook and how to strike a camp so we didn't leave a trace. When Mom couldn't find the first-aid kit, he always knew where it was kept. It was Grandpa who took the time to remove the training wheels from our bikes. Years later, he'd pay for the bus ticket for my boyfriend to come up to Sudbury on Christmas Eve.

He taught us how to find the North Star in the sky.

I'd never properly come out to this man. He simply acted like he always knew. Sometimes what's most important is what we leave unsaid. And if he ever spotted a beer cap in the leaves of grass, Grandpa trusted us kids not to fall into ruin. He trusted that a house in the trees was a place where hearts might grow. He trusted us in our wildness. And he trusted that such moments were ephemeral, that they would shape us the rest of our lives, and that they would never, ever come again.

"What is essential," the Fox said, "is invisible to the eye."

⌒ Early in April, in her battered SUV, Karen drove down to Toronto for her job interview and to find an apartment with her sister Anne. She left Manitoulin before dawn and arrived on our doorstep by noon. The last time I'd seen Karen was at Christmas. This spring, she looked fit in low-rise jeans and a snug Buffy Sainte-Marie tee that showed off her midriff. Her hair was pinned up, and she wore a ball cap with the Ontario Trails logo on the front. She'd brought suitcases and boxes, her books and CDs. I'd store them for her until she moved down in May.

David was at work but I'd tidied the loft and prepared Karen's favourite: Philly steak sandwiches with blue cheese, and tomato soup. I'd also recently bought a used blender off Kijiji and proudly served up smoothies. (The way Karen's old friend Derrick used to make them.) The sunshine poured through our skylight, sparking dust motes in the air.

After lunch, I sat with a coffee as Karen unpacked. "Here." She handed me a mason jar labelled in Mrs. Milton's flowery handwriting: rhubarb strawberry. Last Christmas it had been apple jam.

"Thanks." I turned the jar over in my hands. "So how are your parents doing?"

"Busier than ever, now that they're both retired. They go bowling with your grandpa and Betty every Thursday at Whitewater Lanes. The four of them are planning a road trip this summer."

I looked up. "A road trip?"

"You know," Karen said, "your grandpa and Betty just bought a Winnebago, right?"

"No." I set down the mason jar. "I didn't know that."

"They've got their eye on the Cabot Trail."

"They're driving all the way to Nova Scotia?"

"That's why it's called a road trip."

I reminded myself Karen's parents were seasoned RVers. The road was their home away from home. The Miltons had been regular bloggers on *Campendium* for years. Grandpa and Betty were in good hands. It was time I stopped feeling responsible for everyone's lives.

"Their first stop will be the Blue Mountains," Karen said. "They're going to go zip-lining and tree-top trekking."

"Are you kidding?"

"When I'm retired," Karen said, "I want to have as much fun. Listen, Liam's coming down the first weekend of May."

"But Liam hates the city."

"He coming down with Joan. There's this event called Paddle the Don." Karen pulled her T-shirt off over her head. "They're bringing their canoes. They've invited us to join them, and David and Anne."

"I thought Liam and Joan broke up."

"They did." Karen sniffed at her shirt and tossed it into her suitcase. "Now they're back together."

"Whoa, wait. Hold on," I said. "I have my board exam that weekend. You and Anne haven't even found an apartment yet."

"Daniel, we will have moved in by then. It's just one afternoon." Karen applied deodorant under each arm. "It's the first Sunday of May. When's your exam?"

"Saturday."

"That's perfect then! You'll be done school. It'll be like a celebration. How often does Liam come to Toronto, anyway? And you'll get to meet Joan. She's very nice."

"She's a police officer."

"So she's a very nice person with a gun."

"I thought Joan wasn't a fan of the gays."

"Yeah, well. Her family, they own a lot of land around Ramsey Lake. First settlers, big church-goers—God, Queen, and Country. But Joan's different. She's trying hard and she's come a long way. I know that she's really looking forward to meeting you and David."

"I'm not sure how I feel about this."

"Just be yourself."

"Should I tell her how we shoplifted all that hair dye for Halloween?"

"She's a detective constable, not a priest."

"Karen, I'm joking."

"Really?"

"Okay. Maybe I still feel bad we did that."

"Oh my god, Daniel. That was like in grade ten." Karen held up a blouse. "Get over it. Does this need ironing?"

"No, it's fine. David gets really nervous around police."

"And why is that?"

"C'mon, Karen. Why does anyone?"

"Joan's coming to paddle the Don River with Liam. She's not coming to read you your rights."

"I don't think David's ever been in a canoe."

"So he can go with Liam and Joan. And you can ride with me and Anne. Will you two boys be okay if we break up the set?"

"We'll do our best."

Karen pulled on her blouse. "Bob and Elsie are also coming down with the girls."

"What?"

"Daniel, it's okay. Relax. I'm good with this."

"Are you?"

"Look, I was the one who invited them." Karen let down her hair and brushed it out. "They've always wanted to do Paddle the Don."

"And what about you?"

"What about me?" Karen shrugged, pins in her mouth. "It's been six months. I've moved on. I'm moving on. Listen. Bob's girls and I really bonded. I'm not just going to turn my back and walk out of their lives."

"You were also their teacher."

"I was, yes, in my afterschool program."

"That's complicated."

Karen drew a breath. "It doesn't have to be."

"You've said that before."

"Daniel. I'm really trying, here."

"I'm sorry."

"They're Bob and Elsie's daughters. They're not mine, okay? Did you need to hear me say that?"

"Karen."

She tied back her hair in a ponytail. "Don't give me a hard time."

"Okay, I said I'm sorry already. Zephyr and Sky, right? How old are they now?"

"Eleven and nine. Zephyr just finished this class project on the Toronto watersheds. She made a whole topographic model out of papier-mâché. I got Sky a waterproof camera for her birthday. She's super excited to make a photo journal of the whole trip. Those two know how to handle a kayak better than most adults I know."

"They sound like great kids."

Karen cleared the table. "I know what you're thinking."

"What?"

"That they're just like me and Anne when we were little."

I rinsed out the coffee pot. "I wasn't thinking that."

"Are you sure?"

"Okay. Maybe just a little." I put on David's kitchen apron. "I mean, who wouldn't?"

For once Karen was quiet, her hands on her hips. She reached out and poked me in the chest. "Please don't give me a hard time about this."

I lowered my gaze. "Karen."

"I mean it."

Karen knew me better than anyone in the world but the reverse was also true. I leaned back against the counter. "Come here." I opened my arms.

She stepped into my hug. I rested my chin on top of her head. After a moment, she said: "It is complicated, isn't it?"

"It always is."

"Moving to Toronto will help."

"Yes it will."

"Maybe," Karen said, "I should've moved to Nunavut."

"The hell you should've."

"Wish me luck?"

I wasn't sure if Karen was referring to her job interview, her apartment hunt, or managing her post-breakup relationships with Liam and Bob. All I knew was that it felt good to just hold her in my arms again. "I love you, Karen Fobister."

"I know," she said. "I love you too."

"Good luck."

⌒ At her job interview with the First Nations School, Karen was offered a summer teaching contract on the spot. "I had some good references," she said later. "Also, it turned out, the principal's from Sheshegwaning First Nation. We spent more time talking about the salmon stocks on Manitoulin than teaching. Now, Anne and I just need to find an apartment."

We picked through fruit and vegetable stalls in Kensington Market. The late-afternoon sky threatened rain. Shoppers hurried along the narrow lanes, foraging for Jamaican goods and Middle Eastern foods. Cyclists skirted rumbling delivery trucks.

"You've been at this for a week. Nothing's worked out?"

Karen shook her head. "I was just hoping we'd find something while I was still here, you know?"

The aroma of spices, fish, and fresh-baked pastries mingled on the breeze. Somewhere down the block, a radio played the latest bhangra hit. Karen had insisted on making dinner tonight, bannock and shishkabobs.

"Karen," I said, "are you sure you have to go back tomorrow?"

"I'm sure."

"Anne will find something. You've still got three weeks."

"I hope so."

Seagulls wheeled beneath the low, scudding clouds. Rain drummed an uneven rhythm on the storefront awning. "Hey." I handed Karen a bag of peppers. "At least you got the job."

"I did." Karen surveyed the bustle of Baldwin Street. "Maybe I could still also bartend part-time this summer. It'll be fun."

"Well, we are celebrating." I grabbed her hand. "C'mon."

In search of wooden skewers, we ended up at the Tap Phong Trading Co. Housewares and gleaming restaurant supplies crowded its narrow aisles. Faux Ming vases, rice cookers and racks of bamboo steamers cluttered the back. Karen examined a taiyaki grill. "David's wondering," she said, "if the two of you are going to get engagement rings."

"What?"

"He said you proposed to him a couple weeks ago."

"Proposed to him?" I blinked, taken aback. "What, no. I mean, I just said we were going to get married. He's been asking about it for years."

"And you've never agreed to it before."

"I've never disagreed."

"Well, it was a big deal for him. He was really excited to tell me." Karen turned a corner. "Whatever you said meant a lot."

Red paper lanterns slowly twirled. I thought back to that night, coming home from the Madison. I'd meant what I said. Except exchanging rings hadn't even entered my mind. I hurried to catch up to Karen. "I guess," I said, "this is a big deal?"

"You don't sound so excited."

"Karen, I am. It's just that getting married these days isn't what it used to be. I mean, is there still etiquette around these things?"

"David seems to think so."

Rows of white and golden ceramic cats smiled and beckoned to us, waving their little paws. "All I'm saying," I said, "is that a real, committed relationship isn't always defined by wedding vows, not anymore. Don't half of marriages end up in divorce anyway?"

"Daniel Garneau." Karen snapped open a steel-ribbed fan. "I'm surprised at you."

I shrugged. "Why?"

"I didn't think you were this cynical."

"I'm not being cynical, Karen. I'm just being realistic."

"Listen. No one gets married thinking their marriage will fail. It's still a big deal. It's a public declaration."

I followed her to the check-out counter. I wasn't even the biggest fan of public displays of affection. Announcing a formal engagement just seemed like another box to check on the to-do list of civil obedience.

"It's not like," Karen said, unloading our shopping basket, "he's expecting you to organize some flash mob song-and-dance number."

Before I could answer, someone called out my name. It was my neighbour Liz. Today her cheeks were heavily rouged, her frizzy grey hair piled up in a precarious beehive. Mismatched tea cups filled her basket. She also carried a carpet bag and pushed a buggy spilling over with gigantic plastic flowers. "I've been hired to host a painting party, she explained. "The theme is Alice in Wonderland."

I introduced her to Karen. "Liz is from across the hall. She helped organize David's surprise party."

"It's so nice to finally meet you." Karen shook her hand. "Daniel says you're a designer at the Gladstone."

"Oh goodness no, my dear," Liz said, bracelets jangling. "That's quite an exaggeration. I was just one of thirty-seven artists commissioned to make over their rooms. I called mine *The Butterfield 8*. Did you know Elizabeth Taylor married eight times? That poor girl always did equate marriage with love.

"Now in my day, I had all the boys carrying my books. Except I was saving myself for my sweetheart Richard. As a debutante, I was crowned Miss Congeniality. Back then it was what we young ladies did—parade ourselves about in front of all the young men. All those lovely dresses and ill-fitting tuxedoes. Such a to-do! Not to mention the segregation and even now, the hoopla over same-sex couples. Bless that boy Marc Hall for dragging us kicking and screaming into the twenty-first century. Honestly, I have no regrets. Richard and I were each other's firsts. That will never change. I still love him to this day. We spent our honeymoon at the Gladstone."

At our own high school formal, Karen had worn a lovely dress and I'd had on an ill-fitting tuxedo. I could remember that moment like turning a page in a photo album.

"We were married a whole year," Liz said, "before Richard gathered the nerve to tell me. I'm so grateful he did. Imagine the life we might've had if he hadn't."

"What did he tell you?" Karen asked.

Liz clapped a hand to her bosom. "That he was in love with Sam, our wedding photographer, and that he'd always been! He swore he'd never been unfaithful but he just couldn't keep his secret any longer. Of course, I was heartbroken. But Richard was such a kind and decent man, how could I not forgive him? And honestly, I can't say I was terribly surprised.

"Sam had the most wonderful fashion sense. And excellent taste in men, if I do say so myself. Those two stayed together thirty-five years. Richard and Sam, what a pair! The times the three of us had—quahogging on the

Cape, Broadway shows with all our backstage escapades, all sorts of tomfoolery at The Pines—oh the hully-gullys!—and in Puerto Vallarta con las señoritas. Now they knew how to paint the town." Liz pulled out a handkerchief and dabbed at her mascara. "Those certainly were the days. Heavens, now. I've missed Sam dearly."

Karen glanced at me. "What happened?"

"Oh, the poor soul passed away last summer. Dropped dead right on the dance floor in the middle of Carnival Week. What a shock. Everyone joked: death by glitter. Half of Provincetown came out to the funeral. I organized the reception, of course, at the Atlantic House. Now that, my dear, was a party. They even renamed one of their streets: Sweet Sam's Lane. But Richard's been inconsolable. It just pains me to see him this way. He's even thinking of giving up The Pistachio."

"The Pistachio?"

"Those two ran the Pink Pistachio Ice Cream Parlor for thirty years. It was *the* place to gather. Their lemon sorbet was perfection. Except now, Richard doesn't think he can carry on."

"I'm sorry to hear that," I said.

"Thank you, Daniel." Liz patted my arm. "You and David have always been good boys. Forgive me, I'm not usually this sentimental." She blew her nose. "Que sera sera. That's the truth of it." She thrust out her chin and flourished a fist. "Carpe the fucking diem! That's what Sam would say. Pardon my French. But let me show you something."

Liz beckoned for us to follow her outside. At the corner of Baldwin and Spadina, she pointed up at a metal sculpture mounted high on a red pole: a blue globe or-bited by images of meats and fish, breads and cheese, coffee, fruits and vegetables.

"This was created by my friend Shirley," Liz said. "She made four of these markers, all at entrances to the Market. I was the one who suggested the clasped hands. Do you see them there? It represents our human bonds. We'll always come together, looking for whatever might nourish us. People will travel a world if they have to."

I must have passed this corner a hundred times with-out noticing this sculpture. Now I recalled similar poles elsewhere in the neighbourhood. The rain had ended and blue sky peeked through the clouds.

"The world," Liz said, "is our marketplace. If you're hungry enough, you'll find what you need. Richard, he found his Sam. And I found them." A lump moved inside Liz's carpet bag. A gremlin face poked out, dis-playing bulging eyes and piranha teeth. Karen and I both jumped back.

"Oh, please don't mind Lucille." Liz rubbed the Pomeranian's wrinkled head. "She's just upset because she has to get on a plane." The creature shivered and flat-tened its ears like it was constipated and squeezing out a turd. "Little Lucy-poo here isn't overly fond of flying."

"Where," I asked, "are you flying?"

"Why, down to Boston, of course." Liz tucked a plas-tic flower into her hair. "And then the ferry to P-town. Richard's asked if I could spend the season. The Pistachio could certainly use an extra set of hands."

"You're a good friend," Karen said.

"I," Liz exclaimed, "am a good wife!"

"You two are still married?"

From her bosom Liz pulled a thin gold chain and held aloft a diamond wedding ring. "I don't usually mention it." She sighed. "But Sam's gone now and Richard needs me. Yes, we're still legally married. The truth is, he's always needed me. And a whole summer on the Cape with all the lemon sorbet I can eat? You don't have to ask me twice."

"How long will you be gone?"

"Until August. I'm leaving in two weeks, I meant to tell you. I was thinking, Daniel, you might gather my mail and water my bougainvillea? I just need someone to take in my Frida and Kahlo."

"Who?"

"Oh, my new kittens. I was fostering them this winter and, well, one thing just led to another. When will I ever learn! They're such a delight, but they do need an awful lot of attention. David's allergic to cats, isn't he? Oh, I'd hate to have to give them up." Liz's beehive was beginning to disintegrate. She wrung her hands, the sunflower in her hair bobbing low over her face.

Liz, peered at us. "I don't suppose you know anyone who'd be free to house-sit for three months?"

␁ That evening, it was decided. Karen and Anne would spend the summer house-sitting for Liz. Everyone was thrilled. Someone pointed out that it'd be just like the TV sitcom *Friends*. Karen was Ross/Rachel, while I was Monica/Chandler. That David was Joey Tribbiani wasn't even a point of discussion. Anne stated she'd be Phoebe gone dark-side. David high-fived her while Karen just gave me a knowing look. Tonight, Anne's military haircut was dyed bright blue, and she sported a black graphic tee with a skull and crossbones across her chest. Anne always had a thinner, more angular build than Karen. This evening, in her ripped jeans and army boots, she looked like a teenage boy with make-up. The stuffed giraffe she used to tote around was long gone. It was hard to imagine that little kid who tagged along with us all through our childhood was now twenty-two. While Anne and David shared a smoke on the roof top, Karen and I packed up the leftovers. Close to midnight, Anne fist-bumped the three of us good-bye, and left down the fire escape with her longboard in hand.

The next morning, I got up to fill a thermos with hot coffee for Karen, who left just after sunrise. This time, as I watched her drive off, I didn't feel the usual emptiness in my chest. Karen would be back in three weeks. And this time I'd be helping her and Anne move in across the hall.

When I crawled back into bed, David mumbled from under his pillow: "Is she gone?"

"Yeah." I curled up behind him, wrapping my arm around his chest. "For now." I buried my nose against his neck. I was glad he and Anne had become friends. Luke and Ai Chang might be having a baby, but in our own way, David and I were building our own family.

Before leaving for Sudbury, Karen had made me promise one thing.

The truth was, for the last five years, David had carried our relationship. He did all the heavy lifting. He was the one who'd convinced me to move in with him. He was the one who kept asking me to make room in my schedule for "date nights." He was the one who did all our laundry and spent hours cooking up elaborate meals for just us two. He was the one who started saying "I love you" long before I started saying it back.

And he was worried I was just "putting up" with him?

He deserved better.

I could do better. I wanted to do better. Finishing school and starting my residency was important. But so was David.

We were important.

David had never said anything to make me feel guilty. But Karen never pulled her punches. Sometimes she and I knew each other better than we knew ourselves.

My heart started to race. It thumped so hard, I wondered if David might notice. But he only began to snore.

I squeezed him closer.

I was determined to make it better and I knew exactly what I was going to do.

I was going to propose to David, properly and romantically. I was going to ask him to marry me.

Hell, how hard could it be?

CHAPTER SEVEN

When We Stand Together

That weekend, I met up with Parker Kapoor at the Harbourfront Centre. For months he'd been looking forward to an exhibit at the Power Plant featuring some American artist called Sadie Benning. We spent the afternoon roaming between video installations in flickering, dark chambers. Afterward I sat on a stainless steel bench (first making sure it wasn't a piece of modern art on display) and flipped through the crumpled program.

Apparently, at age fifteen Benning had sparked international attention from videos made with a Pixelvision camcorder, and by age nineteen had received a Rockefeller grant, yada yada. My eyes drifted across their biography and extensive oeuvre. I was stifling a yawn, wondering how much longer Parker was going to take, when my gaze froze over a single line: "... recalling the work of Canadian multimedia artist Marcus Wittenbrink Jr."

At that moment, Parker came out of the gift shop. I quickly rolled up the program and stuffed it into my back pocket. We retrieved our knapsacks at the front desk and escaped from the gallery, blinking in the bright afternoon sun.

The tall ship *Kajama*, a three-masted schooner, was just about to dock. Tourists milled about, taking snapshots of the CN Tower and shimmering city façade. Raucous seagulls swooped low, threatening to snatch food out of the hands of unsuspecting passersby.

Parker was talking but I wasn't listening.

Everywhere I turned, there were reminders of him. Once, Marcus had taken me to a dance party on the *Kajama*. He and I had broken up on Valentine's Day in the CN Tower. This was so pathetic. I was ready to propose to my boyfriend and I was still thinking about my ex. I stared after a shirtless jogger. What was wrong with me?

I noticed Parker had fallen silent for once. He stood with his hands at his side, observing my face.

"You're thinking about him," he said, "aren't you?"

"What? Who?"

"He Who Must Not Be Named."

"And who is He Who Must Not Be Named?"

"You know who."

"Why would you think I'm thinking about him?"

"Because," Parker said, "you have that same look on your face every time you think about him."

"And what kind of look on my face is that?"

"Like you're constipated. And He Who Must Not Be Named was mentioned in the program."

I rolled my eyes. "You can say his name, Parker."

"Us Muggles," Parker said, "dare only whisper the name of The Wittenbrink."

"Don't. I'm not in the mood."

We put on our sunglasses and walked along the bustling boardwalk. Windsurfers and water taxis skirted broad ferries ploughing through the waves. A wobbly plane lifted off from the Billy Bishop airfield nearby.

"Daniel," Parker said. "You're about to graduate from med school. You're about to propose to your boyfriend. These are big changes. It's only natural you'd be thinking back on your old life. Sadie Benning organized a museum retrospective just last year. You can't move forward without looking back."

"I'm not so sure about that."

"All I'm saying is, there's a lot to learn about ourselves when we consider where we've come from."

"I'm pretty sure," I said, "I spend too much time looking back."

Parker exclaimed: "Crouch, bind, set!"

I jumped. "What?"

"It's something I do to ground myself, to bring myself back to the present. I get distracted all the time. But I've also learned ways to reconnect. What do you do, Daniel, to reconnect?"

I made a face. "I don't know."

"Didn't you used to play squash?"

"Years ago."

"Would you be interested in volleyball? I've just joined the Toronto Spartan Volleyball League."

"I really don't have the time right now."

"Have you tried massage therapy? My RMT practically saved my life."

"You get massages?"

"Every month. Deep tissue massages have been part of my care plan since I was twelve years old."

"What happened when you were twelve?"

"I was competing in the Ontario Sectionals when I pulled a groin. Don't pull your groin, Daniel. It is not fun."

"I have pulled my groin before."

"Oh, then you know how awful it can be. I was in so much pain I could barely walk. But the massage therapy helped and there were other benefits. I may be ace, but human touch is really important to me. When Kyle spoons me, it's better than Ritalin. Do you and David spoon?"

"Yeah, we do." We passed two men pushing a baby stroller, bags under their eyes, looking exhausted. "It's great."

"It is great," Parker said. "I love it when Kyle's the big spoon. That's why I also love mosh pits so much. Where else can you get that kind of physical contact? Definitely rugby. But rugby players would snap me like a twig. Did you know, Daniel, there are gay rugby clubs all over the world? I used to think I was attracted to these men. I mean they're like forces of nature. They're like demi-gods. Have you ever watched rugby in slow-motion HD? It's like watching wildebeest battling lions. I can practically hear David Attenborough's voiceover in my head. But really I was just obsessed with the scrummage. All those big burly bodies packed together, all that pressure and tension. For a long time it was my safe-space visualization. I still use it sometimes to calm myself down."

"Your safe-space visualization, Parker, is a rugby scrum?"

"Absolutely. I imagine I'm a second row lock, down on one knee, binding on the prop's waistband, my shoulder butted up with my head wedged in, my flanker's arm tight around me, and my Number 8 driving hard into my bum. My mantra would be: 'Crouch, bind, set!' I know it sounds complex, but it's really quite simple. Daniel, if you want to be the hooker I can demonstrate on you the proper position."

"No. No thanks, Parker. That sounds pretty clear to me."

We passed the Harbourfront Concert Stage where technicians were hanging lights over the amphitheatre. "In real life, of course," Parker said, "there's skating. When I'm skating, I just feel so serene and peaceful. All that noise in my head goes away. Then when I get low and I'm pushing through turns, the wind's in my face, and my fingertips are just skimming the surface of the ice, I feel like I'm Ariel flying through the sea foam!"

"Who?"

"The Little Mermaid," Parker said. "Sometimes, when I'm doing jumps, I imagine I'm Fluttershy."

"Of course."

"And when I'm feeling particularly powerful and bigger than life, I make believe I'm Mothra!"

"Right on."

Parker drew a breath. 'My point is, between spooning with Kyle and my massage therapy, I'm completely off my meds now. Oh, then there are rollercoasters. I can ride those for hours! But it's not like I can jump into a mosh pit or onto the Mighty Canadian Minebuster anytime I want. When I was little, my parents bought me a squeeze machine which helped a lot. I even wrote Temple Grandin to thank her. She and I struck up a correspondence after that."

"What's a squeeze machine?"

"It's a device that provides deep pressure therapy. Everyone needs some proprioceptive input to feel grounded and relaxed. Professor Grandin called it her Hug Box.

Later she built them to help keep cattle calm on their way to slaughter. There's nothing like a good hug to keep the existential terror of death at bay. PETA gave her an award for that. I'm so proud of her. When I was little, my parents and my sisters would give me hugs whenever I asked. Now that Kyle's in my life, it's like I'm a whole new man. When was the last time, Daniel, you went for a massage?"

"Um. Never?"

"You are missing out. Of course, there is Wonderland. Every spring, Father buys me a season pass. Daniel, I can get us discounted tickets! You and David could come with me and Kyle this summer. The Behemoth, it goes operational next month."

"The Behemoth?"

"It's their newest rollercoaster, the biggest in the country. They call it a hypercoaster. Riding the Behemoth will be my birthday gift to myself this year. I can't wait to try it. You'll come and celebrate with me, won't you?"

How could I say no to a rollercoaster ride? "For sure, Parker." I clapped him on the shoulder. "I'm in."

We arrived at the crown of a footbridge spanning the marina. A pair of Canada geese paddled through the weeds below, ignoring the human traffic. Pennants fluttered and somewhere an air horn blasted. Beyond the crowded slips, on the far quay, music and laughter rose from the Amsterdam BrewHouse patio.

"That reminds me, I have something for you." I took a flat box out of my knapsack. The bow was squashed but I was more than pleased with the kaiju-themed wrapping paper. "I know this is early, Parker, but I won't be able to see you next week. It's right before my final exam."

Parker's round eyes bulged. "That's for me?"

I held it out. "Happy birthday."

Parker clapped his hands to his face. "I don't know what to say."

"Open it."

Parker grabbed the box and ripped it open. He held up a blue T-shirt. On the front, two goldfish circled a pink lotus. "O.M.G."

"Do you like it?"

"This," Parker said, "is my favourite flower."

"I know."

And this," he said, "is my favourite colour."

"I had it custom made."

"And are these my Harold and Kumar?"

"They are goldfish."

Reverently, tilting back his head, Parker laid the T-shirt over his face and inhaled. "I love it."

Except for a cross-eyed seagull perched on the guard-rail, no one was paying us any attention. I cleared my throat. "You're welcome."

Parker lifted the T-shirt off his face. "Thank you, Daniel. Thank you." He flung his arms around me.

Parker was the first real friend I'd made in Toronto. Despite appearances, he was one of the smartest, most accomplished people I knew. Even after all these years, he still surprised me with the things he knew and the things he'd done. Even more importantly, Parker didn't have a mean bone in his body. When I'd been at my lowest, Parker had been there to cheer me up, sometimes without even trying. Despite all my hang-ups and missteps he never judged, always accepting me just the way I was.

It occurred to me that of course Parker would be one of my groomsmen when the time came. I was going to get married and all my family and friends would be there, including this guy.

I started to pat Parker on the shoulder as usual but reconsidered. For the first time, with a sudden and delirious abandon, I hugged my friend Parker as hard as I could.

∿ I was eighteen when I gave up skating.

I'd limped away with two black eyes and a pulled groin, my jaw set and my gaze unflinching, my heart beating a funeral march.

Yes, I knew how awful it could be.

At least none of the blood on the ice was my own. In hindsight, it was shocking how simple it was for me to turn my back on the one thing that had saved my life.

On the ice, Parker might imagine he was Ariel or Fluttershy. But when I was skating, I didn't think of anything at all. Hockey had been the one thing that kept me grounded and cleared my head. After my parents died, it was the only thing that kept me from completely falling apart.

But I was also closeted and it didn't help that our enforcer Gary Kadlubek was constantly on my back. Players razzed each other all the time. Locker room talk was normal. But Kadlubek seemed to be on a mission. The day I broke his nose was the day I got kicked off the team.

Years later, we apologized to each other. But by then, skating was already far behind me.

Hockey was something from my old life, from before

I cut my hair and moved to Toronto. Before I came out. I associated it with my hometown of Sudbury, along with all the hurt and grief that came with that place.

But Parker had reminded me skating was still something beautiful and powerful. That it always had been.

Of course, there was also Stephan Tondeur.

Society had an awful lot of rules. Rule #1: don't have sex with your assistant hockey coach. Who the hell made up these rules anyway? The guy was a 27-year-old realtor who coached Junior AA and trained for triathlons on the side. Rule #2: don't have sex with someone who's married with a kid. Every day, I'd see his face on billboards coming home from school. He looked so handsome in his jacket and tie. The RE/MAX colours suited him—same as the Habs.

He also looked good bent over the steering wheel of a Zamboni, his shorts around his ankles, his hands spreading his ass cheeks. He'd worn a jockstrap just for that occasion, because I'd asked him to. That memory alone was enough to fuel jack-off sessions for years to come. But the best part, the part I never told anyone, didn't have to do with the sex at all.

Stephan lived out past South Shore Road and it only made sense he'd drive me home after practices. I'd help him tidy and lock up the equipment, and close up the arena. We'd make sure to clean up any signs of sex on the concrete floor.

Before hitting the lights, he'd give me a friendly pat on the shoulder. Then I'd turn and give him a hug. Maybe I held it a little longer than guys were supposed to. But I didn't care. I felt safe with Stephan. His shirts always smelled of starch, rough against my cheek. I wasn't stupid or naïve. We both had huge stakes in this. If anyone ever found out, if there was even a whisper of a rumour, our lives would be ruined forever. But we trusted each other.

Just giving myself permission to hold this man—and having him hug me back—was the best feeling in the world.

If I lived on the perpetual edge of a panic attack, if nightmares of flaming wreckage haunted all my teenage years, if I missed my parents so much sometimes it hurt to breathe, Stephan Tondeur had been my squeeze machine. He had kept the existential terror of death at bay.

No one ever suspected a thing.

But worry was my middle name and Kadlubek was relentless. Rule #3: Don't let locker room talk get to you. Rule #4: Don't get into fistfights with your teammates if you want to make team captain.

The day I quit hockey, Karen cleaned and bandaged my knuckles. After that, I had her shave my head with Grandpa's clippers.

I stood in my underwear in front of her mirror, eyes swollen purple-black. I looked like a raccoon. I barely recognized myself. But maybe I was actually seeing myself for the first time. For better or for worse, this moment was mine forever.

Rule #5: Keep your eye on the ball, and don't ever look back.

〜 That April, David and I helped Karen and Anne move in across the hall. As the building manager, Rick wasn't happy about the sublet. Liz should've gone through him first. There were procedures to follow, credit and background checks. But Anne spotted the wolf god Moro tattoo on his hairy forearm and let him know she'd watched *Princess Mononoke* eleven times. Then she asked to see his collection of manga comics and it turned out they were both hardcore Motoko Kusanagi fans. By the end of that day, she and Rick were smoking up on the rooftop, debating the merits of sativa versus indica, and trans subtexts in films like *Ghost in the Shell* and *The Matrix*.

That first night, we kept our two doors open and played beer pong in the hallway. Liz's kittens Frida and Kahlo jumped at everything that moved, scattering red plastic cups everywhere. But within a week Anne had trained the two grey furballs to sit on her shoulders.

Liz had also left us the use of her lime green Volkswagen. "That," Karen said, standing next to me with her arms folded, "is a deathtrap." In the alley, Karen parked her own second-hand SUV, which we nicknamed the Mystery Machine.

Karen and I had a secret mission to accomplish. On the morning of her first day back in Toronto, she knocked on my door with two coffees in hand.

I was ready.

Together, we set out to buy an engagement ring.

Karen knew exactly where to go. In a jewellery shop in Chinatown, we picked out a simple, unmarked gold band.

For a small fee, I had an inscription added.

After that, we agreed to celebrate with Vietnamese at Pho Hung. We paused to study the sculpture on the street corner out front: a bronze cat on a kitchen chair, mounted high up on a red aluminum pole. This one was called *Home Again, Home Again.*

"Liz," I said, "should be settling down in Provincetown by now."

Karen cocked her head. "I don't think she's coming back."

"Why do you say that?"

"It's just a hunch."

"You have her cats," I said. "All her stuff is here. Her car is here."

"She just reminds me of me, you know?"

"What's that supposed to mean?"

But Karen was already holding the door open. "C'mon, let's eat. I'm starving." A busboy ushered us through the lunchtime crowd to a tiny table preset with hoisin sauce and sriracha sauce. We sat on red-and-black lacquered chairs, between a tacky stuffed sailfish and a big screen TV playing re-runs of *The Littlest Hobo.*

"This place," Karen said, "hasn't changed a bit."

"We can visit all our old haunts," I said. "Sneaky Dee's, Free Times. We can go back to the Madison."

"We could."

"I still can't believe you and Anne are right across the hall from us. Do you even need to look at that? We can order our usual, right?"

Karen perused the menu. "I think today," she said, "I'm going to try something different."

"Okay. Change is good. Sure." I downed my water glass and refilled it from a plastic jug. "I think I'm going to have my usual."

"Good for you."

I picked out a pair of chopsticks. "It's been a while."

"You do that."

I poked at my ice cubes. "It is good."

"Daniel." Karen squinted. "What's on your mind?"

I drummed on the tabletop. "Did you know," I said, "Marcus was the one who first taught me how to use chopsticks?"

Karen's lips compressed into a thin line. Without warning, she rose from her chair, reached over and slapped me. "Snap out of it!"

Another half-second and my cheek began to sting. I was dumbstruck. Karen sat back down. "I've always wanted to say that."

"What?"

Karen waved at the other customers. "It's okay. We're best friends. He's getting engaged." Nothing to see here, folks. Business as usual. Heads turned away.

"You deserved that," Karen said, taking away my chopsticks and setting them down. "You needed that. Loretta actually slaps Ronny twice."

"Who?"

"Never mind. This is real life." Karen pointed a finger at me. "Daniel, you have a problem. You need to get over your chopstick teacher, like now. And to be clear, this isn't about Marcus. This is about you thinking you don't deserve someone like David. Like you never deserved to be team captain. Like you never deserved anyone's love after your parents went and got themselves killed. You are an amazing and beautiful and awesome human being, Daniel Garneau. And you deserve to be around people who treat you that way. The way David treats you. Not like some fashion accessory man-purse the way Marcus carried you around. Need I remind you? You left him, Daniel, because you knew you deserved better. Remember that? So. Snap. Out. Of. It."

Karen picked up her menu again. She drew a breath and exhaled. "You might consider trying the beef balls soup."

Across the room, a little boy knelt on his chair, peering at me. I imagined one side of my face turning bright red.

"Real family," Karen said, "are people who see you for exactly who you are, and they fucking love you anyway."

"I know that."

Karen bit her bottom lip. "I'm sorry I slapped you." She set down the menu, her hands shaking. "That was uncalled for. Like, holy shit, I am so sorry."

"That's okay." My eyes were still watering. "I think I needed that."

"Daniel."

"Except Parker says you can't move forward without looking back."

"Look back, Daniel. Look back as much as you need to." Karen crumpled up a napkin in her fist. "But listen, make it worth your while, alright? Make it count. And don't get stuck. Trust me, I know."

"It's just that," I said, "I happen to have this ring in my pocket, see? And David, he's the one, I know he is."

"But?"

"But I need to love me first. Isn't that what you're telling me?"

"Is it that hard?"

"I'm working on it."

Karen dabbed at her eyes. "Then we'll be study

partners," she said, blowing her nose. She tossed her napkin aside. "Listen. Hey, look at me. Let's make a deal."

"What's that?"

Now the Littlest Hobo was pulling some drowning kid out of a river. The boy collapsed on the grassy shore, soaking wet but alive.

"You'll be strong for me," Karen said, "and I'll be strong for you. Can we shake on that?"

"Okay."

"We'll work on this together." She held out her hand. "Deal?"

"Deal."

During the final week of school, I stayed late on campus studying every night. After the licensing exam, I'd have two months off before starting my residency. On the last day of April, when I was finally ready to pack it in, I turned my phone back on and noticed David had tried calling twice. Just as I started to text him back, he phoned again.

When I heard his voice, thick and strained, I knew something was wrong.

Ai Chang needed to terminate her pregnancy.

We met at Cora Pizza, not far from the Medical Student Lounge. David was already waiting for me next to his bike. He looked pale and out-of-breath, his eyes red-rimmed.

Some abnormality had been detected. It required what was called a medically-indicated abortion. "These things happen," David said. "We were lucky we even got pregnant the first time, right? What's important is that she's okay. She's fine, she really is. I mean, we'll just try again."

David's face remained flat, expressionless, when I handed him his slice. "Hey," I said. "Look, I'm sorry it didn't work out."

I'd never seen David like this before. When Karen had her abortion two years ago, it'd been an unwanted pregnancy. This wasn't the same at all.

Outside, I sat down beside him curbside. Tonight, the stars were blacked out by the clouds. His pizza lay untouched next to him. "I know," he said, "this isn't the end."

I handed him a napkin. "These things take a few tries."

"Luke says we're just getting started."

"He's the Boss. You should listen to him."

"But do you think it's me?" David ran both hands through his hair. "I mean, I didn't go through any of the expensive testing. I just figured I was healthy, you know. But what if I'm not? Maybe there's something wrong with me. What if it's me?"

"David, it could've been anything. Complications like this are usually random. It doesn't mean it'll happen again."

We faced the concrete façade of the Graduate House, its massive UNIVERSITY OF TORONTO sign marking the western entrance into campus. A police helicopter buzzed overhead. Far away, sirens wailed. At this hour, the few pedestrians and cyclists were indistinct, faceless figures. Cars passed by, their darkened windows reflecting the unsettled night.

"Did you know," David said, "over 95 per cent of sperm donor candidates are rejected because there's something wrong with them?"

"Where did you hear that?"

"I read it on the Internet."

"Well." I sighed. "Sperm banks have really strict standards. They screen for all sorts of things."

"I get all the medical stuff," David said, "the genetic testing, the family history. But they also ask about education and employment, and criminal records. They have all these personality tests, and 'behavioral and social evaluations.' I mean, what the hell does any of that have to do with how healthy my sperm is? Or what kind of life the baby is going to have? All the websites go on about 'finding your perfect donor.' But by these standards, every guy I know would be disqualified, including you."

"Me?"

"You have tattoos, don't you? You've also had sex with a man. Most sperm banks would reject you for those reasons alone."

I was beginning to see where David was going with this.

"So all I got tested for," David said, "was STIs and HIV. And I stopped smoking pot. That's all Ai Chang and Luke cared about. But, I mean, now that you think about it, don't you think they're being a little reckless?"

I did my best to overlook the irony of David's question. Carefully, I considered my next words. "Luke says if you want to live big, you gotta take the big risks. They know what they're doing. You're Luke's brother. I'm sure if it was an anonymous donor, he and Ai Chang would've got all the tests done. But they wanted you."

"Luke and I are half-brothers," David said. "And you thought this was a bad idea from the start."

"Hey." I shifted to face David. "Listen, I never said that. And it was never the baby's health I was worried about."

"Then what? Because you sure as hell weren't the biggest fan when I first brought this up."

I pinched the bridge of my nose. "It was about raising a family. It was about being responsible for another human being. Life decisions don't get bigger than this. But we talked it through and I'm good with it. Hey, really, I am." I reached out and squeezed David's leg. "Listen to me. I'm as disappointed as you are. You'll try again. I want you guys to try again."

"Do you, Daniel?" David stared at the pavement. "Do you really?"

"Yeah. I do."

"You know, I still want us to have our own kids one day."

"I know."

"It comes with getting married. It's like a package deal."

"I know." I gripped his knee. "So." I raised my chin. "How many were you thinking?"

"Kids? Well, on your doctor's salary, let's say three, five." David counted on his fingers. "Maybe an even half-dozen. Come to think of it, seven's a lucky number. That'd be a good start. What do you think? Hey, ow, let go! I'm kidding, okay? I can't help it. It's the Catholic in me."

We both laughed.

"But honestly, choosing to have a baby is an incredible privilege. And yeah, it's hard as hell, and there are going to be sacrifices." David took a bite out of his slice. "You get past all that. It's so worth it. I know it is." He took a second bite. "I want to teach them how to ride a bike. I want to do their laundry and fold kid-sized blue jeans." He wiped his mouth. "I can't wait to pack them their lunches every morning, and read them bedtime stories every night."

The sky had settled. Neon signs hummed.

I remembered Grandpa putting us to bed, a book in his lap, smelling of Old Spice, fresh sawdust and cigarettes.

"My parents never read to us."

"You and me, we'll read to them," David said, "every night. We'll read to them all about pirates and Narnia and hobbits and Hogwarts."

I bowed my head. "And *Le Petit Prince*."

"What?"

"*The Little Prince*, by Saint-Exupéry." I looked David in the eye. "We'll read them that."

"And," David said, "we'll read them that."

Later that evening, David and I sat in bed with our pillows behind our backs. Before turning off the lights, we kissed. Then we kissed again. Soon after that, we took out some lube. After five years together, we could be perfunctory and efficient. Afterwards, I pulled up my underwear and offered him a towel. But David only lay listlessly next to me. We both contemplated the pool of semen on his stomach. Our feet touched. After a moment, I leaned over and kissed his shoulder. Then I kissed the hollow below his breastbone. A drop of cum glistened just above his navel. How much DNA was contained in that single drop? How much human spirit and collective memory? I touched it with my fingertip, and then with the tip of my tongue. It was salty and mild to taste. On an impulse, taking my time, I licked all the cum off David's stomach. Then I pulled back his foreskin and cleaned his head and shaft. He was mostly flaccid by now. It seemed the most natural thing to do. After I was done, I rested against him, one hand cupping the inside of his thigh.

David breathed slowly and evenly. I studied the hard lines and inky shadows over his heart. It was true, our lives were a rainbow of chaos. If my mouth were a womb, I would trade my voice to grow a child for him. But the real world was not so magical. All I could do was offer him my presence, my communion, and my body to hold. Beyond the crumpled edges of our bed, beyond the cinderblock walls of our loft, the city cradled us, soothing our bruised spirits, offering as it always would the promise of a new day and a new hope. Together, in this way, the two of us fell asleep.

CHAPTER EIGHT

Raise a Little Hell

O n the first Saturday in May, I wrote my licensing exam.

At the testing centre I was allowed four hours in the morning, a forty-five minute lunch break, then four hours in the afternoon. No water or food was permitted in the testing area. I found myself taking the maximum allotted time in each session. When I was finally done, I sat back stiffly, exhausted and numb. My deodorant had stopped working hours ago and there were pit stains on my shirt. I'd spent four years of my life preparing for this test.

I was the only examinee left. My chair scraped against the floor. My footsteps echoed as I left the hall.

With the engagement ring in one pocket, I stashed my phone in the other. Even though there would be messages waiting, I kept it on airplane mode. I wasn't yet ready to face the world. But as I stepped outside, squinting into the slanting sun, my mouth fell open.

Marcus Wittenbrink Jr. was waiting for me in the parking lot.

There he was: my ex-boyfriend in a trench coat and Ray-Bans, leaning against a glorious red convertible with cream-coloured bucket seats. I felt like Mia Sara summoned out of school by Ferris Bueller. It wasn't a Ferrari 250GT, but it might as well have been. He was holding up a sign:

DR. DANIEL GARNEAU

I shaded my eyes. "Nice rental."

"You know," someone in the back seat said, "you can rent pretty much anything you want these days." A petite woman in a white dress leaned forward and raised the rim of her sunhat. "Can we offer you a lift?"

"Well, if it isn't the Meatball Queen."

"Hello Daniel the Doorman." She smiled, peering over her sunglasses.

Of course, it would be Marcus and his best friend Marwa. Tweedledum and Tweedledee.

"Dr. Garneau," Marcus said, "I presume."

"I'll find out in seven weeks."

Marcus opened the passenger door. "We'd be honoured if we could take you for a ride."

I hadn't seen Marcus since last summer. He looked older, leaner and more beautiful than ever. His hair had grown out in a Warholian do, stylishly unkempt. When he took off his glasses, I could see the familiar, mischievous twinkle in his eye.

"Am I speaking to The Maleficent or The Marvelous?" I asked.

"Oh, it's The Marvelous, without a doubt," Marwa

said. "Unless it's The Maleficent pretending to be The Marvelous, in which case, sweetie, we are definitely in for a ride."

"Marcus." I squinted. "What are you doing here?"

"We're your ride." He winked. "Don't worry, we're not here to kidnap you, although that would be fun. David sent us."

"I doubt that."

"Well." Marcus opened his arms. "Here we are." When Marcus and I had been lovers, he always knew what to do to my body to keep me just at the edge. It was sadistic and controlling. I'd loved every minute of it. He looked at me the same way now, his lips slightly parted, his fangs just showing.

"Aren't you supposed to be in Montreal?"

"I was." Marcus grinned like a fox. "Je suis revenu. Miss me?"

No possible reply could work in my favour. Marwa saved the moment. "Gentlemen, we really should be on our way. The party awaits."

I massaged the back of my neck. "And what party would that be?"

"Your graduation party," Marcus said. "You've finished med school. It's a celebration."

"Convocation's not until next month."

"Just get in the car."

"David's taking me out to dinner."

"Yes, and where do you think we're taking you?"

On an impulse, I turned on my phone. Sure enough, there were multiple texts from David summarizing dinner plans, and letting me know that Marcus and Marwa were coming to pick me up.

"Do you think," Marwa asked, "we have time to stop by my place, Dum? That wouldn't make us late, would it?"

So I wasn't being abducted after all, and I wouldn't be putting the Stockholm Syndrome to the test. It wouldn't be the first time Marcus had tied me up.

"No," Marcus said, "it wouldn't."

Squeezing past him, I sank into the passenger seat, clutching my knapsack. Marwa took my bag and kissed me on the cheek. "Congratulations, lover." Marcus closed the door, leaned over and buckled my seatbelt. I imagined I was Major Tom getting strapped into his rocket ship. This was the total opposite of a safe space visualization.

Marcus was wearing the same cologne I'd bought him on our last day together, the Valentine's Day we broke up. I tried not to stare at him when he got in behind the driver's wheel.

A champagne cork popped in the back. Marcus tapped his phone and music blasted from the stereo: "Raise a Little Hell" by Trooper. He gunned the motor and skidded out of the parking lot. I could smell the burnt rubber.

Fuck.

I was done med school.

Dark, rebellious Marcus was The Maleficent. Joyful, bright, loving Marcus was The Marvelous. When the three of them—Marcus and The Maleficent and The Marvelous—joined forces, the results were heart-wrenching and spectacular.

Marcus always was the showman. Some things never changed.

He wouldn't tell me where we were going, but the city

was a blur as we raced through the downtown core, the wind in our hair.

When Marwa had me swig from a bottle of Veuve Clicquot, I banged my front teeth and it fizzed and sprayed my entire front.

"Here," Marcus said, "put this on." Marwa handed me a satchel of clothes.

"What is this?"

"You'll need to change. Where we're going it's casual elegant."

"What I need is a shower."

"No time, doctor. Your adoring fans await."

"He could clean up at my place," Marwa said.

"Now, Dee, you would like that, wouldn't you?" Marcus clucked his tongue. "It appears we could all use a shower."

In my lap, I held freshly pressed slacks, a clean pair of socks and my favourite dress shirt. There was also a box containing a brand new pair of Oxfords. David had even packed my deodorant stick. I kicked off my sneakers and unbuckled my belt.

Reluctantly, I changed in the moving car.

We parked downtown by the Distillery District, once a sprawling site of derelict 19th century industrial buildings, now a bustling village of art galleries, boutiques, coffee houses and studios. Fantastical courtyard sculptures drew in passersby and tourists alike.

As it turned out, Marwa lived in a condo nearby. Marcus and I waited for her in the plush, grey-green granite lobby. "Is she okay?" I asked, as she dashed into the elevator.

Marcus whispered in my ear: "She forgot her tampons."

"Oh." I blushed.

After a moment, he added: "Women are taught not to speak about such things."

"Right."

A songbird trilled outside. "Many religions," Marcus said, "label menstruating women unclean. It is manifestly misogynistic."

"Mm."

He examined a thin yonic sculpture on the glass coffee table. "We're taught so much shame about our most basic human nature."

"It's a travesty," I said.

"Yet where resides more truth than in our autonomic functions, our own corporeality?" Marcus shook his head. "Our animal bodies ought to be celebrated."

"I couldn't agree more."

"They're in the wrong holes," Marcus said.

"Pardon me?"

'Your shirt buttons." He pointed.

I looked down. "It's the latest style, Marcus. Everyone in Toronto's doing it. You've been out-of-province too long."

"Call me a traditionalist then. May I?" He positioned himself in front of me. "I should mention, Daniel," he said, unbuttoning my shirt, "you're in my latest exhibit."

"Am I?"

"It's what I've been working on during my residency."

"And how was Montreal?"

"As the Quebecers like to say: C'était l'fun!" When Marcus Wittenbrink Jr. smiled at you, it was like being blinded by a spotlight. With his pale-lashed eyes and flawless features, he had the appearance of an angel. But I knew better. "I spent the winter exploring photomontage," he said, bending his knees. "It was a surprisingly intimate process, and a departure for me." His knuckles brushed against the skin of my chest. "May I show you?" He adjusted my collar and patted my shoulder. "There now, much better." He took out his phone. "I hope you don't mind."

He showed me a picture of himself posed in a gallery lobby. "We staged a private view last month for a few dozen guests." Bone-white walls featured rows of 11"×14" prints. "I called the exhibit *Bodies of Lovers: Canadian Hydrologies.*"

He scrolled through other images: close-ups of mostly male nudes, tangled sheets, a shoulder blade, a woman's breast, masculine thighs, glistening tips of tongues and teeth. All of these were overlaid with ghostly, satellite images of rivers and lakes.

"Our human brains and hearts are composed of 75 per cent water," Marcus said. "We are naturally fluid beings. This series, it is a study of shorelines and embankments."

I was no art critic but it all looked derivative and pretentious to me.

"Here," Marcus said, "these ones are of you."

The framing was tight, capturing the curve of my ribcage, my jaw and matted hair, my chafed wrist, the procession of vertebrae along my spine. I remembered this shoot. We'd been drinking absinthe all afternoon, just the two of us. Marcus had untied me by then.

"As you can see, it's all quite anonymous. I plan to exhibit a smaller selection in Toronto next month, in an expanded, multimedia format."

"These are really nice, Marcus," I said, trying to sound sincere. "Congratulations."

I readjusted the collar of my shirt and checked the ring box in my jacket pocket, probably for the hundredth time.

"Then you have no issue with me using these?"

"Why should I?"

"Thank you, Daniel. I knew I could count on you. I've commissioned your brother Patrick to compose an original score."

"You're putting it to music?"

The elevator doors opened and Marwa reappeared in a hip-clingy, plum cocktail dress. And she had added hair extensions.

"All freshened up, Dee?" Marcus asked.

Marwa twirled. "As a tulip, Dum."

Marcus licked his thumb, reached out and rubbed Marwa's lipstick from my cheek. "I don't suppose," he said, "David is the jealous type?"

"No. He's not."

"Well. Better safe than sorry."

We walked across the broad thoroughfare of Trinity Street and headed down Tank House Lane. Marcus paused in front of an installation where thousands of pad-locks, affixed to a massive metal frame, spelled out the word L-O-V-E. The tradition, he explained, was for couples to write their names on a lock and throw away the key. "As a symbol of their commitment. There are similar landmarks, on bridges and gateways, all around the world. The Pont des Arts in Paris is probably the most famous for its love locks. Or infamous. Many consider it vandalism. Some even call it a plague. But removing the locks has also provoked controversy and even outrage."

Standing between us, Marwa took both our arms in hers. "A plague of love," she murmured.

Marcus kissed the top of her head. "On both our houses."

"Do you think, Dum, people will ever wake up?"

"There's always hope, Dee." Marcus sighed. "How such a pandemic might change the world."

Silently, we observed the installation. Nearby, three laughing girls in party dresses took selfies. It occurred to me that every meeting of one person with another might begin a story, or end it. And that each lock represented a relationship as vivid and complex as my own, an epic narrative in which I was an ignorant bystander, a nameless background figure. I glanced at Marcus. Yet we were, each and all of us, threads in a sprawling, incandescent tapestry. The girls lit sparklers and held them aloft, illuminating his profile.

Marcus checked his phone. "It's time."

We arrived at the Cluny Bistro and Boulangerie. The hostess guided us through a dining room crowded with wine cabinets and resplendent, Belle Epoque décor. Marble counters displayed artful arrangements of freshly-baked bread. She led us into a private back space, where friends and family cheered and clapped at our arrival.

Tomorrow, it was Paddle the Don and everyone, it seemed, was here tonight. The last time I saw my brothers in jackets and ties was on New Year's Eve at Sudbury City Hall. Liam introduced his lady friend Joan (apple-cheeked, with teeth like a horse). Bob introduced his wife Elsie (a shy, pretty woman with dark circles under her eyes). When I waved at Zephyr and Sky, the girls giggled and whispered into hands cupped over each other's ears. Nadia and Ai Chang sat with knees touching, looking radiant, sipping from sparkling flutes. Luke, apparently, was in the kitchen talking to the chef. Parker and Kyle had dressed up in Victorian outfits, complete with coiffed period hairstyles, waistcoats and pocket watches. Anne was enraptured, squeezing her chair in between theirs. Charles insisted on selecting the evening's wine for everyone. Megan was thrilled to have her best friend Karen back in Toronto. David had also invited Gee, who worked as Marcus' stage manager and greeted me with a kiss on the lips (because, of course, that was what gay men did).

Early on, David made a speech and raised a toast. After that, he presented a card containing an Air Canada travel voucher. Everyone, Karen told me, had contributed to this gift. The amount shocked me. (Later I learned Grandpa was responsible for half the sum.) "I don't know what to say."

"You've never got on a plane before," Karen said. "It's about time you did."

David said: "You can go anywhere you want. Anywhere in the world."

After that, everyone started talking at once, pitching their favourite destinations and the perfect travel adventure.

Large dinner parties were always an orchestration of competing voices and eclectic personalities. They could be awkward or dissonant. But sometimes they took on a life of their own, like mountain streams merging with a flowing river.

The night was magical.

Luke, Pat and even Marcus were on their best behaviour. The Marvelous entertained Zephyr and Sky with sleight-of-hand tricks using the silverware. Throughout the evening, people pulled me aside to offer their congratulations. Luke insisted on treating me to a whiskey flight at the bar. Old and new friends alike carried on animated conversations.

I clasped and unclasped the ring box in my pocket.

Tonight, I was going to ask David to marry me.

The only person who knew my plan was Karen.

At this moment in my life, I'd never been in more debt. And I'd never been more happy.

Just before dessert, I joined Liam outside. For this occasion, he'd trimmed his beard and pulled his hair back in an unaffected bun. The Distillery's rustic architecture suited him perfectly. The sinking sun washed the cobblestones and rough limestone in gold. I could easily imagine Liam in shirt sleeves and suspenders, loading whiskey barrels onto giant steam locomotives beneath flickering gas lamps.

Liam lit a joint with a wooden match. He'd left his jacket in the restaurant. His arms were like tree trunks. "Have you been working out?" I asked.

"Yep."

By the time Liam was fifteen, he'd gotten his black belt in kung fu. Once, I'd seen him punch through a cinderblock with his bare fist. Liam was a man who'd haul entire deer carcasses out of the woods on his back.

"Well," I said, "you look good."

"Thanks."

We sauntered past eye-catching displays of gelatos and

chocolate. Flowers burst from planters that lined patios humming with laughter and conversation.

"So, Liam," I asked, "did you know Grandpa bought a Winnebago?"

"Yep."

"Do you think it's safe for him to be driving cross-country?"

"Don't see why not."

"It's just that, you know, handling a motorhome is a big job. And Grandpa, well, he's getting on."

Liam arched one eyebrow. "You going to tell him that?"

"It's a little late now. I just wish you'd told me."

"It's a Sightseer, eight-cylinder Workhorse RV," Liam said. "It has ninety thousand clicks on it. We had to get the front and rear suspensions redone and the fuel line replaced. It's shipshape. Betty and Pépère will be sharing the driving." We paused beneath a flagpole. "He'll be fine."

Grandpa wasn't alone. He was with Betty, and the Miltons. He was going to be fine. Grandpa was going to be fine.

"And what about you?" I asked.

"What about me?"

"Any plans for the summer?"

Liam puffed on his joint. "They've asked me to teach again."

"Hey, that's awesome. Good for you." Last year, Liam had been a guest instructor for Laurentian University's wilderness survival skills course. The Greater Sudbury Police would also sometimes call on him for help with a missing person's case. I cleared my throat. "Detective Joan seems like a fun gal."

"She is."

"She gave Marcus a run for his money."

"I suppose so."

Early in the evening, seated across from Zephyr and Sky, Joan had suspended a spoon from her nose and recited the entire *Jabberwocky* poem while cross-eyed and wiggling her ears. To his credit, the Marvelous had expressed utter amazement and disbelief.

I fussed with the ring box in my pocket. I debated telling Liam my plan. "So the two of you are back together again?"

"For now."

"You're really serious about her?"

"Can't say."

"Liam." I was accustomed to Liam's laconic nature, but something was different tonight. "Is everything okay?"

Tilting back his head, Liam blew out a thin stream of smoke. "I've got cancer."

"What?"

"I'm going in for surgery next week."

The laughter and bright conversation faded into the background. "What?"

"I'm sorry to tell you this during your party."

I observed the milling crowds, their smiling faces. "How long." I swallowed hard. "How long have you known?"

"A while now."

"Why didn't you say something sooner?"

"I didn't want to interrupt your studies."

"For chrissake, Liam."

Pat bounded up between us, draping his arms over our shoulders. "So, did you tell him?"

"I told him," Liam said.

"Did you tell him what they're chopping off?"

Liam handed Pat the joint. "It's testicular cancer. I'm scheduled for a unilateral orchiectomy."

Now I rocked on my feet. What could I possibly say? I wrapped my arms around Liam, my fists clenched against his back.

"Hey. It's okay." Liam gripped my shoulder. "Hey. Dan, listen to me. It's Stage One. I'm going to be okay."

I blinked away the hot tears. "Stage One." It was Stage One. So it hadn't metastasized yet. The five-year survival rate was ninety-five per cent. The sensation started to come back into my hands. This was entirely treatable. I backed up. "You're going to be okay."

"I'm going to be okay."

"Dude!" Pat tousled my hair. "He's going to be okay!"

I rubbed my knuckles across my cheeks. "Give me that." I plucked the joint from Pat's lips.

"Daniel," Liam said, "you know smoking makes you sick."

"This is for medicinal purposes."

Liam looked from one of us to the other. "You both should get checked. Testicular cancer can be hereditary and it affects men our age."

Pat blinked. "What does that mean?"

"It's just a self-exam, Pat," I said, coughing. "It's easy. You can do it in the shower. I'll explain it to you later. Liam, when's the surgery date? I'll come up to Sudbury."

"It's all good. I've got Pépère and Betty looking after me. The recovery just takes a week or two."

"Hold on." Pat had gone pale. "Liam, will you still, you know, be able to get it up?"

"I shouldn't have any problems in that department."

"And what about kids?"

"Pat," I said, "he'll be fine. Liam, what did the doctors say?" I took one last drag before handing him back the roach.

"That this shouldn't affect the testosterone in my body," he said. "And that I can still get someone pregnant."

"Okay. Right on." Pat grinned shakily. "I mean, gotta keep the family tree going, y'know?" He pulled out a flask. "Here's to keeping it up."

I took a swig, but Liam waved it aside.

"You're still not drinking?" Pat opened his arms. "Seriously, dude. I'm proud of you. Did you know this used to be the biggest distillery in the world? Gooderham & Worts. Back in the 1800s, they used to produce over two million gallons of whiskey a year, right here on this spot."

"Pat," I said, "how the hell do you know that?"

"One of my students wrote an essay on it."

Liam folded his arms. "I'm impressed."

Growing up in Sudbury, us Garneau boys had practically been raised on whiskey and beer. Except Liam always drank more than anyone I knew. There were some dark episodes in his past.

Liam examined one callused palm. "Daniel, Pépère sends his regards. He's looking forward to seeing you at your convocation. He's really proud of you. We all are."

"Our brother the doctor." Pat elbowed me in the ribs. "You know what this means? Now you can prescribe us all sorts of shit."

"I still have to get my exam results."

"What grade do you need?"

I leaned against the flagpole. "It's my licensing exam, just a pass or a fail." I was starting to feel sweaty and dizzy. "We should get back. They're probably wondering where we are."

I'd forgotten how strong Liam's weed was. I made it as far as the front door. "I think," I said, "I'm going to be sick."

"Aw, no." Pat stood back. "Liam, why'd you let him toke?"

"You," Liam said, "gave him the joint."

"Liam, Patrick!" Karen appeared at the front entrance. "Did you just smoke Daniel up? You know how he gets when he smokes up!"

Bile rose in the back of my throat. I closed my eyes and swallowed hard. My stomach was a carousel.

"He's turning green," Pat said.

"I can see that." Karen took me by the elbow. "I'll take care of this. Go back inside. Tell David, okay? Go!"

In the men's washroom, Karen had me splash cold water on my face. She soaked a handful of paper towels and pressed it against the back of my neck. I gripped the edge of the marble basin. My head was spinning. How many times in my life had I overdrunk or over-smoked or over-binged? How many times had Karen come to the rescue?

"I'm sorry," I mumbled.

"Don't be."

"It wasn't their fault."

"Just take some deep breaths. In through your nose and out through your mouth. That's right. This will pass. You'll be okay." She rubbed my back. "How much did you have to drink tonight?"

"Half a bottle of Champagne in the car. A sambuca

shot with Pat. A flight of whiskey with Luke. A few glasses of wine, maybe. I'm not sure." Now my eyes were red and my nose was runny. "Someone ordered me a cognac. It wasn't that much."

"Right. Well." Karen stood back. "Do you still have the ring?" I nodded. "Are you still planning on proposing to David?"

"Liam's getting a testicle removed."

"What?"

Marwa appeared at the doorway. "Is he okay?"

"No," Karen said. "No, he's not. Apparently he was drinking before he even got here."

"Oh. Well." Marwa cleared her throat. "Well, I have just the thing." She rummaged a small tincture out of her crystal hand purse. "Just a few drops under the tongue."

"What is that?"

"It's pure CBD. It'll counter the psychoactive effects of the THC."

"Are you kidding me? You want to give him more drugs?" Karen wasn't quite shouting but Marwa still flinched. "He's not high. He's just having an allergic reaction."

Marwa stiffened. "I was just trying to help."

"Don't."

David rushed into the washroom. "Is he okay?"

Now here, I thought, was the guy I was going to marry. This was the man I loved. I'd padlock myself to him any day and throw away the key. My heart swelled. "Surgery," I said, "is next week."

"What?"

Violently, and without warning, I threw up. Medium-rare filet mignon and French onion soup with melted gruyère and escargot tartine, all over the Mediterranean-themed tile floor.

David jumped forward and caught the vomit dripping from my chin. "Sink's this way, mister." Both he and Karen manoeuvred me around.

"But," I said, "he's going to be okay."

David gripped my shoulder. "You're going to be okay."

I looked up. "He passed the test, Karen."

"Yes," Karen said. "Yes, he did."

When Karen and I were in high school, we came up with the Vomit Test. It was really simple. If you threw up in front of someone, did they jump forward or did they jump back? (It was, I supposed, what Marcus might call an autonomic response.) The first time we noticed it, Janet Leibowitz had gotten sick on some fumes in art class and Mr. Arbuckle had jumped forward. He was right by her side, holding her hand as she heaved over the garbage bin, aromatic chunks of snot streaming from her nose. The cafeteria had served mac and cheese for lunch that day. It was not a pretty sight. But Arbuckle hadn't flinched. That made a big impression on the whole class.

After that, Karen and I started observing other incidents more keenly. When our quarterback got sacked during a homecoming game and puked all over the twenty-yard line, Coach Van Dyck just stood back on the sidelines, fists on hips, shaking his head. You saw it every time babies or toddlers threw up, in the mall or at the park: moms diving in with wipes and face cloths the way firefighters run into burning buildings. No hesitation.

Pure instinct. In our senior year, when Kadlubek tossed his cookies at the prom after-party, everyone had jumped back. The entire basement, in fact, had cleared out faster than you could say Purple Jesus Jello Shot. To be fair, most people jump back. I mean, who can blame them?

That was the Vomit Test.

And David had passed.

∽ I lay beneath the cool, freshly laundered sheets of our bed, my body a dead weight. I was exhausted but I couldn't sleep. The day had been a rollercoaster. I should've been mortified getting sick at the party. But the truth was I didn't feel anything at all.

Flickering light outlined the staircase. I could hear the TV playing. I sat up in the dark, pulled on a T-shirt and made my way downstairs.

"You're up." David was boiling water in a kettle.

"Yeah." I rubbed the bridge of my nose.

"You want some chamomile?"

"Sure." He poured us both a cup, adding honey to mine and milk to his. "Thanks."

David flopped down on the couch.

"Thanks," I said, "for taking care of me."

"No problem."

At the restaurant tonight, David had been so proud. When he gave his speech and raised a toast, I'd never seen him so happy. Tonight, I'd been ready to propose to him: to get down on one knee in front of strangers, friends and family alike, and ask him to marry me. After I got back from my walk with Liam, I was going to do it. I'd planned it as the highlight of the evening. How could things have gone so sideways? I had no one to blame but myself.

The TV bathed David's face in a pale light. "David," I said, "are you mad at me?"

"What? No, of course not." He sipped his tea. "I'm glad you're feeling better."

"Thanks for coming to my rescue."

"You'd do the same for me." He flipped through the channels. "And I'm glad Liam's going to be okay."

"Me too."

"That news must've been a shock for you."

"It was." I picked at a loose thread in the band of my underwear. "And what about you?"

"What about me?"

"How are you?"

"Me? Daniel, I'm fine. Why do you keep asking?"

"I'm just checking in."

"Look, it's all good." He set his tea cup aside. "Ai Chang just let me know she's still not pregnant."

"I'm sorry to hear that."

"We'll try again. We've got time." David turned off the TV and set aside the remote. "C'mere." He sat up and opened his arms. Gratefully, I lay down in his lap. "Don't ever worry about us, okay?"

"Okay." I pulled my knees up to my chest, and closed my eyes. I wondered if Karen and Anne were already asleep across the hall. Tomorrow was a big day, and an early one.

Somewhere in the building, water pipes groaned and rattled.

"David, can I ask you something?"

"Sure."

"Why did you invite Marcus?"

"What?"

"You invited Marcus," I said, "to dinner tonight."

Well." David pressed his cheek against the top of my head. "I mean, all these people from Sudbury were already in town. When I invited Pat, he told me he had plans with Marcus, so I just invited the both of them. Marwa was already meeting Marcus at the airport. Then those two offered to pick you up from your exam. I mean, it's not like I wrote out any official guest list or anything. Tonight just kinda came together on its own, you know?" David studied my face. "Was it weird to have Marcus there?"

"A little bit."

"Last year, the guy had us over for dinner. He really wanted to celebrate your graduation."

"I know. It's okay. You don't have to explain."

"I don't want things to be weird between us, Daniel."

"They're not." I took his hand in mine. "You have no idea."

"About what?"

"About how important you are to me."

David stroked my hair.

"I mean it," I said. "I love you. You stuck with me all through med school. And I know you've been handling a lot more of our bills than I have. But I'm not a student anymore, and I'm going to start making a real income, and it's going to be different from now on. I promise."

"Why," David said, "are we talking about this?"

"We're talking about this because when couples fight and break up, a lot of the time it's about money."

"Have we ever fought about money?"

"No. But it's important to discuss these things." I turned to face him. "I just want to start off on the right foot. I just want us to be good."

"Daniel, we are good."

"Right! And I feel that way too. All I'm saying is you've done a lot, and I'm grateful for it. And it gets better. It starts now, trust me. I mean it."

"So serious. You've never talked like this before."

"We're about to begin this whole new chapter of our lives, right? And we are serious, aren't we?"

"Daniel, I was serious about you after our first date."

"I know that. I just needed some time to think this through."

"It's been five years, mister."

"Yes it has."

"Alright. So what's so funny?"

"I'm just happy," I said. "When you came into the washroom tonight and I puked all over you, it was the best, most romantic moment in my life."

"It was?"

"It just meant a lot to me."

David nodded. "Okay."

"Hey you." I raised my cup. "Cheers to us."

"Cheers to us."

CHAPTER NINE

Waiting for the Miracle

Early in the morning, we all prepared to drive up to the launch site for Paddle the Don. I kept David's ring box safe in a zippered pocket of my cargo shorts. After last night's debacle, I had no plan for another proposal, but wondered if the right moment might reveal itself.

David had borrowed a two-person canoe from a colleague. As Karen and I tied it to the roof of her SUV, Pat and Nadia arrived bearing coffees for everyone. Anne kept her sunglasses on all morning, but seemed a little more approachable after she'd had a smoke.

After a hearty breakfast, we all piled into the Mystery Machine. It was a half-hour drive to Ernest Thompson Eton Park where we met up with Liam and Joan. Scores of canoes and kayaks already crowded the parking lot. At this point, the river was fast-moving, narrow and winding, its green banks shaded by budding trees. Joan, in a Tilley hat and with a whistle around her neck, waved at us from across the parking lot, looking more like a camp counsellor than a police detective. Liam's dog Jackson, a big golden lab, greeted us with his tail thrashing wildly.

Bob and Elsie were later to arrive with Zephyr and Sky. They'd also brought their German Shepherd Gracie, a dark and gigantic beast who never ventured far from the girls' sides. Another man accompanied them whose own daughter, apparently, was best friends with Sky. When Bob introduced us, I shook his hand. After that, I turned my back and busied myself with our safety equipment. It was Anne who commented a minute later: "Hey, Daniel, wasn't that your old hockey coach?"

"Who?

"Bob's friend. Wasn't that Stephan Tondeur?"

"Now that you mention it." I double-checked the straps on my life preserver, tight across my chest. "Yeah, I think it was."

"Hey, Anne," Karen called out, "I need your help with this."

Volunteers with the Toronto Conservation Authority lined us up along the launch point. Officers with the Police Marine Unit checked the readiness of each vessel. Out of the corner of my eye, I caught Stephan watching me.

It'd been a long time since I'd been in a canoe but once we slipped into the water it all came back.

The south-flowing Don bisected the city and our course was a 10K stretch ending where the river entered Lake Ontario. Nadia would drive Karen's SUV down to meet us at the landing site in two hours. Upstream, dams had been opened to raise the water level. Liam warned us there were rocks and sharp turns along the way. Every year a few canoes capsized.

As it turned out, finding our cadence took no time at all. David had a sharp eye for upcoming obstacles and was a natural with the cross-bow draw. "Are you sure," I asked, "you've never done this before?"

"Never!" he shouted. "This is awesome!"

Last Halloween, David had finished building a tandem bike which we rode around town, taking it to the Pumpkin Parade in Sorauren Park where over a thousand jack-o-lanterns decorated the pathways. Likewise, this spring David was the perfect paddling partner, happy to provide the hard labour up front while I steered from the stern.

Entering a calmer bend, we drifted with the current, gliding past shorelines tangled with low-hanging branches filled with songbirds.

"He was a hottie," David said.

"What?"

"Bob's friend. That other dad. What was his name?"

"Stephan."

"I mean, total DILF. What did you think?"

A drake chased a hen across our path, bobbing his iridescent head, pausing to show off his colourful plumage.

"That," I said, "was him."

"Who?"

"The guy I did it with in the Zamboni."

"Shut up." David looked back at me. "You mean your hockey coach? The first guy you ever had sex with?"

The canoe pitched precariously and we spent the next minute navigating a stretch of light rapids. "At the time," I said, "he was the new second assistant coach."

"That was, what, like eight years ago?"

"I guess so."

"So, how was it seeing him like that?"

"It was weird."

"So what'd you do?"

"Nothing. I mean, neither of us said anything." The hull scraped a log and I worked hard to steer us clear. "I guess we both figured it was easier that way."

Nadia once stated that Marcus was my first great romance. But in truth it had been Stephan Tondeur while I was a senior in high school. I wasn't the best scorer or the toughest player on the team. But Stephan saw something more important in me. He was the one who convinced the head coach I might make a good team captain.

I absolutely and totally fucked that up.

The first day he arrived in the locker room, it was like this man had stepped off the cover of a Harlequin romance. I happened to be dripping wet and clutching a towel around my waist. Most of the other guys were still showering. I knew he was married and expecting a baby but I'd flirted outrageously with him anyway. I wasn't proud of that, not by a long shot. But I didn't regret it either. The simple truth was I was eighteen and horny as hell. I knew what I was doing. And so did he.

Seeing Stephan today was a shock. He was in his mid-thirties now, tall and fit, with the same dimpled smile and crinkled blue eyes. It was an instant hard-on the second I shook his hand. The last time we met was in a bathhouse in Toronto. But ours was a sordid past, and I meant to leave it that way.

His daughter's name was Ella-Grace.

During the rest of our route, David and I portaged

around three small weirs. We lost sight of Liam and Joan ahead of us. White high-rises appeared beyond the tree line. A hawk circled in the sky. Soon we approached the enormous Prince Edward Viaduct. Forty metres above, subway trains, cars and trucks rumbled past across the Don Valley.

"So who was the first guy," I asked, "you ever slept with?"

David glanced over his shoulder. "What do you mean?"

"Did it with. You know."

David's paddle dipped in and out of the water. "This really hot French-Canadian guy. His name was Daniel."

"What?"

"It was you, dumbass," David said. "You were the first."

I was stunned. "I didn't know that."

"I was saving it for someone special."

"But that night we met, you were, I mean, you just seemed like you knew what you were doing."

"Picking up a guy at a bar?"

"Sex, you idiot."

David laughed. "We were both drunk."

"Sure. All I'm saying is you seemed really confident."

"Yeah, and? I was. Douche kits, condoms, lube. Lots of lube. Mouthwash. I was ready. Bring it. Just because I hadn't actually done it yet doesn't mean I didn't know what I was doing. Did I mention lots of lube?"

"And how was it?"

We manoeuvered around a sandy shoal strewn with driftwood. "Sex with you, the first time?"

"Having sex with a guy," I said, "for the first time."

David leaned into his stroke. "Well, five years later, I'm still with the same guy. What do you think?"

"I don't get it." I was the sheltered kid from hick town Ontario. David was born and raised big city. His mom called him a Don Giovanni. "I always thought you'd had sex with lots of other guys."

"There's a lot of ways two guys can get it on, Daniel, without full-blown penetrative sex. I was a good Catholic boy. I saved my virginity."

"Seriously?"

David rose up on his knees and pulled down his shorts. "See this?" He slapped his firm ass. "No one's ever tapped this except you."

"Um, say that again? I didn't quite catch that."

This time, David bent over the bow and twerked. "Oh yeah baby!" Our canoe rocked. On the Lower Don Trail, joggers stumbled. A cyclist swerved and crashed into a ditch.

"You boys want a room?" Karen and Anne pulled up behind us. "Ahoy, me hearties!" Pat called out, perched between them in a straw hat.

"Buongiorno!" David pulled up his shorts. "How you ladies doin'?"

"Us ladies are doin' great!" Pat clambered to his feet with his ukulele and started belting out Bryan Adams' "18 Till I Die."

"What the hell?" Anne clutched the gunwale.

"Pat," Karen shouted. "Sit down. Now! Honestly, it's like having a five-year-old in the boat."

Pat sat down with a mischievous grin, his tongue between his teeth.

Expertly, Karen manoeuvered their canoe alongside ours. "We," she said, "are doing just fine. Bob and Elsie are behind us. I see you two boys are having fun."

David and I nodded. "Not-in-front-of-Bob."

"Or," Anne said, "your old hockey coach."

"Hey, you guys know why," Pat asked, "American beer is like having sex in a canoe?"

Everyone replied in unison: "Because it's fucking close to water."

Soon the grassy embankments gave way to steel piling, and we traversed a canal parallel to the Parkway. We paddled beneath the Queen Street Bridge, its underbelly splashed with neon graffiti. The green banks of the Don River gave way to transmission towers, condo buildings, and luxury car dealerships. Under an echoing overpass, Anne and Pat hollered at the top of their lungs and we all joined in: "Woohoo!"

Finally, we reached the Keating Channel and hauled ourselves ashore. The landing party was already in full swing. Bright banners fluttered, a live band was playing and there were hotdogs and lemonade for everyone. Every few minutes, more paddlers disembarked. Kids and barking dogs chased each other through a field of sparkling kayaks and canoes.

Joan stood in the beer tent, waving an arm and blowing her whistle. "You made it!" she shouted.

"Is it me," Anne said, "or does Joan look like a big beaver?"

We all joined Joan and Liam with beers in hand. Jackson sniffed at our crotches before laying down beneath our picnic table.

Joan slapped Liam on the arm. "Tell 'em about the ducks."

"Well." Liam scratched his beard. "I was just telling

Joan how male mallards have external penises. Most birds don't have penises at all, just a sensory spot called the cloaca. The more time the drakes spend around each other, the larger their penises grow."

"What?" David sat back. "Like, literally?"

"It's their way of competing with rival males," Liam said, "the way bucks grow their antlers."

"Or the way boys," Anne said, "soup up their cars."

"Their sex organs also have a corkscrew shape that locks a mating pair together. The hen's twisted vagina actually has some dead-end pockets she can use if she doesn't want to be fertilized by the drake mounting her."

"Like built in birth control?" Karen said.

"That," Joan said, "is fascinating."

Sitting cross-legged on the table, Pat sang: "My girl from Regina, she gave me angina, with her twisted vagina, oo oo ooh!"

I rested a hand across his ukulele strings.

"Then, at the end of the breeding season," Liam said, "the male's penis shrinks and wastes away."

"No ways." David sat back.

Pat stared. "Dude."

"It's just a natural cycle." Liam sipped from his water bottle. "It regrows when the next season begins."

Joan shook her head in awe. Apparently, she'd shot and eaten many a mallard over the years without knowing these extraordinary facts. A moment came when the two of us went to grab burgers.

"You must've heard," Joan said as we made our way through the crowd, "your brother and I broke up for a while last fall. I don't suppose he told you why?"

"Um, he might've mentioned something."

"Well." Joan made a face. "I hate to admit it, but it's all true. My family was saying some pretty darn ignorant things, and I wasn't calling them out on it."

"Okay."

"I might not be able to change what they believe, but I can change what I put up with. So I did. And I let them know." We joined the line-up in front of the barbeques. "I owe you and your boyfriend an apology. I know better now. And I have Liam to thank for that."

"Okay."

Joan raised the brim of her hat. "Now, I'm as straight-shootin' as they come. But as a woman in uniform, I've been called a few choice words in my time, if you get my meaning. I know how it feels."

"Alright."

Joan cocked her head. "Do you mind if I ask a personal question?"

"Sure."

"Liam tells me there're all sorts of animals, hundreds of species in fact, who have, well, who display homosexual behaviour. Mallards, bison, dolphins. I mean, honestly, who would've thunk? Penguins, giraffes, lions even. Those bonobo chimps, why, I hear, they just, well, go right at it." She rested her fists on her broad hips. "Marmots, for cryin' out loud. Heck, you name it."

"Those marmots," I said.

"So I got to thinking. I mean, why would God put all these animals on Earth if there wasn't some purpose to it, right?"

"I guess so."

"You know, Daniel, your brother Liam, he's just got big country love and respect for you. And you and David seem like an awful sweet couple. The truth is, you're the first gays I've ever met! And to be honest, I have to say you're not what I expected at all."

I did my best to keep my mouth shut.

"And I was just wondering," Joan said, "what does it all mean?"

"What does what mean?"

Joan clutched the back of her neck. "I've been asking myself, why the heck are there gays in the world? Not to mention mallards and marmots. I mean, there must be a good reason, right?"

Before I could even try to reply, I spotted Stephan, barefoot and soaking wet, marching toward us. I imagined him in slow motion, muscles rippling beneath his tank top, haloed in lens flares, the band striking up a "bow chicka bow wow" backing score.

"Hi. I'm Stephan."

Now he was standing in front of us. Joan, wide-eyed and slack-jawed, shook his extended hand.

"I'm sorry to interrupt," Stephan said. "Daniel, can we talk?"

"Why are you all wet?"

"Some kid fell out of their canoe, I just jumped in to help them out." Stephan cleared his throat. "Look, do you have a minute?"

"Um, sure." Stiffly, I turned to Joan. "Excuse me."

Following Stephan, all I could do was stare at his perfectly formed, muscular calves.

He drew me into a shady patch beneath a tall cedar.

"Look," he said, turning. "I wanted to tell you I'm divorced. No wait. Wait, Daniel. Let me finish, please." I buried my fists in my pockets. I couldn't look at him. The world was spinning again. "My ex-wife," he said, "I came out to her. I owed her that. We still go to counselling. She's home right now with our six-year-old, Hadrien. I've got Ella-Grace this weekend."

I focused on his big pale feet in the grass. They were enormous, like the feet of a giant. "I'm sorry," I said, "about your marriage."

"It was tough for a while." Stephan wiped the water from his face. "But we got through it. It's behind us now. She's getting married again, to our accountant. He adores her, the kids like him. He's lousy on the green and can't barbeque a decent rib-eye if his life depended on it. But he's a good man." Stephan searched my face. "I wanted you to know, Daniel, that if it wasn't for you, I'd probably still be living a secret life. I'd still be hiding, hitting up bath houses during trips out of town. I'd still be lying to her. Who knows where that would've led. Now every-thing's in the open. Now we're completely honest with each other. Now our relationship's better than ever. I don't think you can understand how important that is to me. I just wanted to say thank you."

"Why," I said, "are you thanking me?"

Across the field, the band struck up a Blue Rodeo hit. We watched as a single bright balloon floated away across the sky.

"I thought." Stephan drew a breath. "I thought sex could be just sex. I thought I could keep it separate and in this box. And I did that for a long time. Some people,

they do it their whole lives. But after what happened between you and me, I realized I couldn't anymore. There
came this moment when I realized if things had been
different, if I'd just let myself, I could've fallen in love
with you. I didn't, Daniel. I never did, I never let myself.
But just that feeling, just realizing the possibility that I
could fall in love with another man, it was like this window smashed open, and all this light, the whole world
came rushing through.

"It changed everything. Now I can be a real father, a
real role-model for my kids. I can't imagine how any of
this might make sense to you. But I've wanted to let you
know, for a long time. I even thought of writing a letter.
And then seeing you today, well. I just had to talk to you.
Bob says you're a doctor now. Congratulations. That's an
incredible achievement. That takes a lot of discipline and
hard work. Well done. And thank you, Daniel Garneau.
I just wanted to say you changed my life."

Now the balloon was a tiny point in the sky. All I
could feel was the enormous gravity of Stephan's presence
before me.

Far across the field, David was watching us.

Joan clapped David on the back, handing him a burger. At the picnic table, Liam and Pat were arm-wrestling.
Outside the beer tent, Karen and Anne welcomed Bob
and Elsie, laughing in their bright orange life jackets,
three girls and two dogs underfoot.

Stephan gestured. "Is that your boyfriend?"

I imagined the band, and all the people, the banners and
the trees vanishing, the city skyline and the music fading
away. I pictured David standing alone in an empty field.

The details of David's face astonished me: the tiny lines of his lips, the individual lashes of his eyes. The sunlight shone through him. I saw myself reflected in his gaze.

"That," I said, "is the man I'm going to marry."

Now the sky was empty.

I raised my hand and waved. David waved back.

"Can I introduce you?"

"You want to introduce me?"

"You were my hockey coach." Beneath the evergreen branches, I looked up at Stephan. "You believed in me. Of course I want to introduce you. You changed my life. I want to introduce you to everyone."

⌒ A week after Paddle the Don, I went for a bike ride at Tommy Thompson Park, what the locals called Leslie Spit, a narrow peninsula reaching out into Lake Ontario, ten kilometers of winding paths and dirt trails for hiking and cycling. The park was also a bird sanctuary, with no dogs or motorized vehicles allowed. Near the entrance, I spotted a great blue heron. Between tracts of wetland, the flora was dense and overgrown. I rode hard without a break, only stopping when I finally reached the westernmost point. Here an automated lighthouse directed marine traffic into Toronto Harbour. The shoreline was a sprawling swath of cinderblocks, bricks and twisted metal. Technically, the park wasn't a spit at all, but an urban wilderness resulting from decades of landfill from city and harbor construction.

Dismounting to catch my breath, I gulped some water. Across the waves, the Toronto skyline gleamed. With my bike on my shoulder, I descended the grassy embankment and carefully picked my way through the rubble to the edge of the lake. On this terrain, a person could easily twist an ankle.

"Hey buddy," a voice called out.

A guy in a Raptors jersey reclined on a slab of concrete, his arms covered in tattoos, a pair of rollerblades at his feet. He was chewing gum, the muscles flexing in his jaw.

There was no one else in sight. "Hey," I replied.

"Number 305."

"Excuse me?"

He pointed. "You're 305."

I squinted. "Sorry?"

"S'okay, man. It was a long time ago."

He grinned up at the sky, a gap in his front teeth. I wondered if he was entirely sober. I began to retreat, but there had been something familiar about his voice.

"Hey." I looked back. "Why'd you call me 305?"

"That was your room number."

Two eagles circled over the lighthouse. "You," I said, "used to work at Spa Excess."

"Yeah. That's right."

My heart thumped in my chest. I'd hooked up once with this guy. I'd given him a blowjob on his front porch. He'd been a lot skinnier then. "You were on chemo."

"Taking off his ball cap, he ran a hand through his thick, unruly hair. "I told you I was gonna grow it back."

"You were going to grow your mohawk back."

The guy's mouth twisted in a lopsided smile. "Yeah, well, that's the old version of me. What you got here is version 2.0. I just got the 'all clear' this morning. It's been five years. That cancer shit is done."

"Congratulations."

"Today, my friend, is the first day of the rest of my life."

The sweat prickled, drying on my skin. I picked at the handlebar tape on my bike. "My brother, I said, "has cancer."

The guy whistled.

My lips tasted like salt. "They operated on him yesterday."

"Is that right?"

"He's going to be okay."

"You sure about that?"

"Yeah." My brow knit. "I'm sure."

"Good to hear."

"Look, I'm sorry," I said. "I don't remember your name."

The guy sat up, peeled his jersey off over his head, and tossed it aside. His torso was toned and smooth, his nipples pierced. The last time we met had been outside Fly Nightclub. He put his ball cap on sideways and leaned back on his elbows. "I never told you my name."

"Alright."

Now ragged V-shaped waves of cormorants crossed overhead like war planes. "So here's the thing," he finally said. "My stage name's Axel."

"Your stage name?"

"Yeah. But that's just an anagram."

"Of your real name?"

"My old man, he named me after the Russian tsar. But nobody calls me that, not anymore. You can call me X."

"X?"

"That's what my friends call me."

"Just X?"

"X marks the spot, man. This is where I've signed on, y'know?" He tapped his fist against his chest. "Right here."

"X is where the treasure's buried."

The guy chuckled, like he'd never heard that before. "Right on."

"I'm Daniel."

"Pleased to meetcha, Daniel."

I remembered pulling X's torn jeans down in the dark and holding him in my fist, one hand splayed across his stomach, my knees bruised against the hard steps of his porch. I remembered his saltiness and muskiness. I wondered if he tasted different now that he was no longer on chemo. We'd shared a cigarette then. "You still living with your sister?" I asked.

"Yeah, well. She's in rehab. Right now it's just her kid and me."

"Sorry to hear that."

"Shit, man, don't be. I've been trying to get her into rehab for years. She's doing a whole lot better now. We all are."

"Where is your nephew?"

"Where do you think he is? The kid's in school."

"Right."

"He's in grade two. I pick him up in a couple hours." X studied the sailboats in the distance. "A while back, he starts calling me Daddy. I mean, what the yowza! That just happened? So, I remind him: Look kid, I'm your Uncle Al. But he hears all the other kids talking, y'know?"

"A boy wants a daddy."

"I suppose so." X sniffed. "So after a while, I just stopped correcting him."

"It's a big job."

"Yeah, well. Let me tell ya. For a couple months there I was on disability. Sis hooks up with this crackhead and starts using again. She loses her job. Then child welfare comes snoopin' around and starts leaning on all three of us."

"That's tough."

"I was ready to shit a motherfuckin' brick." X reached into his shorts and adjusted himself. "But things are lot better now. Now I'm dancing."

"Dancing?"

"At Flash on Church. You know it?"

I nodded.

"It's good money, if you know what you're doing." X tapped his head. "Now me, I gave up drinking, cut back on the darts. Even got myself a gym membership. Who'd ever thought I'd be one of those gym rats? Check out these guns." He flexed his biceps. "I figure I got a few years in me still." He stroked his six pack. "The regular customers, they like me."

"You're a likable guy."

"So I've been told." X winked. "So what do you do? You a student or something?"

"Yeah. I mean, no. Not anymore." I propped up my bike against a concrete block. "I'm a doctor."

"Shut the fuck up. What kind of doctor?"

"I start my residency this summer in community medicine."

"You with St. Mike's?"

"Yeah, actually, I am."

"They treated my lymphoma at St. Mike's. They got

some good people there." X pulled his ball cap low over his face. "So how's your brother doing now?"

"Liam? They sent him home already. He's staying with my grandpa. We'll just have to wait and see."

"He with St. Mike's?"

"No," I said. "He's up in Sudbury."

X nodded.

I picked up a rounded brick, worn smooth by decades of pounding surf. "He's going to be okay."

"If you say so."

"You don't sound so sure."

"Look." X shook his head. "I don't know your brother. Alright?"

Now I was silent.

"I met a lot of other patients at St. Mike's," X said. "Not all of them are around anymore. That's all I'm sayin'."

I weighed the brick in my hand. "That's kind of an asshole thing to say, don't you think?"

X regarded me sidelong. "It's what I told my nephew."

"You told a little boy that?"

"He's a smart kid. He can understand a lot. They got him in a gifted class." X cracked his neck. "But today, my friend, is a whole new day."

"Five years."

"That's right. Now you," X said, "are going to save a lot of people's lives. The world needs people like you."

"I can see why the regulars like you."

"You ain't seen nothin'."

"Look." I cleared my throat. "I'm just out here for a bike ride."

"S'okay." X smiled. "I'm just killing time before I pick up my kid from school." He sat up and took out his phone. "Check this out, I want to show you somethin'. Come on over, I won't bite."

Cold, clear water lapped at the shoreline. X watched me as I picked my way across the rubble. I imagined draping myself over his shoulders, inhaling the smell of him, kissing his neck, gripping his jaw and scraping my stubbled cheek against his own. His lips were full and sensual. I imagined doing everything I hadn't done the last time we'd met.

X showed me a photo of a boy in a cowboy outfit flourishing a pair of plastic six-guns. "He says here he's Calamity Jane." X swiped left. "So this one's from last Halloween." Now the boy was decked out as a robot fairy, complete with a tiara, laser pistols and sparkling wings. This close, I could feel the heat radiating from his body. "The kid," X said, "loves to dress up. So this year, he tells me he wants to be Chris Hadfield. So then I go: 'Who the hell's Chris Hadfield?' and he says: 'The Spaceman, Daddy.' So I Google this Hadfield guy, and it turns out he's a real fucking honest-to-god spaceman. Then I ask this nut job seven-year-old if he wants to fly to the moon. But he shakes his head and whispers in my ear: 'No, Daddy, I want to fly to the stars.' And that, my friend, is why I'm dancing, see. I need to save up enough to get this dumbass kid into university. Because this little guy right here, he's got big dreams. And he's going to need all the help he can get."

He put away his phone.

"X," I said, "marks the spot."

"You know it."

"He's lucky he's got you."

"He's got the both of us. Me and sis, we're going to this kid's graduation. I made that promise to all three of us."

I took out my wallet. "I want to make a donation." I pulled out a bill. "To his college fund. Here, take it."

X took the bill between two fingers. He turned it over in his hands. After a moment, he folded it and slipped it under his waistband. "Alright."

His eyes were green beneath his bangs, his lashes dark. He took off his ball cap, and beckoned me closer. "C'mere."

I stepped up next to him. He took my hand in his, and rested it on top of his head. "Last time," he said, "you thought I was some skinhead."

"Yeah," I confessed. "I did."

"S'okay. Me? I just thought I was dying."

"Yeah, well."

"We was both wrong."

Tentatively, at first, I ran my fingers through his hair. I thought of Grandpa pushing my brother out of the hospital in a wheelchair. I imagined Liam punching through cinderblocks, stalking deer barefoot with his crossbow, smoking venison beneath towering red pines. I remembered Liam hauling a canoe on his back and turning to smile over his shoulder at me. He was always the youngest, the biggest and the strongest of us.

"Your brother," X said, "he's gonna be okay. He's a fighter, ain't he?" I nodded. "He's gonna be alright."

X took my hand in his and squeezed it tight. He patted my hip.

I blinked, backing away. My nose was runny. I wiped at it with my wrist. I picked up my bike and turned to go.

The tall grass quivered between the rust-stained, sun-scorched rubble.

"I'm really glad," I said, "you're alive."

"Hell." X flashed his gap-toothed smile. "You ain't the only one."

"Good luck."

"You too, my friend. You too."

CHAPTER TEN

Heart in Two

Late in May, Karen and I headed over to Sneaky Dee's. It happened to be the first Pedestrian Sunday of the year in Kensington Market. Food stalls, vintage clothing racks and art displays had taken over the streets and alleyways. A rock band played the local brewery patio. Buskers sang and danced. The Garden Car, a refurbished four-door sedan sprouting spring flora like a moveable feast, made its annual reappearance on Augusta Avenue. Karen insisted we take a selfie with the expansive Alphonse Mucha-inspired mural in the background, a beautiful young woman wreathed in flowers.

We dropped into Bikes on Wheels, but it was their pre-summer inventory and David and Anne were too busy to join us for lunch.

"So how is Liam doing?" Karen asked.

I'd just returned from a visit to Sudbury, where Liam was recovering from surgery. I hadn't minded the drive up on my own. After Port Perry, I put on Three Dog Run's EP, and listened to it on repeat the rest of the way. I'd been ready to take Liz's car, but Karen had insisted I borrow the Mystery Machine. "Liam's doing okay. He and Joan are spending a week up at the cottage."

"Well, your grandma didn't call it the Good Medicine Cabin for nothing. That place has a lot of healing energy."

When I'd arrived in Sudbury, Liam was waiting for me on the front stoop of our home. We hugged and he handed me a cold beer.

"Doctor," he said.

"Professor," I replied.

Grandpa and Betty had already left for their summer-long road trip with the Miltons, and Liam was house-sitting for both couples. Dirt covered his big, callused hands. He'd started working on rebuilding the flagstone path to the garden.

"So." I gestured, as politely as I could. "How're you feeling down there?"

"Swelling's gone down." He tossed a shovel into a wheel-barrow. "It's still a little tender. It gets better every day."

I glanced toward the pile of gravel in the drive. "Shouldn't you be taking it easy?"

Liam shrugged. "I'm being careful. The stiches are starting to dissolve. I think the incision's okay. You want to take a look at it?"

"What? No. I mean. You'll see Dr. Barr about that, right?"

"Dr. Barr died last year."

"He died?" The man had been our pediatrician. He'd been our family doctor our whole lives. "Liam, why didn't you tell me?"

"I guess I forgot."

"He couldn't have been that old, what, maybe sixty? He's younger than grandpa."

"It was a skiing accident. He got caught in an avalanche."

"Oh my god." These things happened. The truth was I hadn't thought about Dr. Barr in years. "He knew us as babies. He knew Mom and Dad."

"He knew pretty much everyone in town, Dan. He was a popular guy. People miss him."

"Did you miss him?"

Liam shrugged, hooking his thumbs into his jeans. "The new doctor's not so bad."

"Is that all you have to say? Did you even go to his funeral?"

I hadn't come up to Sudbury to pick a fight. I'd come up to check-in on Liam, to offer my support after his surgery. Except I hadn't been home five minutes and here I was, right at it again. You'd think triplets would get along. But nothing was further from the truth. All the locals knew who the Garneau boys were. Pat's ex Blonde Dawn had called me the angry one.

I hated being the angry one.

"No," Liam said. "I didn't go to the funeral."

Of course he hadn't. Why had I even bothered to ask? "Well." I examined the beer in my hand. "I'm sorry he's gone."

"It's still Dr. Barr."

"What at you talking about?"

"His son took over his practice. I still go to see Dr. Barr. It's just a younger version. He's a decent guy, a lot like his dad."

I shook my head. Honking geese passed low across the neighbouring field, heading north. "Well, I'm glad you're seeing someone."

"I'm glad to see you, Dan."

"Why?" I glanced up. "What is it?"

"I'm just happy to be alive."

For a second, I wondered if Liam had started drinking again. His sun-weathered face was flushed, his eyes bright in a way I hadn't seen in years. Liam used to be obsessed with collecting bones and antlers. I still remembered his excitement when he showed me a whole moose skull he'd found out in the bush, my first Christmas home from university.

"Dan." He gestured. "I have to show you something." He led me past the woodshed and pointed up at our maple tree, its far-reaching branches in full bloom.

I shaded my eyes. "What is it?"

"There's rot set in. We need to take it down."

"What? It looks perfectly healthy to me."

"No. The treehouse."

In a graffiti-stained booth at Sneaky Dee's, Karen sat back as the server set down a cast-iron plate of sizzling onions, peppers and steak. "So." Karen nodded. "The pirate ship treehouse, eh?"

"Yeah." I'd followed Liam up a ladder to check it out. "It was all covered in moss and mould. Liam even ripped out a few planks with his bare hands to prove his point."

"I remember," Karen said, "when your grandpa built that."

"Twenty years ago."

Karen handed me a fresh flour tortilla. "So what's the plan?"

"Well, Grandpa had asked if Liam could take it down."

"Oh, that reminds me. My mom sent this last night.

Check this out." Karen poked at her phone and set it in front of me.

It was a video of Grandpa and Betty in full safety harnesses and helmets, flying overhead, spread-eagled against the sky.

"Oh my god."

"Swipe left, there's more. Pass the guacamole. So, is the treehouse gone now?"

"Well, it's totally fallen apart, if that's what you mean." There were photos of the Miltons and Grandpa and Betty splashing about the beach, Betty in a hot pink floral print, Mrs. Milton in a ruffled two piece. "Your parents are in really great shape."

"They go to Pilates and spin classes three times a week. It makes me dizzy watching them. Wasn't your grandpa a boxer?"

"Yeah, in the merchant navy, back in the day. He taught all three of us how to throw a punch. That's how Liam got into kung fu."

Karen took a bite of her tortilla and chewed thoughtfully. "So you said he's doing okay?"

"What? No. He's on all this cholesterol medication. He still refuses to get a hearing aid. He thinks he can drink and smoke and eat whatever he wants. I don't think he realizes how old he is."

"I meant Liam."

I handed back the phone. Wasaga Beach was just the first leg of a cross-country journey to the East Coast and back. The four seniors in their Winnebagos were acting like kids on this road trip.

"Liam doesn't complain."

"It's weird to think," Karen said, "he has only one testicle now."

"His surgeon offered to put in a prosthesis, but he said no. He didn't see what the point was."

"Tell that to women with mastectomies."

"He asked if I wanted to look at it, to see how it was healing."

"So, how did it look?"

"Seriously?"

"I thought you boys checked out at each other's junk all the time."

"Ha-ha. Funny."

"Daniel, you're a doctor. Why so squeamish?"

"Karen, this is my brother's junk you're talking about."

"It's Liam's junk. Trust me, I have a lot more history with it than you do. He can still make babies, right?"

I reached for the chipotle sauce. "Yes, he can. Why is everyone so interested in this?"

"Who else was asking?"

"Pat. It was almost like he had this panic attack when he thought Liam might not be able to have kids."

"Has Pat ever wanted to be a dad?"

"Pat loves kids. But he's got Three Dog Run, right?" Carefully, I wrapped my tortilla. "His last girlfriend called him a man-child. If he ever settles down, that's still a long ways away."

"I'm not sure, Daniel, if anyone's ever ready."

"David's ready."

Karen licked sour cream from her fingertips. "And how are the monthly deposits coming?"

"After the abortion, they took a break. They're trying

again this month, except Ai Chang's three days late and David's a nervous wreck."

"Just three days?" Karen refilled both our glasses. "David needs to relax. Are you still doing the fluffer thing?"

"The what?"

"You do realize," Karen said, "I looked up 'spit-roasting'."

"Oh, that." I gulped from my pint. "I don't know. I mean, we haven't talked about it."

"I thought," Karen said, "you'd have proposed to him by now."

"I keep trying. I was thinking about it at Paddle the Don. But then the whole Stephan thing went down."

"Daniel, about that." Karen sat back. "I'm sorry. I had no idea Bob had invited him."

"It's okay. I mean, it was totally awkward at first. I hadn't seen the guy in years. Then he basically tells me I broke up his marriage."

"He said that?"

"Well, no. He put it differently. He actually thanked me. But the whole time I just kept thinking about us having sex. And I still had David's ring in my pocket. How messed up is that?"

"You wanted to have sex with him?"

"I was thinking about how we used to have sex."

"That's completely different. Or did you actually really want to have sex with him?"

"With Stephan? No! I mean, I don't think so. No?"

"Having an erotic fantasy," Karen said, "about an ex-lover is the most normal thing in the world. Daniel, you told me that. I'm glad you introduced him to us. I was wondering when you would."

"You recognized him?"

"Stephan Tondeur? Of course, I did. We all did. Your old hockey coach who you did it with on a Zamboni?"

"Who's we? Who else knows what happened?"

"Daniel, relax. No one knows about the Zamboni, I promise."

I studied the tabletop. "I know coaches can take advantage of players. You hear about it all the time. It happens. And that kind of abuse is awful. But this. This was different. You'd think I'd be in therapy about this. But it's the opposite."

"You miss him."

"I did, for a long time. But you move on, right?"

"That's right." Karen looked me in the eye. "And I've kept your secret."

I bit my lower lip. "I might've told a few people."

"You boys do that, don't you? You just can't help it."

"Hey, if everyone talked more honestly about sex, then people wouldn't be left guessing and making assumptions and getting all sorts of things wrong."

"True." Karen pointed. "Did you know abstinence-only education is proven to be totally ineffective?"

"I'm not surprised. Did you know David was a virgin when we met? He'd never done it with another guy."

"Really?"

"I mean, I just found out. We've been together five years. How come I didn't know that?"

"You told me he was this Don Corleone."

"Don Giovanni."

"Whatever." Karen scraped up the last of the mole sauce. "So, what does it mean to lose your gay virginity, anyway?"

"What do you think it means?" I lowered my voice. "It means, you know, fucking. Anal penetration."

"Giving or receiving?"

"Either I suppose."

"So you say."

I shook my head. "What else could it mean?"

"Well, I think," Karen said, leaning forward, "it might mean different things to different people. For instance, does getting fingered or fingering someone else count?"

"Um. I think a penis needs to be involved."

"And what if it's two girls?"

"I hadn't thought about that."

"Some girls," Karen said, "let themselves get fucked up the ass by guys (with their penises, to be clear) just so they can still call themselves virgins."

"What? No."

"And some people think you lose your v-card when you have any kind of sexual intimacy."

"What counts as sexual intimacy?"

"Exactly." Karen made a face. "This whole antiquated concept conflating 'purity' with what we do with our genitalia is ridiculous. You lose you virginity when you feel you lose your virginity."

"Well, as far as I'm concerned," I said, "I lost my virginity when I topped Stephan."

"I wonder," Karen said, "if he ever thought to buy his wife a strap-on."

"I never asked."

"It might've saved their marriage."

"I'm not so sure. They broke up because he cheated on her for years. Now he's dating some older guy from

Vancouver, someone he met at a conference. They're planning a trip to Puerto Vallarta this fall."

"Well good for him," Karen said. "I'm glad he got his happy ending."

"I'm not sure I'd call it that. It's more like a new start."

Karen peeled apart two tortillas and handed me one. The Cowboy Junkies played in the background, something melancholy about Sweet Jane.

"Thank you," Karen said.

"For what?"

"For convincing me to come back to Toronto."

I studied Karen's face. We weren't children anymore. But her eyes were the same: dark golden-brown and quick. "I'm glad you're back."

"Did you know," Karen said, "Bob and Elsie threw me a going-away party? Bob took us out on his boat to this secret picnic spot. There was a waterfall and an osprey nest on the side of a cliff. Did you know ospreys mate for life? We brought everyone's favourite food. Zephyr had Cheerios in chocolate milk. Sky had spaghetti and meatballs. Bob made me grilled cheese and tomato soup over the fire. We lit sparklers and watched the sun set. The whole day was beautiful. It was perfect. The girls made me goodbye cards."

"You mean a lot to them, Karen."

"You know what Elsie said to me? She said I'm like family, and that their home on Manitoulin would always be my home too."

"She said that?"

"And she'd baked me a cake. That woman has never baked a cake in her life. I think it was the girls' idea."

The song was over now. On the ceiling, a yin-yang symbol, a peace symbol, and a bright yellow happy face framed the words: "GET IT?" Karen drew a deep breath. After a moment, I said: "You okay?"

"Yeah." Karen reached across the table and squeezed my hand. The dimples showed in her cheeks. "Yeah, I am."

After lunch, we walked together to The Beguiling, where tables piled with discounted comics lined the sidewalk. Behind the glass front, books and graphic novels crammed the tall shelves.

"He asked about you," I said.

"Who?"

"Liam."

Karen paused, rifling through the white cardboard boxes. "What did he want to know?"

I toed the sidewalk. "He just asked how you're doing."

"What did you tell him?"

I set down my gym bag, and pushed up my ball cap. "I told him how it was great having you and Anne living right across the hall."

"What else did you tell him?"

"I told him you'd started your summer teaching job and that you really liked it. He was happy for you."

Karen studied a copy of *Black Widow*. "Did he actually say that?"

I leaned against the brick wall. "You know how Liam is."

"Yeah."

"Since when were you into comics anyway?"

"I'm not." Karen moved on to another box. "Anne's always on the lookout for back issues of Marvel's Tsunami imprint."

"You're a good big sister."

"Tell that to Anne." Karen worked her way through multiple issues of *Tank Girl*. "So, did he say anything else?"

"Why're you asking?"

"I'm just asking. Hey, look at this." Karen held up a comic in a plastic sleeve with a tattered Superman cape on the front. "It's #75."

I read the cover. "'The Death of Superman'?"

"Back in the '90s," Karen said, "sales were down. So the writers got together and decided to kill him off."

"Just like that?"

Yeah. Just like that."

I buried my hands in my pockets. "Karen, what's going on between you two?"

"Between me and Liam? Daniel, we're fine." Karen thrust the comic at me. "Look, I'm just taking some time."

"Are you even talking to him right now?"

Karen shrugged. "I'm not sure what good that would do. I mean, Liam's got Joan now, right? Detective Joan's a terrific gal. Gotta love them Birkenstocks. I'm pretty sure they deserve each other."

"You said Joan was a nice person."

"Yeah, and?"

"So why am I detecting this note of hostility?"

"What?" Karen threw a copy of *She-Hulk* back into its bin. "Anne," she said, "gets hostile. When do I ever get hostile?"

"You don't, not normally. It's been a while."

"Tell me, when was the last time?"

"I dunno. When I broke up with Marcus. You called him a narcissistic prick."

"I did? Okay maybe I said that. That was a long time ago."

"Like I said."

"I was protective of you."

"Who are you protecting now?"

"I'm protecting me, Daniel. Okay? Does that work for you?"

"He asked me if you were happy."

Now Karen straightened. "Liam asked that?"

"Yes, he did."

"Do you realize," Karen said, "in twenty years, he's never asked me if I was happy?"

"Well. That's just Liam."

Karen folded her arms. "And what did you tell him?"

"That you two are miserable apart from each other."

"What? You didn't." Karen's expression went completely blank. "Tell me you didn't say that."

"Hey. It's the truth, isn't it?"

Karen's eyes were round and bright. Finally, she said: "I should slap you again. I'm not kidding. I mean it."

"Look, hey. At first I thought I was being selfish, wanting you two back together. I mean. Karen, listen to me. He's my brother and you're my best friend. But you've always told me it hasn't worked. Except people change. Liam's changed, you said so yourself. After his cancer scare, he told me he woke up. He's woken up. He said he realized he'd been sleepwalking pretty much through most of his life. Karen, he's going up to the cottage to break up with Joan."

Karen's mouth formed a thin line. "He told me already."

"What?"

"Before the surgery," she said, "he told me he was ready to end things between them. I told him not to."

"What? Why?"

"Why do you think?"

"Karen, listen to me." I drew a breath. "Liam told me that he loves you. He told me that he's in love with you, and that he's just realizing this now."

"Yeah." Karen glared. "He told me that too."

"He did? And what did you say?"

"I told him it was over. I mean, I mean what the fuck? I just moved to Toronto to get away from him, for chrissake. I was ready to move to fucking Nunavut! And after twenty years, he decides to tell me this now? He had his chance. I'm done. Holy shit. I just want to be done, you know?"

"'I wish,'" I said, "'I knew how to quit you.'"

"What?"

I cleared my throat. "It's what Ennis says to Jack."

Karen just shook her head, open-mouthed.

"Never mind. Look, you keep thinking you're okay with this, Karen. But you're not. And I can understand why you might think this is what you need to do, after all this time. But Liam, he's just had this near-death experience. He just survived cancer. That really genuinely can change a person, you know? He's changed. He's a new man. He's coming."

"What?"

"He's coming after you. He told me not to say anything, that he wanted to do this himself. But Liam's coming to Toronto."

"And you encouraged him?"

"I didn't encourage him. I just …"

"You just what?"

"I dunno. I didn't discourage him."

"Are you insane?" Karen stared at me. "Daniel. You're supposed to be my friend. You of all people were supposed to get this. But you think you know better than me when it comes to Liam? Fuck!" She raised her arms and dropped them again. "Fuck!" She started to walk away, but then whirled about. She marched up and punched me in the chest, hard enough for it to hurt, and hard enough to make me take a step back. "Fuck you!"

"Karen."

"Daniel Garneau." Karen's face was all twisted. I'd never seen her this upset before. "This was supposed to be a whole new beginning. You promised me. You promised me it would be! You've ruined everything. How could you? No. This conversation's over. Stop, don't. Don't talk to me. And by the way, it's what Jack says to Ennis, you fucking idiot."

Now she did walk away. I watched her turn the corner. I wanted to follow her, but my feet felt like they were planted in cement.

If Karen had superpowers, there'd be flaming, blackened footprints left in her wake.

And a hole in my chest.

A white ice cream truck trundled past, its bright bells jingling, the first one I'd seen this year. I felt dizzy again. How could this possibly have happened? One moment you're cruising along casually on a pleasant Sunday afternoon. The next second you hit a bump, and the whole world's careening. Everything was carnage, and everything was burning. This was just like my parents all over again. It didn't feel real. It wasn't right. Karen and I had got into arguments before, but not like this. I couldn't accept this. But she was gone. And I was left standing alone, ditched, clutching a comic book in my hand.

And Superman was dead.

∽ I wore my best underwear.

Weeks earlier, Parker had invited me to Wonderland, but I cancelled last minute, having scheduled a massage that same day. A classmate had recommended a cousin of hers and scribbled down a number. I booked a session right there on the spot. I'd never had a massage in my life. Before the appointment, I got a haircut, and then spent an hour in the bathroom manscaping. I ended up showering twice. When David asked if I was going to also bring flowers, I threw a magazine at him.

The Queen Street address turned out to be a wellness clinic tucked in between Ali's Roti Shop and a vegan Danish bakery. The waiting room smelled of cedar, and a bouquet of dried lavender adorned the wall. A receptionist with a French manicure had me complete a medical questionnaire. Afterwards, I sat on a chair beneath a series of Edward Burtynsky prints.

When my massage therapist appeared, I tried not to stare. He introduced himself as Ryan. I couldn't decide if he looked more like Ryan Reynolds or Ryan Gosling. All three buttons of his polo shirt were undone, his chest hair poking through. I observed his enormous, thick-veined hands. They were like the hands of a CFL quarterback or

Michelangelo's *David*. I was mortified. Following him down a narrow hallway, I wondered if it was too late to cancel. I could check my phone and explain there was an emergency.

Before I knew it, we were in a dimly-lit chamber with soothing music playing and white towels laid out. Scanning a clipboard, he asked what had brought me there. What was I supposed to say? That I lay awake at night panicking over my crushing school debt? That I was terrified my boyfriend was making the biggest mistake of his life donating his sperm so his brother could be a dad? That I'd just had the hugest fight with my best friend and now she wasn't even talking to me?

Stress, I managed to say. He nodded (as if he'd heard that maybe a thousand times), asked a few more questions, instructed me to remove my clothes and left the room.

I took off my shirt. Then I unbuckled my pants. I folded both as neatly as I could, tucking my socks into my shoes. I was still sniffing my underarms, when he knocked on the door and asked if I was ready. I jumped up onto the table, flung the sheet over me and told him I was.

I lay on my stomach, my face in the cradle, arms at my side. I watched his feet like I was observing the approach of an axe-wielding psycho killer. I reminded myself Ryan was a professional, a certified healthcare provider belonging to a regulatory college. This thought was helpful, until he placed his hands on me.

An hour later, when I left the clinic, I did feel more relaxed, relieved and faintly nauseous.

Back home, climbing the stairs to my loft, I ran into Karen coming down with a laundry hamper. "Karen!" I wanted to tell her everything: how I'd just got a full body deep tissue massage by Gosling-Reynolds with his mutant Michelangelo hands and had almost thrown up as he worked on my psoas muscles.

But Karen walked right past me without a word, descending the stairwell to the laundry room.

"C'mon, seriously?" I shouted after her.

Later, when I knocked on her door, it was Anne who answered, eating Ramen in a styrofoam cup, with pink highlights in her hair. Before I could open my mouth, Anne said: "She doesn't want to talk to you."

"I know she doesn't." I held out a note. "Just give her this."

"She also told me not to pass on any messages. Sorry." She closed the door in my face.

The next day, I knocked again. This time when Anne answered, her hair was bright purple. "This isn't for Karen." I thrust out a comic. "It's for you."

"What is it?"

"It's a Tsunami imprint."

"Really?" Anne chewed on her lip ring. "Why're you giving me this?"

"You follow *Runaways*, don't you?"

"Yeah. That and *Mystique*. Nico Minoru and Raven Darkhölme are badass. Where'd you find this issue? Never mind, okay." Anne flipped through its pages. "She's still not going to talk to you."

"Help me out here."

"I'm not," Anne said, "even supposed to be talking to you." But she didn't close the door. "Look, she's pissed. What'd you do, anyway?"

"She didn't tell you?"

"No. But, I don't want to know." She glanced over her shoulder. "She hasn't been eating. Have you thought about making her some food?"

The next day, David asked why I was making so many grilled cheese sandwiches. "They're for next door," I said.

"Is Karen still mad at you?"

I nodded, wiping my forehead, spatula in hand.

"And this is your peace offering?" David stood next to me over the hot stove. "Daniel, you can't give her these."

"What's wrong with these?" I exclaimed. "I make great grilled cheese sandwiches."

David's jaw was set. Taking me by the shoulders, he looked me in the eye. "Because," he said, "I love you."

The next day I texted Anne and she was waiting for me when I stepped into the hallway. Today her hair was spiky blue with orange streaks. "It took you long enough," she said. "What's that?"

I held out a glass dish wrapped in tin foil. "This," I said, "is Apulia Panini grilled cheese, with a walnut and arugula garlic pesto, sundried tomato compote, and a black olive tapenade."

Anne's eyebrows rose. "Okay."

I handed her the dish. "Will you make sure she gets that? There's enough for both of you."

"Sure. She should be home soon."

Footsteps thumped up the stairwell but it was only Rick. Today, he was wearing eyeliner and black lipstick, and his long hair was bound up tightly in two horns. When he saw me, he froze on the top step.

"Hi," I said.

Rick blushed and made a growling sound.

"It's his wrestling persona," Anne said. "I'm helping him develop a character."

Rick looked between Anne and me. "I've enrolled in the spring intensive training program with Superkick'd."

"Really?"

Rick's eyes narrowed. "It's a sport."

"We're deciding," Anne said, "what his wrestling moniker should be. It's either Doogie Devil Dog or Beelzebub." She leaned against the doorframe. "We're working out a back history. We figured his time with the Hells Angels could come in useful."

"You," I asked, "used to belong to the Hells Angels?"

Rick grunted.

I cleared my throat. "That's cool."

"No." Rick glowered. "It wasn't. They were assholes."

"But he left in good standing, didn't you, Devil Dog?"

"I kinda like Beelzebub," Rick said.

Anne nodded at me. "It's a work-in-progress."

"That smells really good." Rick gestured. "What is that?"

"It's grilled cheese."

Anne hefted the glass dish. "It's Karen's favourite."

Rick jerked his thumb in my direction. "She still mad at him?"

"Mm-hm."

Rick scowled at me. "What'd you do, anyway?"

"Um. It's kinda personal." Now both of them were looking at me like I'd just drowned a bagful of kittens, or voted PC in the provincial elections. "Anne, will you just keep that warm in the oven?"

"Sure. I can do that." She stepped aside and gestured Rick in. "Here, take this, will you?" She handed him the foiled dish, and patted him on the back. Since when, I wondered, did Anne become such good buddies with our ex-Hells Angel metalhead building manager?

"Hey look." Anne hesitated before closing the door. "Daniel." I fully expected her to tell me not to get my hopes up. But she only said: "Whatever's going on between you and Karen, good luck."

CHAPTER ELEVEN

La Fin Du Monde

"**D**aniel, you're telling me, you actually came during your massage session?"

I raised a finger. "Hold on."

"Goodness gracious." David splayed a hand over his chest. "I didn't know it was going to be *that* kind of massage."

"It wasn't that kind of a massage! The guy was a registered professional. And I didn't come. I just kinda … leaked."

David laughed and threw himself onto the couch. "You do leak, Daniel. It has been oftentimes observed."

"Semen leakage is common. It's normal." I rummaged in the kitchen cupboards. "It happens to guys."

"I didn't say it wasn't."

"I mean, take wet dreams."

David flicked his beer cap so that it bounced off the head of the male mannequin in the corner. "I haven't had one of those in years."

I rolled my eyes. "I wouldn't expect you to."

"This guy was that hot, eh?"

"He was working on my hip flexors." I poured chips into a bowl. "He was going right at it. It was actually really painful."

"I wonder," David said, smiling and sipping on his beer, "if Charles and Megan might enjoy the marvellous manual manipulations of this magical masseur of yours."

"He's not my magical masseur. His name was Ryan and he was my classmate's cousin."

"You think," David said, "I could book a session with Magic Ryan before my next visit to Ai Chang and Luke?"

"Ha-ha. Funny."

The buzzer rang and David jumped up to let in our guests. I'd spent the morning cleaning and tidying our loft, picking up David's empty pop cans, pizza boxes, and scattered magazines. Bicycle tools and chains littered the kitchen table. Under the couch, I discovered our Cherry Scented Vibro Dong (missing for months), covered in dust bunnies. I stood holding it at arm's length, deliberating whether to just throw it in the trash, when David snatched it.

This afternoon, Parker's boyfriend Kyle was going to lead us all on a Dungeons & Dragons adventure. I'd never played D&D before, but I felt I owed Parker one after bailing on his Wonderland outing.

I was fully expecting the two to show up in cosplay outfits, but Parker was only wearing over-sized aviator glasses and a T-shirt featuring Audrey Hepburn from *Breakfast at Tiffany's*.

"How was Wonderland?" I asked.

Parker and Kyle clutched each other's arms. "Deep within the valley," they whispered, "lies a mythical creature with enormous strength. Those brave enough will set out on a quest to conquer … the Behemoth."

"That good, eh?"

Parker nodded. "Oh, 'twas a monstrous beast."

"A wild ride," Kyle said.

"We rode it seven times." Parker and Kyle high-fived.

"I'm impressed."

"And Daniel," Parker asked, "how was your massage session?"

"It was a wild ride," David yelled from the kitchen.

Today, Kyle was sporting cargo shorts, and carrying his official sailing club tote bag. The soles of his feet were black. When I asked him why he was barefoot, he said that it helped him with earthing. Before I could ask what "earthing" was, Anne and Rick appeared at the front door. Parker greeted them as if they were old friends.

"Parker said we needed a fourth player," David said, melting butter in the microwave, "so I suggested Anne. Then she asked if Rick could join us."

To add to my confusion, it turned out it was Anne leading the game not Kyle. "And what's 'DMing'?" I asked.

Parker had brought his own battery-powered sharpener, and was sharpening pencils one after another. "Someone has to be the Dungeon Master," he said, flourishing a Staedtler graphite HB. "Kyle really prefers to play, and Anne already had this one-shot adventure prepared, involving goblin pirates and merfolk! How exciting is that?" He blew on his pencil tip and lined it up next to five others.

Kyle untied a leather bag and dumped a set of crystal dice onto the table. After that, everyone took out their dice. I felt like I was the only one who'd forgotten to bring his stick to a game of pick-up. "Don't worry," David said, "you and I can share."

Everyone sat around discussing artifacts, alignments and spell books, scattering popcorn everywhere. Rick had brought his own snacks: a jumbo bag of McSweeney's beef jerky and two cans of Moosehead in his tool belt. When David commented how he looked like Blackbeard in his red bandana, Rick showed everyone a skull-and-crossbones tattoo he had on the back of his neck. Rick, it turned out, had been playing D&D over twenty years.

Anne, for her part, sat at the table with her feet on her longboard, poring over books and notes like she was preparing for her MCAT. Eventually, she pulled out a number of sheets and handed them to us. We were to choose from a set of pre-generated characters, each with their own list of attributes, class, weapons and armour. Except she also wanted us to pick our own secondary skills and back history. "I'd like to remind you," Anne said, "you don't need to be confined to binary notions of sex and gender. And you can be whatever race you want to be."

Incredibly, a whole hour passed before we settled on who everyone was and their backstories. I turned out to be the only human in the party, a penniless paladin named Sir Danton De Villiers, the long-lost brother to David's half-elf rogue, Fausto Fandahk the Feckless, our common mother being a disgraced lady-in-waiting to the High Queen of Albion. Rick chose to play a bearded female dwarf fighter, and Kyle a halfling druid. Parker landed on a gnome bard he named Winkle the Wary Wise. When David announced that Danton and Fausto were also lovers, Anne didn't blink an eye.

A week later, I met Nadia over cake on the terrace of Casa Loma overlooking the city. Beyond the parapet, brilliant beds of rhododendron bordered the garden paths. Wildflowers and roses were just coming into early bloom. I learned that Casa Loma was a century-old, Gothic Revival style mansion, once a private home and now a popular museum and historic site, restored by the city at great expense to its original Edwardian splendour. With its soaring turrets, castellations, leaded windows and secret passageways, it was no surprise the building was billed as Canada's foremost castle.

"And you've never played D&D before?" Nadia asked.

"No, never. But Anne was really great. Apparently, she's been running her own campaigns for years. There was a sunken galleon, these really scary sea zombies, and a mist dragon that helped us escape. Rick played his dwarf Maewyst Flintbeard as this pansexual character—that was a lot of fun. Oh, and none of us died."

Nadia sipped her Earl Grey. "Well done."

Below us, a vast fountain pool gushed and sparkled. "Right at the end, David was hit by a poison arrow but I saved him with my healing hands. Except the arrow was also cursed, and Fausto lost all his memory of me. Now he has no idea who I am."

"Weren't you two lovers?"

"We were! Now I have to go on this quest to lift the curse."

"Or," Nadia said, "you could have Fausto fall in love with Sir Danton all over again."

"Did I mention we're half-brothers?"

"How very dramatic."

"We have a follow-up adventure planned next month. Parker says, at least it's not like I'm a fairy in love with a giant."

"Now that," Nadia said, "would be an unconventional romance."

Today Nadia was wearing a lace sundress, and multistone earrings that matched her slim sandals. For years, we'd met over cake in different parts of the city. Now that Nadia was seeing Pat, I wondered if anything would change between us. I was grateful to receive her invitation. I'd never been to Casa Loma before and wondered what other landmarks in Toronto I'd overlooked all these years.

"Parker," I said, "told me D&D allowed him to discover he was neuroqueer. He says RPGs gave him a safe space to think and feel and act in different ways."

"RPGs?"

"Role-playing games. People, I'm told, use fantasy role-playing to figure out all sorts of identity issues."

"Do you think, then, your friend Rick might be transgender?"

"Because he played a female dwarf? Oh, no. I mean, I dunno. I never thought about it. I don't think so. I think he was just having a lot of fun. There was this moment when Maewyst was flirting with the one-legged barkeep. Anne had Rick roll for seduction, and he got a natural 20! You don't want to know what happened after that."

"It sounds like you enjoyed yourselves."

"Well, that got us the treasure map and the whole adventure started. I always thought of Rick as this big, scary-looking guy. He actually used to belong to the Hells Angels, can you believe it? His dad and uncle were founding members of the Montreal chapter. But Rick's super nice and funny when you get to know him. He was the one who befriended the mist dragon and convinced her to help us."

"It sounds like these games can allow us to escape the persona we play in real life."

"What do you mean?"

Nadia poured the last of her tea. "In our everyday lives, we all perform roles. We go to great lengths to conform to people's expectations."

"Rick told David he never wanted to be part of a motorcycle gang. He just wanted to be close to his dad."

"And in our time we may play many parts." Nadia set down her silver spoon, observing the bright fountain water. "The front stage is where we follow our scripts. But there is a back stage."

"A back stage?"

"It's where we can relax and set aside our masks. In those moments we can be vulnerable, and show our true, honest selves."

An iridescent hummingbird hovered about Nadia's brow. "And are we backstage now?" I asked.

Nadia smiled over her teacup. "I'd like to think so, Daniel."

Later that afternoon, we strolled past suits of armour and coats of arms, exploring Casa Loma's imposing chambers: the Great Hall, the Oak Room, the Library. We paused in the spacious Conservatory beneath its magnificent stained-glass ceiling. Banners of light from the ornate windows unfurled across the pink and grey Italian marble floor.

"His dad," I said, "got shot in the Quebec Biker War. After that, Rick was done. He said he'd had enough, and just walked away. I didn't even know members could leave the Hells Angels. But Rick did."

Drops of water trickled into a small fountain basin. "This Rick," Nadia said, "he's your building manager, the one I met at David's birthday outing?"

"Yeah, that's him."

"I remember he was very shy and polite with me." Nadia ran her fingers through glistening ferns. "He seemed like a sweet man."

"Are you kidding?" Rick acted the part of a surly metal-head. But over the years, he had in fact helped us out a lot, installing our claw foot bathtub, fixing our keg at a party once. As the manager of Graffiti's Bar & Grill, he'd arranged for Three Dog Run's first real gig.

"Sometimes," Nadia said, "a boy just needs to be given a chance to let down his hair."

"Did you know the Hells Angels greet each other by kissing on the lips? I mean total, full-on making out."

"No, I did not know that."

"They're this hyper-masculine motorcycle club, right? But Rick says he saw his dad and uncle kissing other guys lots of times. He says it's common among biker gangs, that it's all done on purpose, to shock the public."

Nadia laughed and shook her head. "Then they perform their outlaw role well."

From the third floor, we climbed a spiralling iron staircase, and stepped out onto the rooftop of Casa Loma's Norman tower. Beyond the broad crenellations, the vista of Toronto was breathtaking.

"There was a time," Nadia said, "not long ago, when men in society might commonly embrace, hold hands in public, or even share a bed."

"Straight men?"

Nadia nodded. "They would speak and write to each other with sentimentality and tenderness, and share their innermost thoughts and emotions."

"And this was normal?"

"No one considered this conduct unmanly, if that's what you mean." Nadia gazed over the battlement walls. "Romantic male friendships are well-documented throughout history. The ancient Greeks called this *philia*, and considered it the highest and most noble form of love."

I imagined grown men holding hands, expressing their affection and love for each other. How different would the world be if no one cared?

"There are many cultures in the world today," Nadia said, "where this kind of intimacy is still commonplace."

"Nadia." I hugged my chest. "I want to tell you something." I studied the hillside. "I went," I finally said, "for a massage a couple weeks ago. I had this male RMT. He was really attractive and it was my first time, and I got, well, excited."

"You mean sexually aroused?"

"Something like that."

"I suspect," Nadia said kindly, "that's not so uncommon."

"That's what I told myself. David didn't care. He just thought it was really funny. But what I didn't tell him was how it actually happened."

"Oh?"

"The session was really uncomfortable actually. I was sore the whole next day. But there was this moment when I was lying on my back, and the guy—his name was Ryan—he picks up my hand. That took me off guard. I wasn't expecting to be holding another man's hand in my own. And suddenly there's like this electricity that flashes through my whole body, up into my throat and down into my stomach. He starts working on the inside of my forearm and my wrist. Then he's got my hand in both of his, and he's massaging the pads of my palm, and even my individual fingers. It was really personal. I mean, it was shocking how intimate that felt."

I lowered my gaze. "Then he switches sides and does the same with my other arm. That's when it happened. That's when I kinda leaked." I didn't dare look at Nadia. "You'd think," I said, laughing, "I'd never been touched by another guy in my life."

"And have you?"

Now I glanced up at her. But Nadia's face was open and sincere. She brushed her hair back, observing me.

"Nadia," I finally said, "I've had a lot of sex with a lot of guys. But this. This was different. It has happened a few times. Once it happened with a total stranger at a bathhouse. I'll never forget that."

"And at other times?"

"It happened the first time I met David. We were at this punk bar, a band was playing. We were standing next to each other. The sides of our arms touched, and he didn't pull away. I felt him lean into me. I felt it then. With David, when we touch, I still feel that spark, that connection."

"Even after five years?"

"It's just different now, more familiar."

I remembered the first time David and I had sex without condoms, the moment I felt myself inside of him. It was a sensation I'd never experienced before in my life. I hadn't lasted a minute. After that, David asked if I would bottom for him. He had me lie on my back, and rimmed and fingered me a long time, before he finally stood and repositioned my hips with a pillow.

"'And your very flesh,'" Nadia said, "'shall be a great poem.'"

I drew a breath.

"It's something Walt Whitman wrote." Nadia's lips parted. "And this Ryan, will you go back to him?"

"Part of me wants to. For sure. But I dunno. I don't think so. I mean, I wouldn't want to go back on purpose, you know? Not just for that. David says he can give me a massage the next time I wanted one. This time with a happy ending. If that's all I was after, I think, Nadia, I'd just rather do it with my boyfriend."

I recalled David's grip on my ankle, the angle of his hips, the expression on his face as he entered me. I looked down upon the flight of birds. How orderly the world seemed from this distal vantage point. How simple and stately the skyscrapers appeared on the horizon. A jet traced its graceful, perfect line across the sky.

"Parker's boyfriend Kyle," I said, "told me there are electrons that flow through the earth, and that he goes barefoot whenever he can so that energy can flow up into him, so that his body can be in balance with the universe. It sounds crazy, right? But then I remembered I actually felt it once myself, when I was camping last year, this connection moving through everything."

"In yoga," Nadia said, "it is called *prana*. It is a life force energy. It flows around us and inside of us."

"And between people?"

"Between all things, Daniel."

I could always tell when David was close. In the set of his jaw, in the rhythm of his breath. He crushed his mouth to mine, and his whole body shuddered. In that moment, I could feel him come inside of me. "Parker says human touch is the most important thing to him in the world."

"Prana is in our breath and in our being. When we touch each other, it moves between our skin. You're a doctor, this need not be mystical. Our bodies are charged with electrical currents and magnetic fields."

"And neurotransmitters and hormones."

"We can learn a lot from our natural energy and our bodily fluids. Our saliva yields a painkiller six-times more powerful than morphine. Tears also help to reduce pain and stress. Our sweat is a carrier for chemical signalling."

"Now you sound like Charles."

"Your friend Charles Ondaatje is trying to understand the world the best that he can, the way he was trained, the same way a musician might learn how sound waves move through metal or wood."

For years, Charles in his research had tried to reduce human love to biochemical processes. But even I knew this was like trying to reduce a novel to mere syntax, or a symphony to the vibrations in a catgut string.

Nadia was a poet and she was a blues singer. I'd even attended a few of her yoga classes. I imagined her intimate with my brother Pat. She'd told me once that he took his time as a lover, that he paid attention. I'd watched Pat once having sex with a girl. I knew what his body looked like aroused. He'd held my hand when that same girl made me come. These kinds of experiences were not easily forgotten.

"'Love the earth and sun and the animals,'" I said.

Nadia's thin, dark eyebrows rose. "'Despise riches, give alms to everyone that asks.'"

"'Stand up,'" we said, "'for the stupid and the crazy.'"

Now Nadia studied me with a discerning gaze, her dress fluttering in the breeze. "You surprise me constantly, Daniel Garneau."

"My grandma," I said, "was an English teacher. The dementia ruined her, but she never forgot her poetry. It was like these words were kept in an entirely untouched, perfect part of her brain. I spent a lot of time with her before I moved to Toronto. I always felt safe when I was with her. Sometimes she'd just sit and recite poems for hours from memory."

"By heart."

"Whitman was one of her favourites. When I was younger, I always thought that last line meant standing up for myself."

"You'd think of yourself as stupid and crazy?"

"There have been moments."

"Have you ever considered, Daniel, that perhaps we're all of us just stupid crazy at heart?"

"Even you?"

"For dating your brother Pat, maybe I am."

"I won't argue with that."

"Would you believe me if I told you it's the most frightening thing I've ever done?"

"Boys in rock bands," I said, "can be dangerous."

"Yes, they can."

I reached out and took Nadia's hand in my own, on this high, windblown tower overlooking the world. "Well, in that case," I said, "then I'm okay to be just stupid crazy together."

⌒ Graduation day.

Eight long years of university was done.

I should've been over the moon. But all I could think of was Karen. She still wasn't talking to me, and I wondered if she would even show up. But she did, along with the rest of our families.

Liam had driven down from Sudbury in his battered Jeep (conspicuously alone this time). Grandpa and Betty and the Miltons arrived from the Blue Mountains. They'd parked their Winnebagos at Yorkdale Mall and taken the subway down to St. George Campus.

Our parents had dressed up for the occasion. I shouldn't have been surprised. They looked great. Grandpa seemed ten years younger. (Had he dyed his hair?) They were like royalty taking a break from their grand tour, coming down to honour me. I felt honoured. Betty was thrilled just to be visiting Toronto. Mr. and Mrs. Milton couldn't stop taking pictures. Pat had brought corsages and boutonnières for everyone. "Pat," I said, "it's not a wedding."

"Dude, it's an occasion," he said. "It's your convocation, man! And these are a gift from Sara-Lee."

"Who?"

"Sara-Lee. She comes to every Three Dog Run gig there is. She's an artist. She loves making stuff with her hands. She's got amazing hands."

"She's a groupie?"

"She appreciates great music."

"And how are you and Nadia?"

Pat straightened his tie. "We're doing great. Nadia and me, we're spifftacular. She's like my sistah."

"You and Nadia," I said, "were having sex."

"Yeah, about that. We're going through a cooling off period. Now that we're band mates, she wants us to be serious, y'know? About the band, I mean. We're working to cut a new EP. We're writing a lot of new songs together. We can't be messing that up. It's all good." He finished pinning a boutonnière to my jacket label and punched my chest.

"Don't do that," I said.

Pat punched me again with his other fist. "C'mon, man, loosen up, this is your big moment. Today, you are officially Dr. Dan the Man!"

"Seriously, Pat. Don't."

Pat laughed, took aim and jabbed again.

Today, I was about to take the Hippocratic Oath. I breathed in deeply through my nose, the way Nadia had taught me. I supposed it wouldn't look good if I put Pat in a headlock at this moment. Also, I had to admit, the boutonnière was a nice touch.

In front of our parents, Karen smiled and chatted politely. But we both knew it was all a show. Today, she wore a thin, slate-coloured dress, her hair in a bun. With the bouquet on her wrist, she looked beautiful. I remembered the corsage I'd got her for our senior prom. Karen and Liam were a couple at the time. But Liam avoided these kinds of events. It only made sense that Karen and I would go together. I was pretty sure Liam wasn't in Toronto today just for my convocation.

Yesterday, a card from Liz had arrived in the mail, a cat in a mortarboard exhorting me to "seize the day!" I wondered how Liz was doing, helping her bereaved husband in Provincetown with his ice cream shop. That woman was a lot more than she seemed. It was Anne who'd pointed out that Elizabeth McLaren was, in fact, a popular supply teacher at the Ontario College of Arts and Design. People in my life kept surprising me. Or maybe I was just surprising myself by how little I knew about them.

Mr. and Mrs. Milton were both retired college professors. In his bow tie and suspenders, Mr. Milton looked the part. "Today, Daniel," he said, firmly shaking my hand, "is the first day of the rest of your life." If a good cliché worked for the man, he wasn't one to reinvent the wheel.

This morning, a misty rain silvered the parked cars, iron lampposts and brass building plaques. Hints of sunlight sparked and glowed. The moment came when I parted ways to join the other graduands. But by the time the ceremony was over, the morning drizzle had turned into a steady downpour. Outside the domed rotunda of Convocation Hall, families spilled out onto the vast, soggy lawn inside King's College Circle. It was a chaotic sea of umbrellas, graduates in sodden academic regalia clutching their parchments and hitching up their gowns to avoid the puddles and tracts of mud.

Beyond the Medical Sciences Building, the distant CN Tower was a familiar sight. How often had David and I emerged from some seedy establishment long after midnight, stumbling in the dark, only to orient ourselves by its blinking lights to find our way home? Suddenly, I felt a deep and painful nostalgia, a yearning to reconnect with all of Toronto's ramshackle neighbourhoods, its dive bars and hipster cafés, its theatres and broken-down clubs.

Karen and I had spent our first three years in Toronto together. The city transformed people. Life changed people. From this point onward, I would never ever be the same again.

"Ground control to Major Tom?" David nudged me. "You okay?"

"Yeah."

"C'mon, mister. It's photo-op time."

Today was my rocket launch moment, my stepping up to the starting line. Today was, in fact, the first day of the rest of my life.

Pat and Liam crowded next to me, Anne and Karen on David's other side. Betty and the Miltons huddled behind Grandpa as he raised his camera. Lightning flashed and a crack of thunder split the sky.

So why did I feel like the world was coming to an end?

David's ring in my pocket was hard and bright. It was a ticket to a new life, a golden key. What if I took it out right here, got down on one knee and asked him to marry me?

But the rain now was torrential and everyone was running for shelter. David was shouting, beckoning me to follow. I looked for Karen but she was already walking away, head bowed, arms wrapped around her chest, her bra straps showing through the thin, soaked fabric of her dress. Liam walked behind her, a stoic and silent hulking figure.

Grandpa raised his umbrella over me. Today, he'd worn his favourite burgundy tweed jacket and tie, with a golden seahorse pin. His sterling silver hair was neatly parted and combed. "Daniel," he said, "your parents would be proud of you."

Now the whole world had become like the Mirror of Erised. On the far side of the field, Mom and Dad stood beaming at me. I'd started seeing visions of them at every turn—in the deep summer forest, in a snowy city park, poised behind veils of springtime rain.

Pat and Liam and I weren't identical triplets, but anyone could tell we were brothers. Everyone always said how Liam looked like Mom, and Pat took after Dad. Our grownup selves lived inside each of us, behind our eyes, just waiting to emerge.

Over Lake Ontario, thunder boomed and rumbled. I swallowed, and stood as straight as I could. "I miss them," I said.

Grandpa squeezed my shoulder. "Ils me manquent aussi."

"And I miss Grandma."

Grandpa nodded, his heavy hand a reassuring weight. Now I was grateful for the rain.

"I'm so scared," I whispered, "I'm going to lose you too."

Grandpa looked me hard in the eye. "Oh, one day, Daniel, I will be gone. Ça c'est la vie! But you will never lose me."

Great edifices of knowledge, wreathed in ivy, imposing and steadfast, encircled us all. I breathed in the earthy scent of the rain, the raw odour of stone and new green leaves. The air itself seemed charged with electricity. I wiped the water from my eyes, and looked again to the needle spire of the CN Tower, dim but still visible down the avenue of King's College Road.

"I am very proud of you." Grandpa gripped the back of my neck and pressed his forehead to mine. "Mon petit prince."

When he extended his hand, I held onto it like I was a kid heading to his first day of school. Walking together in this way, we crossed the sea of green. I knew, in Grandpa's eyes, my life was just beginning.

I wondered what waited for me on the opposite shore.

CHAPTER TWELVE

In Praise of the Vulnerable Man

I stood in the middle of the Allen Lambert Galleria.

Its soaring architecture formed an arched, parabolic roof six stories high, a majestic, pure white latticework of glass and steel. It was clear why this atrium was called the "crystal cathedral of commerce." As a pedestrian thoroughfare in downtown Toronto, the cavernous space connected Yonge Street to Bay Street, the heart of Canada's financial district. Building façades along the sides of the structure evoked a museum-like atmosphere. It was the perfect location to showcase the newest exhibit by Marcus Wittenbrink Jr.

The installation was curated by Luminato, Toronto's celebrated international festival of arts and culture. The introductory labels on either ends of the galleria described the exhibit as the most ambitious project of the artist's career.

Twelve massive projections, six on each side, depicted satellite images of shorelines and waterways. These were the historic routes of Cartier, Champlain, Mackenzie and others—legends and heroes of Canadian exploration, and harbingers of colonialism and genocide in the New World. The contours of the landscape were carefully superimposed over close-up, black-and-white topographies of human nudes. The haunting soundscape evoked an eerie diorama of lapping canoe paddles, political speeches, train whistles and steamships.

The exhibit was titled: *Bodies of Lovers: Canadian Hydrologies*.

And there was my butt.

I'd recognized it instantly, displayed in high resolution (captured by a Fuji FinePix 2600 Zoom). I lay partially on my side, legs splayed, Highway 69 traversing the inside of my thigh, my left knee touching the town of Whitefish Falls. The French River (called *Wemitigoj-Sibi* by the Ojibwa) ran precisely down my crack, from Lake Nipissing to Georgian Bay, a transportation corridor for the Algonquin peoples, and a vital route for the logging industry in the nineteenth century. My perineum overshadowed the French River Provincial Park, a backcountry oasis of glacially sculpted gorges and waterways. This particular piece was titled: *Daniel/Canadian Shield*.

The image was over six metres high.

Parker stood next to me. After a moment, he said: "I suppose it's an ironic critique of power and desire."

Kyle nodded. "It's a commentary on broken dreams."

Megan gazed upwards. "I think, Daniel," she said, squinting, "I can see your butthole."

"I believe," Charles said, "that's just Hartley Bay Marina."

"And these," Megan asked, "are all real-life photos of people he's had sex with?"

"Apparently," Charles said.

"How many lovers," Kyle asked, "has Marcus had?"

"A very great many," Parker said, "by the looks of it."

Marwa peered down the row of us. "Marcus is bisexual. He's had sex with gay men and straight men."

"I thought," Megan said, "Marcus was pansexual."

"He is, sweetie." Charles patted her arm. "Marwa is just making a joke."

"I had sex," Kyle said, "with a straight guy once."

Parker's protruding eyes swivelled.

Charles put on his reading glasses. "It says here in his Artist's Statement he's had over a hundred lovers."

"Do you think," Kyle said, "he's just being figurative?"

Parker winced. "I don't think so."

Collaborators were also credited: Ghazwan Al Numan (he/him) as the designer, and Patrick Garneau (he/him) as the audio artist. (What the hell was an "audio artist"?) A heartfelt debt of gratitude to the creative team at Luminato, and a very special thank you to L'Oréal for sponsoring this world premiere. A statement by the Artistic Director:

> *Wittenbrink's* Bodies of Lovers *gallery project depicts shorelines and waterways where French and English voyageurs penetrated the Canadian landscape, heralding centuries of invasion and dispossession. By juxtaposing intimate photos of his own past lovers, Wittenbrink offers an eroticized confessional, a commentary on both colonial exploitation and his own existential exploration of sex and love. Human secretions and fluidity have featured prominently in all of Wittenbrink's work.* Bodies of Lovers *elevates these themes to mythic proportions.*

Eroticized confessional? Mythic proportions? What was this pseudo-intellectual hipster bullshit crap? I closed my eyes and sighed.

"This is amazing."

"He's a genius."

"He's in my PhD thesis."

This was *déjà vu* in the worst way.

"Marcus," David said, standing next to me, "should be selling prints of these."

"No," I said. "He shouldn't."

Farther down the galleria, there was an oblique photo of Marwa's demure naked breast, superimposed over a low satellite shot of Toronto itself, its taut nipple perfectly outlined by the Toronto Islands. A bright red arrow, labelled YOU ARE HERE, pointed to our location.

"That's a bit distracting, don't you think?"

"He's making a statement," Parker said. "This one's called *Marwa/The Breast We Suckle*. You do realize, we're literally standing in the lobby of the global headquarters of the Toronto-Dominion Bank."

"How do you know that?"

"It says so right here in the caption, from the man himself: 'Boasting six towers and a pavilion, the TD Centre is a fortress of blackened steel and bronze-tinted glass. Erected on the former site of the Toronto Stock Exchange, it is the largest commercial office complex in Canada.'"

"Sexy."

"Money talks."

Marwa plumped up her cleavage. "Marcus," she said, "promised me a hardcopy print of this one."

After that, Parker and Kyle left us. They had tickets to

an all-Indian cast production of *A Midsummer Night's Dream*. "My auntie tells me," Parker said, "the play is ravishing! Daniel, please pass on our congratulations to Marcus."

Luminato was a ten-day festival that assembled visual and performing artists from around the world. Wittenbrink's name had been announced back in December, along with scores of others: American choreographer Mark Morris, British director Tim Supple, Canada's own Joni Mitchell. On the schedule were free events citywide, artist residencies, and outreach projects. Yesterday, Marcus had taken Marwa to the VIP opening-night gala at the Royal Ontario Museum, sponsored by Giorgio Armani. Tonight, he was pre-recording a one-on-one interview with Ismaila Alfa at the CBC Broadcast Centre. This was his moment.

"This," Charles said, "is Marcus' moment."

Marcus had taken photos of me six years ago. I'd given my consent then, and I'd given him my consent to use them now. He'd explained to me his plan to incorporate them in an expanded, multimedia format and had even commissioned Pat to provide the score. But I hadn't really been listening, had I? It had been my graduation dinner at Cluny. I'd had half a bottle of champagne. All I'd been thinking about was my proposal to David.

Of all the photos he'd taken of me, why this one?

Now my gigantic, French-Canadian derrière was going to be on display to the world for another eight days. I suppose there could've been worse locations than the crystal cathedral of commerce. Hell, my butt even had corporate sponsorship. Once again, somehow, Marcus Wittenbrink Jr. had managed to tap my ass.

I had no one to blame but myself.

I wondered what Karen would say if she were here.

"Daniel," Megan asked, applying lip gloss with an applicator, "is that photoshopped, or are you really that smooth?"

Charles, Marwa and David replied: "He really is that smooth."

"I'm always getting pimples on my tushie," Megan said. "Daniel, what's your secret?"

"Actually, sweetie," Charles said, "what you have isn't acne, but folliculitis. We just need to find you a new hypo-allergenic body scrub that doesn't aggravate your eczema."

Marwa's heels tick-tacked across the gleaming floor. Planting one hand on her hip, she thrust out a business card.

Megan read out loud: "'Cherry Bomb Beauty Care'?"

"Darling." Marwa tossed back her hair. "May I recommend an exfoliator I've created myself? It's a vegan scrub made with creamy shea butter, soothing aloe vera, finely ground walnut, ginger, and several secret extracts that's guaranteed to leave your tuchus tight, soft and glowing. I call it the Cherry Bomb Booty Blitz. You can order it off my website."

"Daniel," Megan asked, "is this what you use?"

"Well, actually." David cleared his throat and patted my behind. "Daniel uses a roux-based poutine gravy blended with cretons made with minced shallots and several secret spices—very similar, Megan, to classic French rillettes. The gay boys can't get enough of it. I rub it into his ass every night." He snapped his teeth and growled.

Megan's eyes widened. She handed back Marwa's card. "Thank you. But I'm going to try what they're using."

"I need a drink," I said.

The five of us walked east along the tree-lined avenue of Front Street past statuesque brownstone storefronts. Summer was around the corner, and the fresh, fragrant air helped cool my mood. We paused by the Berczy Park fountain where two dozen cast-iron dogs gleefully spouted water up at its giant bone. Beyond the skyscrapers and the city's radiance, scattered stars twinkled. We ended up crowded around a table on the patio of the Flatiron & Firkin pub.

"So, Daniel, where's Karen tonight?" Charles asked, draping an arm around Megan.

"Karen's not talking to me right now."

Megan sipped from her daiquiri. "That's not like Karen."

"They had a fight," David said.

"We had a fight."

Marwa glanced up from her phone. "I'm sorry to hear that."

"When did that happen?" Megan asked.

"A couple weeks ago."

"And she's still upset with you? What were you fighting about?" Megan bit into her lime slice.

"Just family stuff. You know." I bowed my head. "I don't need to talk about this right now."

"Oh no, that's alright, sweetie." Megan waved her napkin. "Of course, no, we don't have to talk about it at all."

"I mean, she was really upset," I said. "She even hit me."

Megan's face puckered. "Did she have your consent?"

"What? No. To hit me? No. In fact, since she moved back to Toronto, she's hit me twice."

"This friend of yours," Marwa said, "has issues."

"Marwa, Karen's a really old friend. She's my best friend. Except, you're right, it's not like her. I mean, she's never not talked to me. We always talk. I don't think we've stopped talking in twenty years. We've had fights before, but this is different. I mean, as if not talking about something is going to solve anything, you know? She hasn't even given me a chance to fucking apologize. But you know what the stupid thing is? I'm not actually that sorry! I meant what I said. We just have to agree to disagree, right? Giving someone the silent treatment, that's just so juvenile. I mean, c'mon, we're adults here!" I hit the table, rattling the drinks. "We've all got issues, but this is real. This is important! Jesus fucking Christ."

I hadn't realized how much I'd been holding in. When I got stressed, I always felt horny. And right now I was horny as hell. I wanted to jack off right then and there. I wanted to smash the nacho plate the server had just set down. I wanted to throw back a whole beer in one gulp.

Then I did grab my pilsner. I pushed back my chair, and I drained it in one go. Chug. Chug. Chug.

Breathlessly, I set the pint glass down hard and wiped my mouth on the back of my hand.

White foam slid down the inside of the empty glass. Everyone stared.

Do you," David asked, "feel better now?"

"David." I stood up. My chair scraped. "I have something I've been meaning to ask you. I've been wanting to ask you for a while now." His phone started ringing but I kept talking. "It was Karen who really got me thinking about this. Sometimes you just need a good kick in the pants to see things straight. And that's what Karen did for me. And honestly, that's all I was trying to do for her, right? But Karen she made me promise. And the truth is none of this is about Marcus, but it's always been about me. My own family trauma and my own fear of commitment. Except things are different now. I'm different. And yeah, it's still scary as hell! But I want this. I really do. And I want to do this right. What I'm trying to say is there's something I've realized, something that's more important than anything in the world." *Riiing.* "Look, are you going to get that?"

"No. I wasn't planning to."

"Can you please, David, just answer your phone?"

But his phone had fallen silent. Other patrons were looking our way, but I didn't care. I thrust my hand into my pocket.

My pocket was empty.

My heart skipped a beat. Palpitations, according to medical science, happen for a variety of reasons, none of them good.

"What is it?" David asked.

"It's gone."

"What's gone?"

David's phone started to ring again. Now I started to sweat. I patted down my whole body. After a few seconds, I found it where I'd put it, in the inside left pocket of my blazer. But this time David had picked up. I waited for him to finish his call. Uh-huh. Uh-huh. "Okay," he said, "I'll be right over."

He hung up.

"It's Ai Chang." He stood, his face flushed. "She's ovulating. She's been late. But it's happening now."

"Who's ovulating?" Megan asked.

"Now?" I said.

"Yeah." Sitting at the next table, Mom and Dad winked at me. David's Adam's apple rose and fell. "Daniel?"

I felt the hard edges of the ring box in my fist. I remembered to exhale. "Yes," I said. "Go."

"Are you sure?"

"Of course, I'm sure. What are you waiting for?"

Grabbing my arm, David planted a kiss on my cheek. He shouldered past the server and hurried through the crowded tables. When he got to the sidewalk, he stopped and looked back. "Daniel, you were saying? You were going to tell us something?"

"It can wait. Go."

A cab pulled up and passengers disembarked. David ran around the other side and jumped in.

"Where's he going?" Megan asked.

"We're trying," I said as calmly as I could, "to have a baby."

Megan hiccoughed. "Oh my god."

I sat back down. "It's David. He's the sperm donor. It's for someone else, a couple we know."

Marwa sipped her merlot. "Luke and Ai Chang?"

Megan looked bewildered. "Who's Luke and Ai Chang?"

"That's David's older brother and his partner." Charles said. "You propositioned them at the Gladstone, remember?"

Megan gripped his arm. "Those two want to be parents?"

"Yes," I said. "They do."

"Congratulations." Charles raised his Guinness.

"We haven't done anything yet. She's not even pregnant."

"I beg to differ," Charles said. "This is an extraordinary psychological and emotional investment you and David are making."

"We weren't planning to tell anyone. Not until it happened."

"Of course," Megan said. "We understand completely. But this is just so exciting, isn't it poopsie?"

"Daniel." Marwa said. "Am I mistaken, or were you about to propose to David just now?"

I nodded. I couldn't trust my voice not to shake.

I set the ring box on the table.

Megan squeaked.

Marwa bit her lower lip. "I'm so sorry, darling."

"I've been trying to propose for weeks. I think I'm not very good at it."

"No," Marwa said. "You're not."

I swallowed down the hard knot in my throat. There was absolutely no way I was going to start crying. Not here. Not now.

"Perhaps, Daniel," a voice from behind me said, "you just need a little help from your friends?"

⌒ This weekend in June, Luminato wasn't even over yet when Toronto's North by Northeast Music Festival launched into full swing. The free concert line-up at Dundas and Yonge included a NXNE Festival Village that closed down two blocks. Hundreds of young bands and new talent performed across the city, from sweaty holes-in-the-wall to legendary venues like the Silver Dollar and Horseshoe Tavern. On Friday night, Three Dog Run played a whole new set-list at the Bovine Sex Club, and announced their upcoming second EP.

Afterwards, while David chatted up a couple of old acquaintances, I withdrew to the bar where they had Jägermeister on tap. Post-apocalyptic décor covered every surface in a Dadaist tangle of junkyard debris and fairie lights. I ordered a round of shots for the band. Pat and Nadia and the others were still on stage packing up their gear. They had killed it tonight, as usual.

I tucked my hair behind my ears and pulled my toque down low. Long ago, in dive bark rock clubs, I'd learned I could be comfortably invisible. In gay bars, I often felt on display. Later, when I mentioned this to David, he pointed out how the Bovine in June would feature all sorts of Pride events, whether it was transgender karaoke or dyke bands or punk acts in drag. Maybe this was why the Bovine had lasted as long as it had. And maybe, he suggested, I just needed to explore more diverse queer spaces.

It was Karen who'd held my hand and walked me into my first ever actual gay bar on Church Street in Toronto. I'd been simultaneously terrified and thrilled. We'd waited in line for what seemed like forever. I was ready to piss my pants. When I finally crossed the threshold and stepped inside, it was like Dorothy stepping into Oz.

Karen loved live music.

I wondered where she was tonight. I took out my phone and texted her: *Miss you—wish you were here.*

Many people were sporting NXNE festival passes on their wrists. This weekend, venues had last call extended until 4 a.m. Late night DJ sets and after-parties would have festival-goers up until dawn. I spotted Pat signing a girl's bare shoulder with a Sharpie, while Nadia chatted up some Nordic-looking hippie clutching a sitar. Up on stage, a glam rock band called Semi-Precious Weapons was just setting up. A glass broke close-by. Someone sloshed their drink onto my arm. The jam-packed space was sweltering, and I was glad when David and I finally said our goodbyes.

Just as we were manoeuvering our way to the door, a fight broke out. A stool got knocked over but it was more of a scuffle and didn't last long. The bouncer ejected some-one, and returned a minute later. As I made to squeeze past, his hand landed on my shoulder. "Hold on, doc. Just one minute."

I realized, with a shock, that it was my old friend Robert Burns. He'd been homeless when I knew him, and in rough shape. I barely recognized him now.

"Hey, Robert Burns," I shouted over the din. "How's it going?"

"Keepin' it real, doc, keepin' it real."

He'd grown out his hair in a glossy braided ponytail, and wore an embroidered leather vest over a black tee. He was shorter than David, but solid as a truck. He'd clearly been working out. He wore blue-tinted glasses in black wire frames.

"Robert Burns," I said, standing back, "you look fuck-ing great."

"Got no complaints."

"I thought you might've moved back to the States."

"I did." He shrugged. "Settled some debts." He shrugged again. "Came back." He gestured with his scarred chin. "Who's your friend?"

"This is David."

"He your boyfriend?"

"Yeah." I rubbed my nose. "He's my boyfriend."

Robert Burns stared at David, deep crevasses in his pock-marked brow. "He treating you right?"

I tried not to smile. "He treats me right."

Robert Burns squinted, then extended his fist. "Pleased to meetcha."

David fist-bumped him. "Nice ring."

Robert Burns examined the ring on his little finger. "Funny you mention it. This morning, eh, I woke up. Spirit in my head, tellin' me about this ring. Had this vision, y'know." He looked hard at me. "Now, here you are, doc, after all this time."

Semi-Precious Weapons started their sound check. Robert Burns worked the ring off his finger and placed it onto his fleshy, upturned palm. The band was silver and gold, set with multi-coloured stones in a quartered circle.

"Doc," he said. "Thanks, but I won't be needing this anymore."

Years ago, this ring had been my parting gift to Robert Burns, before I left Regent Park to move into David's loft. "You sure about that?"

He held it out. "Did the trick."

I took back the ring.

Robert Burns pointed. "Lot of medicine in that."

"You sure," I asked, "you don't want to hold onto this?"

He rested both fists over his chest. "Medicine's in here now."

"Okay."

"You a doc yet?"

"Yeah." I nodded. "I am."

"Hunh." Robert Burns studied the burnished tips of his cowboy boots. "Well, keep on truckin'." He looked me in the eye. "Remember, ya got Indian in you."

"I won't forget. Hey, can I show you something?"

He peered over his glasses. I reached under my collar and pulled out a tiny, wooden eagle feather. Its original leather thong had frayed long ago, and I'd replaced it with a metal chain. "David," I said, "this guy made this feather."

"No kidding."

"You still carving, Robert Burns?"

"Nah," he said. "I'm not carving anymore. Been too busy to carve. Don't need to carve no more."

"I'm glad to hear that."

"It sounds like," David said, "that's a limited edition now."

Robert Burns regarded David sidelong. "This guy why you moved away?"

"Yeah, actually. He was."

"No regrets?"

"No." Now I laughed. "No regrets at all."

Robert Burns looked us both over. Finally, he straightened. "Keep it real." He fist-bumped us and held open the door.

Outside, David paused to light a cigarette. A mass of industrial scrap metal and bicycle parts encrusted the Bovine's front façade. A line-up was already forming to get in. We walked up Ryerson Avenue and into Alexandra Park. Away from the bright traffic of Queen Street West, the night deepened into a cool darkness.

"No regrets?" David asked.

"Nope."

We sat on a park bench while David finished his smoke. Sadly, both our flasks were empty. We shared our last piece of gum.

"That's the ring," David asked, "Karen gave you, right?"

"Yeah it is."

"I thought I recognized it."

NXNE was a vibrating, incandescent presence, a scattering of bonfires across a vast, labyrinthine landscape. I took the ring out of my pocket. "I never thought I'd see this again."

"It found its way back to you."

"It did."

David finished his cigarette. We got up and walked side-by-side, farther into the dark until we stood opposite the red-pillared Ching Kwok Buddhist Temple. It was long after midnight and the stars glinted above the monolith trees. The haloed streetlamps posed like sentinels. I inhaled the fecund moisture of the earth.

"Did Karen ever find out you gave it away?" David asked.

"I don't think so."

"Will you tell her?"

"Yeah. Now, I think I will."

I turned the ring over between my fingertips. It'd been Karen's gift to me after our time together in Toronto. She'd finished teacher's college, and was heading back home. It was the first time in our lives we'd ever parted ways. She explained to me how each of its stones had a different meaning: resilience, calm, courage and clarity. Together they formed a Medicine Wheel. When I gave the ring away, it was because I felt someone else needed it more than I did. I never regretted that decision. But I was also thrilled to have it back.

"Will you," I said, "marry me?"

"What?"

Wreathed in shadows and firelight, I knelt down on one knee. I held out the ring. "Will you marry me, David Gallucci?"

David stared. "Shut up."

"I mean it."

"You're proposing to me now?"

"Actually." I sat back on my heel. "I had planned to do it tomorrow. The truth is, I've been trying for a while."

"You have?"

"David, I was going to propose to you at my graduation dinner."

"Look." To my utter amazement, David also got down on one knee. "I have to tell you something." He dug into his pants pocket. "I had their kitchen staff put this in your dessert."

He held up a band of pure white-gold, delicately etched, glowing like a tiny comet. "I ordered you a slice of cake. I had them hide this inside."

"You did?"

"They had it served on the table already, waiting for you."

"Holy shit."

David sighed. "Yeah."

We breathed in unison. The bonfires were burning everywhere now, like shooting stars crashed into the beautiful, ancient world.

"I don't know what to say."

"When," David asked, "were you going to propose tomorrow?"

"Tomorrow afternoon, at Yonge-Dundas Square. It's all planned out. Everyone's going to be there. There's even going to be a flash mob."

"Fuck off. You, Daniel Garneau, organized a flash mob?"

"Um, no."

"So who did?"

I cleared my throat. "Marcus did."

"I see." After a moment, David rested his chin on his knee. "Everyone's going to be there?" He looked up.

"Yeah."

Well." His eyes twinkled. "We better not disappoint them then."

〜 On a Saturday afternoon in June, David and I made our way down to Toronto's Yonge-Dundas Square.

Beneath a carnival sun, thousands milled through the Festival Village, a thrumming symphony of art installations, beer gardens, food trucks and eSports events. Massive flickering billboards and corporate logos towered over the crowds.

At the allotted time, David and I made our way to the precise spot where I'd been instructed to stand.

Then, as promised, Marcus held up his end.

Long after it was over, David and I would dispute, assemble and reassemble a kaleidoscopic montage of what happened next. What we did agreed upon was how it began —with a glorious Bellagio burst of fountains. Then my brother Pat's voice reverberated over the sound system. My jaw dropped. It was Three Dog Run on the Festival Main Stage launching into an original song. How Marcus managed to squeeze TDR into that exclusive line-up I'll never know. When the chorus kicked in, people started to run. At first they raced in circles, then they ran towards each other. Like dominos toppling, couples embraced, spinning in the air, and started to kiss. Many were obviously trained dancers, others actors in outrageous costumes: Antony and Cleopatra, Batman and Robin, Tarzan and Jane. I spotted Marwa with her assistant Brody, and Megan and Charles in full fetish gear. I saw Luke and Ai Chang in each other's arms, and Frederic twirling Rebecca in a magnificent red dress.

When Nadia and Pat started kissing on stage, the billboards lit up like fireworks. After that, laughing teenagers threw down their knapsacks and started to kiss. A grizzled couple on a Harley made out with flowers in their hair. As David gripped my hand, a river of cyclists poured through the intersection of Dundas and Yonge, a mass of flying bodies stark naked as newborns, waving at us and cheering us on, Parker and Kyle among them, their arms in the air. People started pointing and raising their phones. Friends turned to kiss each other on the cheeks, and mothers their babies, and husbands their wives. School girls kissed their little beribboned dogs, while turbaned Mounties blew kisses to cab drivers honking their horns. Amidst all of this stupid and crazy spectacle, I saw my parents again. And Mom and Dad were with me, and they were everywhere, inside and out, in the whirling dervish of this one life, in the groundswell of this multitude, in the faces of strangers and friends alike. And David was by my side, my lover, my man.

It was wonderful to look into his face and to have him look into mine. I held him by the waist as he held me by mine.

"Hey, mister."

"Hey."

We slipped our rings onto each other's hands.

And just like that, like a home run driven high up and out of the park, we leaned in and shared the best kiss we'd ever had in both of our lives.

CHAPTER THIRTEEN

Very Good Bad Things

Bodies of Lovers was going on tour.

Marcus himself was staying in Toronto to focus on Three Dog Run's upcoming EP. In recent months, Pat had taken to starting each gig with a call-out to the crowd: "Heeeeey puppy lovers!" That always got the fans going. The flash mob Marcus had engineered was all over social media. I had to give him credit. It was a genius piece of marketing. Now the band's five minutes on the Festival stage was blowing up. Marcus must have had started planning this months ago. I wondered if Nadia knew about Sara-Lee and her amazing hands. Later I learned that Kyle had participated for years in the World Naked Bike Ride, an annual protest across the world to raise awareness of oil consumption and urban pollution. "Less gas more ass!" was their motto.

My own gigantic ass was soon to be on display at the National Gallery of Canada in Ottawa.

But none of that mattered.

Megan had texted with an urgent message. She absolutely needed to talk and she'd tell me more in person. I

wondered if, once again, there was a terrible misunder-
standing between her and Charles. Their six years together
had been a rocky road. So I agreed to meet at the Toronto
Reference Library where Megan worked part-time during
the summer. It was the launch of Pride Week and rainbow flags and diversity posters decorated the lobby. I
passed a murmuring waterfall and ornamental pool. The
theme this year was "Unified" and visitors were greeted
by a prominent display of LGBTQ literature, from children's books to classics by James Baldwin, Yukio Mishima
and Virginia Woolf.

Taking the glass elevator up to the fifth floor, I found
Megan in Special Collections.

Karen was with her.

I could tell right away Karen was as surprised to see me
as I was to see her. Megan showed no remorse whatsoever.

"You two," she said, "need to work this out. You're best
friends, and it's silly you're not talking. See this?" She
pointed at a poster pronouncing: LOVE IS LOVE. "Karen
and Daniel, I'm leaving you now. I expect you both to do
the adult thing."

After that, Megan marched into the elevator and was
gone.

Karen adjusted the knapsack on her shoulder. For a
second, I was afraid she might walk away. Instead, she
said: "Congratulations."

"Thanks."

"Let me see." I held up my left hand. "It looks good on
you."

"Did David show you his?" I asked.

"Yes, he did."

"Is it weird?"

"That he's wearing the ring I gave you? No." Karen leaned over the parapet. "I'm flattered. The truth is, I thought you'd lost that ring."

"Why would you say that?"

"You stopped wearing it."

"I never lost it."

"Okay."

"I still have the ring," I said, "we bought in Chinatown."

"It's not too late to return it." Karen's brow furrowed. "People return engagement rings all the time."

I followed her gaze down to the main space where some kind of tour was assembling. "Look, Karen. I'm sorry."

"I'm still upset with you." Karen set her knapsack down. "But I understand. You thought you were doing the right thing. And what you said, about us being miserable, it was the truth."

"It was?"

"Of course it was. It's been really hard."

"But Karen, if that's the truth …"

"You want there to be a happy ending to this. But it's not going to work out that way. Liam and I talked. We're not getting back together. I'm sad it didn't work out. We tried our best. But just because I'm sad about Liam and me, it doesn't mean I can't be happy about life, Daniel."

"Are you?"

"Am I happy?" Karen glanced at me. "Of course I am! I'm happy to be back in Toronto. I love my new job. I'm happy to be living with Anne, across the hall from you boys. I'm happy Liam's surgery went well, and that you're a doctor now. Seriously, I'm proud of you."

I swallowed hard. "Thanks."

"I've always thought of Liam as fragile," Karen said. "Yes, Liam. He was always the most sensitive of the three of you. He feels things differently. This world we live in, it can be a really painful place for him. But Liam's also strong. And now he's stronger than ever. And do you want to know why? You think it's because he's a recovered alcoholic, or because he's lived through cancer?" Karen shook her head. "It's because he did it without me. I've been there for him, Daniel, since we were seven years old, propping him up. I know that sounds grandiose but it's the truth. I've always been his support, and his safety net. You have no idea how often I've held him in my arms while he just cried and cried. But this time, he survived on his own. And now he's full of hope and love and lust for life. And it reminds him of the good times we shared. He told me we could go back to the way things were. But I don't want to go back. I want to go forward. And that's the difference between Liam and me. Liam became the best version of himself long ago. I haven't even started."

If I stood still enough, I might hear the whisper of a volume being drawn from a shelf, the turning of crisp pages, the clicking of keyboards. Far below, a drag queen led a group of children and their parents through the lobby. How many stories were told and retold every day? Growing up, I couldn't ever remember seeing Liam cry. Not even at Mom and Dad's funeral, or when Grandma died. I'd never thought of him as fragile but in this moment it made sudden, perfect sense. It was like a flare gun Karen had fired off with her words.

In that light, Karen's face glowed. "I got over Liam,"

she said. "He'll get over me. We'll always be family. And I know we'll still be friends. I just need you to trust me. I need you to trust the both of us. Alright?"

"I trust you."

"It's not your job to save the world, Daniel. People need to learn to save themselves."

I just really didn't like it," I said, "that you weren't talking to me."

"Yeah, well. You can't always get what you want."

"I know that."

Karen's face softened. "Even friends and family sometimes need space from each other, okay? But I am sorry I stopped talking to you. That wasn't very adult of me."

"We're here now."

"A great relationship," Karen said, "is a co-operative endeavour."

"Did Megan tell you that?"

"Something like that. She had some choice words to say. I've missed her. She's changed a lot. She's really taken charge of her life."

"I think we're great together."

Karen looked me in the eye. "Remember that vision board we made, before we came to Toronto?"

"Yeah."

"Well, we did it. We did everything we set out to do. We did it together."

"I passed," I said.

"Your qualifying exam?"

"I got the results this morning. It's official. I have my medical license."

"I knew you would. But that's great news."

"I have so much I want to tell you."

"You want to go get a coffee at Balzac's?"

I nodded.

And so we did.

⌒ That Pride Weekend we threw a rooftop party.

We hauled David's mannequin and my palm tree up from our loft, along with a couple of old couches, and decorated with all the plastic flamingos we could find. Anne brought in her graffiti artist friends and turned the rooftop into a tropical lagoon. We hung up a disco ball. Karen spiked a gigantic cooler of pink lemonade. David served up home-made bacon ice cream. Three Dog Run dropped in to play an unplugged set, all on tiny instruments: a kazoo, a kalimba, a toy piano rescued from a dumpster. After the Egster served up an astonishing handpan solo, everyone burst into applause. I started to worry the rusted fire escape would collapse from the amount of people. At one moment, it was shoulder-to-shoulder, and I was hard-pressed to spot a familiar face. While emptying the recycling bin, I overheard a lavender-haired kid declare: "I'm queer so I don't judge. I push every way. Love is love, dog. It don't matter!" I waved to Parker and Kyle who arrived in boy scout uniforms with colourful queer flags stitched into their sashes. Then Marcus and Marwa appeared bearing an enormous bouquet of pink carnations and two dozen rainbow cupcakes. Gee was also with them, wearing cut-offs and a cowboy hat. He set up a body painting station, and soon everyone was dancing under the hot afternoon sun with flowers on their cheeks and limbs.

In the stairwell to our loft, I bumped into Marwa wearing a black ball cap with pink rhinestones spelling out CHERRY BOMB. "Marwa! Thanks again for the cupcakes. They're all gone. People loved them."

"I saved two for you and David," Marwa said, adjusting her bikini straps. "They're in your fridge."

"You're the best."

Marwa twirled and struck a pose. "I'd like to think so. Look what Megan gave me. I think I'm going to try to make my own."

"What is it?"

"Lift up your shirt."

"What? Why?"

"Daniel the Doorman, just trust me. All the way up." Marwa dipped her pinky finger into a tiny container and rubbed something cold onto my nipples. "It's called Nipple Nibblers! Now how does that feel?"

I blushed despite myself. "Really weird."

"Every-sing," Marwa said huskily, her pinky in the air, "starts viz a tingle."

"Whatever happened," I asked, "to Cherry Bomb Bakery?"

"Oh, I'm still baking. Business is better than ever; we're very high-end now. We cater to an exclusive clientele."

"And who would that be?"

"Corporate clients, industry people, York Mills moms willing to take out a second mortgage for their kid's bat mitzvah. Last year, I invested in a booth at the Food & Wine Expo. That really paid off. Now I'm diversifying. Your friend Kyle and I might partner up in fact."

I wondered if Kyle knew Marwa's catering company

was financed by years of drug dealing. But Marwa was always on the move and she'd assured me how she'd left that part of her life behind.

"Well, congratulations," I said. "I'm excited for you."

"Thank you, Daniel. I'm excited for me too. I'm building Cherry Bomb as a lifestyle brand. Don't underestimate this goth girl from Burlington."

"I never have."

"Remember Marwa the Mutt? She's come a long way in the world. I have Marcus to thank for that."

"You don't think you did this on your own?"

"Daniel. There are always people who help us. Think of all the people who helped you become a doctor."

I wanted to say no one helped me, that I'd saved up and paid my own way through med school. But then I considered my professors; mentors like Stephan Tondeur; all my friends and family who'd supported me along the way. I hated to admit it, but it was in fact Marcus who first encouraged me to consider the MCAT.

"They might not be in our lives anymore," Marwa said, "but they're still with us. Isn't everyone we're close to a part of us forever?"

"Yeah." I picked at a rusty nail stuck in the sole of my flip-flops. "I suppose they are."

"And you, Daniel the Doorman," Marwa said, tapping me on the nose, "are a wonderful part of fabulous me."

"Marwa. When I broke up with Marcus, you wanted to throw a brick through my window."

Marwa giggled. "Well, deep inside I'm a mama bear." She growled and bared her teeth. "But Marcus, he's a pacifist. He doesn't believe in anger or violence."

"That's very noble of him."

"Hey! I was angry a long time with the world. I'm done with that. I don't want to be that girl anymore."

I sat down on the landing floor. "Is it that easy?"

"No. But I'm worth it." Marwa perched on the stairs opposite me. "We deserve to be anything we want to be. That's what Marcus taught me."

"That's what family's for."

"I chose my family." Marwa sipped from a heart-shaped flask. "I'm glad Marcus chose you. See this?" She pulled out her keys.

"Pussy Power?"

"No, not that. This." Attached to her keychain was a thin metal tube. "When I step out, I bring one cigarette. And I'm good with it. I used to smoke a pack a day. I have you to thank for this."

"How so?"

"Last summer, you reminded me why I started smoking in the first place. When high school's just one long, drawn out torture session putting up with fuckhead jocks and queen bee bitches, what's a chubby brown girl with bad hair and acne supposed to do? She self-medicates, with sugar, caffeine, nicotine. Why do you think I started cooking and baking? Then I got into the diet pills and, well, you know the rest. But life's different now. Smoking was just a habit left over from an extinct and shitty past. Honey, that is over. Now, I enjoy my one super slim menthol at the end of the day. I've joined a gym. And I've started working as an escort. I'm really loving who I am. Cherry Bomb Bakery & Beauty Care is my glow up. I'm in a great place."

"Um, what did you say?"

"My glow up. This is my celebration of myself, my—"

"Marwa. Did you say you're working as an escort?"

"Mm-hm. Yes, Daniel, I know what you're thinking. People judge. But I've been dealing with judgmental pricks all my life. I'm making ten times more money now than when I was working with RentAFriend. And it's tax deductible. I'm just doing sex work part-time to finance my beauty line. Brody doesn't approve but he still supports me."

Shrieks of laughter echoed up the stairwell. Half-naked partiers, tangled in boas and wielding enormous plastic water guns, charged past, shedding glitter all the way.

"If you need money, Marwa," I said, brushing sparkles off my face, "you could go to the bank."

"Unh-uh." Marwa wagged a finger. "Not this girl. I was in debt once, never again. Brody offered to loan me the start-up capital, but that would've been his college tuition and he's in his final year of culinary school." She opened a compact and examined her makeup. "Also, it's important for me I do this on my own."

I dangled my drink between my knees. "Whatever happened to getting by with the help of others?"

"Yes. And we should also get to decide when we go it alone." Marwa snapped shut her compact. "I, Daniel, am choosing fiscal responsibility."

"Does Marcus know?"

"About the escorting? No! Marcus wouldn't understand. This is just between you and me, alright?"

"And Brody."

"Brody's my sous-chef and personal assistant. I also think he might be in love with me. I'm telling you this,

Daniel, because I trust you. This is what I'm choosing to do right now. Don't worry. Marwa's in charge."

I swished the dregs of lemonade around my plastic cup. "I'm surprised you think Marcus wouldn't understand."

Marwa studied my face. "Here's the thing. Did you know when Marcus was fifteen he ran away from home?"

"No. I never knew that."

"He doesn't talk about it. But Marcus was on the streets a whole year before they brought him back."

"Why'd he run away?"

"Herr Marcus Wittenbrink Senior. That man was a monster. When Marcus was younger, his father sometimes locked him in the attic, just to make some kind of bizarre point. One day, he'd had enough and we planned his getaway."

"You helped him?"

"I wanted to go *with* him." Marwa sat down and pressed up next to me, smelling faintly of cherry cola. "But this was a solo project. Marcus felt that he was wasting his potential. He said he wanted to make himself a poet, a visionary. Like Rimbaud."

"That sounds like Marcus."

"Marcus," Marwa said, "plans out his life like it's a Gus Van Sant film. But I think the truth is some awful things happened during that time. He's hinted at things he'd done, that were done to him. A boy has to eat and sleep somewhere. Marcus is protective of me. So, no. He wouldn't understand."

"I had no idea."

"Daniel, don't look so shocked. Marcus accomplished what he set out to do. He got what he wanted."

"I guess he did."

"His father hired a private detective to find him. When they finally brought him home, Marcus was different. He was brighter, more focussed—there was an edge to him.

"I'm the closest he has to family. But there was this part of him that didn't need anyone at all, including me. That's what Marcus discovered about himself when he was living on the streets."

"Then I really feel sorry for him."

"Why? I don't. And he definitely doesn't feel sorry for himself. His parents brought him up to believe in respectability. That was their entire world. But Marcus threw that back in their face. Marcus was in rehab and therapy for three years after that. That's when he started calling himself Max, King of All Wild Things."

"Max," I said, "was an angry little boy."

"Yes, he was."

"You two had a lot in common."

"Yes we did. For a long time."

"But you said Marcus doesn't believe in anger."

Marwa plucked a pink feather from my arm. "We'll always be soulmates. But these days, we don't always see eye to eye. Please don't tell him I told you all this."

"Marwa, I don't talk to Marcus anymore, not really."

"Did you know he's considering moving to Berlin?"

My breath caught. "No. Why?"

"The city offered him a grant, a big one. Also, he has relatives there. But he hasn't decided if he wants to go."

"He should go."

"You don't need to be afraid of him, Daniel."

"I'm not afraid of Marcus."

"Then why do you avoid him? He misses you. He loves you. He'll love you and David together if you let him. You do know that, don't you?"

"I know."

"Then what is it?"

"I just don't like who I am when I'm around him."

Marwa frowned. "I don't understand what that means."

"I don't think Marcus ever cared whether or not I loved him. When I was around him, I was just another one of his adoring fans. It made me, well, feel diminished, less than me."

"You think Marcus doesn't see you?"

"I think he sees his reflection in me. He sees you, Marwa. Like you said, you're his only family. Maybe you're the only person in the world he really does see."

"He better see me." Marwa rested one hand on her hip. "I run three businesses. I'm fucking incorporated."

"I'm being serious."

"Okay."

"He loves you," I said.

Marwa drew a deep breath. "It's nice to hear someone say it." She uncapped her flask. "Because of Marcus, Daniel, my tits and your ass are on tour across Canada. Can we toast to that?"

"I just have one question."

"Ask me anything."

"Did he really suckle your breast?"

"Yes." Marwa laughed. "Yes, he did, once. We were on Molly, in my basement. Marcus told me his mother never breast fed him. He said he wanted to know what that was like. So I had him curl up in my lap. I told him I loved

him, and that he was a good boy. He needed to hear that.
It only happened once. We've never fucked, in case you're
wondering. Everyone thinks we have. I go along with it.
I'm fine with that."

"He put you in his *Bodies of Lovers* exhibit."

"I know." Marwa smiled. "He says I'm his honorary
lover."

"Not a bad thing to be."

"True. But can I tell you something?"

I rested my head against the wall. The spiked lemonade
was gone and I tossed my plastic cup down the stairwell.

"I used to have a lot of misconceptions about what it
meant to be a sex worker. But I had a good talk with your
friend Megan and she helped sort that out."

"Megan's a kindergarten teacher."

"She's also a domme. You know she's starting to make
a name for herself? She goes by Mistress Grey."

"After," I asked, "the Duchess of Grey?"

"Oh, then you do know all about it! Megan said to
me that a woman shouldn't be ashamed to feel pleasure
or to have power. We're taught that's not what respectable
women do. But fuck that. Mind you, I got the pleasure
part down long ago. But owning my power, that's something I'm still learning. Hearing Megan say that meant a
lot to me. When I'm working as an escort, I feel powerful." Marwa regarded me. "You know, Daniel, maybe I will
tell Marcus. I want to tell him. The funny thing is, I'm
not that into the fetish or kink. Believe it or not, I'm
pretty vanilla between the sheets."

"But you're comfortable doing what you're doing?"

"I am. I feel really confident about it. I'm not just a

pretty face, you know. I can read people's energies. Most people are just lonely. I've been there, I know what it's like. I give them what they need. There's one couple who reached out to me because their therapist told them to experiment with a third. Now that therapist is referring other couples to me. Most of the time, Daniel, I'm teaching my clients how to love their bodies, and how to trust and be intimate again."

"Okay."

"I know, eh? I was a bitch for the longest time. But it was exhausting. And it was never fun. That old Angry Marwa, she protected me for years. But now it's time for her to retire."

"What about Marwa the Mama Bear?"

"Oh, she's still got her claws, honey. Don't you worry."

"I just want you to be safe."

"You're sweet. If it makes you feel better, Brody watches out for me. I have a lot of affection for that boy. He's come a long way."

"You said he's in love with you?"

"Yeah, well. You have one taste of Marwa's meatballs, there's no going back."

"I've tasted your meatballs."

Marwa wrapped an arm around my knee. "I rest my case." After a moment, she leaned in and kissed me on the lips. "You really are sweet. And I like this look on you." She stroked my jawline. "Very rugged. Have you ever thought about growing this out?"

"I start my residency in two weeks. So, no. In fact, I'm going to have to shave this off and get a haircut. I need to, well …"

"Look respectable?"

"Yeah."

"What is respectability anyway?"

"I'm not so sure these days."

"Well." Marwa kissed me again. "As long as it works for you."

⌒ As Marcus was leaving he told me he'd left something for me on my bed. We were on the rooftop, where I was starting up the barbeque. I thanked him for coming, and we hugged. I wanted to ask him about Berlin, but the timing didn't seem right. There was a weird moment when David suggested we invite Gee to stay. But Gee and Marwa left with Marcus. Parker and Kyle headed out to some Queer Slowdance event, leaving me to cook hotdogs and veggie burgers for a crowd of strangers, mostly Anne's art school friends. Just as the sun was going down, a bunch of rough-looking guys showed up carrying their own cooler and a two-four of beer. From the way they were talking, they were into street racing. I overhead one of them ask what the fuck was with all the pink flamingos. I spotted Anne arguing in hushed tones with a classmate in the corner. Where was Karen when you needed her? For a while, things seemed to settle. Pat had left us a couple mix tapes. At least they didn't seem to mind the playlist. This Saturday, Rick was working a double shift at Graffiti's down the block. I texted David and told him to get his ass up here. Where the hell was everyone?

Finally David showed up. I could tell right away he was stoned. "Where were you?" I asked.

"Getting stoned." He grinned, chewing his gum open-mouthed. He was shirtless, wearing a rainbow *lei*, with pink rhinestones and tropical flowers painted on his cheeks.

"Where's Karen?"

"I dunno. She was on her phone a minute ago." Playfully, he leaned into me, grinding up against my hip.

Now the Racing Guys were getting loud again, talking over each other, gesticulating and punctuating every other statement with a "yo!" I overheard how members of Canada's Armed Forces would be marching for the first time in tomorrow's Pride Parade. People were laughing, but not in a nice way. I turned down the barbeque and closed the lid.

Then someone chucked a flamingo over the edge of the roof. David walked up to him. "Dude," he said, "this is a Pride party."

The guy had a black eye. His neck tat was a pit bull. "Yeah?" He butted out his cigarette on an empty beer keg. "Do I look queer to you?"

Now Anne's friends were telling him to chill. Apparently, his name was Stan. "Stan, cut the crap. Relax, alright?" But Stan wasn't ready to relax. He got up off his cinder-block, stood up and looked down at David.

David flashed a lopsided smile and pulled out a joint. You could disarm Mad Max with a smile like that. "Smoke up?"

Stan rested his hands on his hips and cocked his head. "I asked you a question, faggot."

I stopped the music.

"No," I said. "No, you don't look queer. You look like an asshole. Party's over. And I'd like my flamingo back."

David glanced over his shoulder. "Right on, lover boy." He raised his fist. "It's morphin' time!"

Then Stan shoved him, hard enough for David to stumble backwards and fall on the gravel rooftop.

In superhero movies, you get to see in bullet time how the protagonist takes out the bad guys, defying the laws of physics, haloed in lens flares. But this was real life. The truth was, I had no idea how I crossed the space between me and Stan. One moment, I was tossing aside my BBQ apron, the next moment I was throwing a punch. I think I might've jumped a couch to do it. It wasn't the best shot. But it connected and it was enough to knock him down. I think the guy was more surprised than hurt. He was up in seconds and his buddies now were also getting to their feet.

Both my fists were clenched now. They were fucking sledgehammers. I had no helmet or pads on but I was ready.

I was Pussy Pierogi at Sunday dinner. I was Marwa the Mutt taking on the whole football team. I was Godzilla ready to rumble with King Ghidorah. I was Daniel the Doorman ready to show these boys the door.

But to my surprise, none of them came at me. They just stood eyeing each other and shifting uneasily. Stan looked embarrassed and confused. His nose was also bleeding. I must've hit him a lot harder than I thought.

I was aware of David climbing back to his feet. But my eyes never left Stan. Stan the Dog Man. Why'd he have to chuck the flamingo off the roof anyway? What kind of asshole crashes a party and does something like that?

Stan and his buddies exchanged words. They gathered up their cooler, muttering and scoffing, and departed down the fire escape. One of Anne's classmates hesitated, then hurried after them. Anne stood beneath the disco ball looking pleased as fuck.

The hairs on my neck prickled. When I turned around, everyone was lined up behind me: Karen and my brothers Pat and big Liam, all of them looking steely-eyed and ready to rock 'n' roll. Rick the ex-Hells Angel stood with them, hefting a baseball bat.

Electrons glittered and snapped between us.

Pat pointed sideways. "Liam's in town."

"I can see that."

"Thought I'd swing back," Pat said, "and hang out with my bros."

"Surprise." Liam said. "Happy Pride."

Behind them, a man in a gimp outfit emerged from the stairwell onto the roof. I could tell from his big cannelloni arms that it was Charles. Megan was holding his leash and gripping a riding crop, decked out in a pleather cat suit in candy-apple red. "Did we miss the party?" she asked, looking from one of us to the other.

"No," Karen said. "It's just getting started."

CHAPTER FOURTEEN

Unholy, Dirty and Beautiful

A week after our Pride party, Pat wanted to take me to a mystery concert for our birthday. It was just before the start of my residency. The timing wasn't the greatest, but David said the distraction would do me good and was more than happy to make us dinner and send us off.

Pat insisted we show up early at the Opera House to get a spot close to the stage. The venue was once a vaudeville theatre offering up circus and cabaret acts. Its classical architecture featured a tiered balcony and an elegant proscenium arch. Performers like Nirvana and Eminem had all played the Opera House. Tonight it was an eclectic metal crowd and I was glad I'd brought ear plugs. I'd never heard of this band but Pat told me I was in for a treat.

An hour later, Vulvatron, war-painted and roaring like a Valkyrie, activated her blood-spewing prosthetic breasts. Twin geysers drenched the audience as Pustulus Maximus ripped into a wailing thrash guitar solo. The rain-gear worn by security guards at the front suddenly made sense. Blothar the Berserker proceeded to dismember and decapitate an army of gigantic, heavy metal Muppets on-stage, complete with fake brains and gory entrails, as lead singer Oderus Urungus flailed about with his pulsating, malformed phallus. This, I discovered, was GWAR, Scumdogs of the Universe. By the end of the concert, half the audience was dripping in a purple mixture of fake blood and black alien semen. The band closed with an encore cover of "West End Girls" by the Pet Shop Boys.

On the streetcar ride home, I had no words for Pat.

Fortunately, we'd found seats in the very back. I sat with my hands on my knees, and ignored the stares of the other riders. Pat took a selfie of us and, before I could stop him, giddily posted it on social media. I resisted an impulse to put him in a headlock and chuck his phone out the window.

Later that night, after I'd showered and thrown my clothes into the dumpster, David reported how the band even had its own comic book imprint, and promptly or-dered on-line a copy of *GWAR: Orgasmageddon*.

After that, David had me sit on the couch and turned off all the lights. The front door opened and Karen, Anne and Rick walked in bathed in golden candlelight, singing happy birthday.

Technically, my birthday was over since it was after midnight. But nobody cared. Over cake there were gifts. Karen got me a bottle of Sortilège maple whiskey. David presented a monogrammed briefcase. Rick and Anne bought me my ticket to Fan Expo in August. I learned that the five of us would be attending together. "We," David said, "are going to cosplay our favourite characters!"

"And who would that be?" I asked.

"We haven't decided yet."

"But," Anne said, "it's going to be epic."

After that we stayed up debating our options, polishing off shots of Sortilège. We lit more candles. Anne crossed the hall to retrieve a tin of tealights. Rick reported his Superkick'd training was going well and that his wrestling moniker was going to be Boss Brony.

"Whatever happened," I asked, "to Devil Dog or Beelzebub?"

"It wasn't me," he replied.

"Boss Brony," Anne said, lighting a dozen new candles, "is so much better."

Bronies, I knew from my time with Parker, were male fans of *My Little Pony*. Why couldn't an ex-Hells Angel love the magical flying denizens of Equestria? I'd remember to mention this to Parker at our upcoming D&D session. Karen had no interest in joining but said she'd drop by to watch. When Rick and Anne went topside to smoke a bowl, David chased after them. Karen poured the two of us the last of the Sortilège.

"I know why," I said, "you got me that."

"I'm sorry we drank your birthday gift." She passed me my glass. "I'll get you another bottle."

"You don't have to do that."

"No, I want to. I'm counting on you putting it to good use." She curled back up on the couch. "So, you had a good time with Pat tonight?"

I wasn't sure how to answer this question. Pat always had the best of intentions. GWAR should have been offensive to me on every level. Except not far from us there had been a lanky, long-haired boy having the time of his life. His joy was infectious. I couldn't keep my eyes off him, especially after he peeled off his shirt. The way he was pogoing up and down, drenched in fake blood with the biggest smile on his face, was just incredibly sexy and strangely beautiful. And there I was with him along with my idiotic brother Pat and nine hundred others cheering on this over-the-top, shock rock band that had sold out shows for decades without any sign of slowing down. Like the Hells Angels, everything GWAR stood for was about rebellion and transgression. Pat reminded me how Rob Halford, the reigning god of metal, had come out as gay years ago to an enthusiastic and supportive community.

I squeezed shut my eyes. "I can't believe I'm saying this."

"What?"

"Yeah," I said. "I had a good time."

"You know," Karen said, "Pat's not ever trying to impress or offend you or anyone. That's the last thing on his mind. He just likes to have fun."

"I know."

"And he really, genuinely loves hanging out with you."

Now I felt a pang of guilt. "I know he's my brother. He's just hard to put up with sometimes."

"Remember when he lit the dumpster on fire behind the school?"

"Or got caught spying on the girls changing room?"

"Or when he skitched that police cruiser in your grandfather's roller skates?"

"He was such a little shit disturber."

"But Daniel, would you change Pat if you could?"

I cracked my neck. I'd spent my whole life putting up with Pat's goofball antics. It was painful growing up with him. "I just wish," I finally said, "he wouldn't get into trouble all the time, you know?"

"Is he in trouble now?"

"No." I savoured my drink. "No, I don't suppose he is."

"Then enjoy this moment." Karen raised her glass. "Life's too short."

Life was short. Sometimes it seemed to be flying by at breakneck speed and it was all I could do to hold on.

"And," Karen said, "'life moves pretty fast'."

"'If you don't stop and look around once in a while,'" we said in unison, "'you might miss it'."

"I know, I know." I sighed.

"Mind you," Karen said, "you were pretty fast on your feet there last week. It felt like we were at Daniel Garneau's Rock'em Sock'em Party."

"I just don't want to be that angry guy, y'know?"

"You weren't angry," Karen said. "You were awesome."

"I still can't believe Liam came down for Pride."

"I guess this is the new Liam we have to get to know." Karen hugged her knees to her chest. "He had a good time."

"Joan's taking him out to Red Lobster tonight."

Karen nodded.

We regarded each other gravely, before bursting out in laughter. "Can you picture him in a lobster bib?"

"I don't think," Karen said, "they actually give those out anymore."

"Then I'm sure, golly gee whiz, Joan will bring her own!"

"I bet she's a fan of the lobster nachos."

"Very romantic."

"Do you think she'll ask for twenty-six candles on it?"

"Thar she blows!"

I lay on my back, resting my head in Karen's lap. "I'm kinda glad," I said, "those two are still together."

"Me too."

"Detective Joan's not that bad when you think about it."

"Not at all."

Our glasses were empty. I got up and retrieved a mickey of Crown Royal from David's Tardis cookie jar. I lined up five shot glasses and topped them up. "Here's to good times."

When I knocked over a candle, Karen picked it up, still burning. Turning my palm upward, she dripped wax onto it. "Did that hurt?"

"A little."

"Here. My turn." She handed me the taper and I tipped it over her outstretched hand. "Megan's been telling me," Karen said, touching her palm, "how she's been getting into the BDSM scene."

"Did she tell you about Mistress Grey?"

"She did. So, like, is it something you and David have ever tried?"

"No, not really."

Karen played with the candle flame. "Megan told me how, when she was little, she watched *Sleeping Beauty*. Seeing Prince Phillip bound and gagged and then chained up and helpless in Maleficent's dungeon—that was, shall we say, strangely intriguing for her."

"A Disney movie? Christ. How old was she?"

"Old enough. It has to start somewhere. What about you?"

"What about me? Alright, um. *The Princess Bride*?"

Karen sat up. "The torture scene."

I nodded. "When Westley's tied down and half-naked and they've got him hooked up to the Machine with all those suction cups. I saw that as a kid. I'm pretty sure that was my first ever boner."

"You do realize," Karen said, "the whole point of that movie is that life is painful and unfair. Westley dies in the Pit of Despair."

"He only mostly dies. The power of true love saves him."

"So the movie's about pain and true love?"

"Something like that."

"I'm sure David loved that scene."

"David likes his role-plays. The other day in bed he kept calling me 'milord'. He said he was my squire, and that it was his duty to oil and clean my sword. That was a big turn-on for him."

"And for you?"

"It was pretty silly. But I have fun when he's having fun."

"So." Karen nudged the bottle of maple whiskey with her toe. "Are you going to do it?"

"What? Spit into David's mouth?" I dripped more wax onto myself. "I dunno. Maybe." I laughed out loud. "I think I might. It is kinda hot when you think about it."

Now Karen regarded me sidelong. "He's just a kinky little Italian-Catholic motherfucker, isn't he?"

"Yes, he is."

"And you two boys are getting married."

"Yes, we are."

In that moment, my love for Karen felt bigger than

ever. Maybe it was because we'd just got over our fight. Or maybe it was because she was there last week on the rooftop when I needed her the most. Or maybe it was simply because we were a part of each other's lives again.

All our friendships were changing. Each one of us was transforming into something new and a little bit unexpected. We were all having an impact on each other whether we meant to or not. Whether we realized it or not. As our relationships evolved, so too did our sense of self, and our place in the world. But instead of finding this sad or bewildering, I was starting to appreciate the wonder of it all.

The forest of candles blazed on the steamer trunk, melting, blending and fusing, a golden bonfire.

Karen held out her hand, covered in wax. "Do me again."

Because we were changing together. Because none of us was alone. Because no one judged us, no matter how crazy or queer or perverted we seemed. This was our glow up.

"As you wish."

Because, of course, as everyone knew, friendship was magic.

"Our friendship is over," Parker said.

At Jimmy's Coffee, the barista served us our drinks and we headed past the gas fireplace and bookcase of leather-bound tomes.

Today, we were both in shorts and sandals, Parker in a lime button-down with an eggplant print, while I had on a plain white V-neck. Sunlight splashed the back patio, lush with cycads and climbing vines. Planters spilling over with wildflowers hung from the broad trellis. Someone had parked their orange scooter next to the fire escape. All the tables were taken, but thankfully a couple with a sleepy spaniel was just packing up.

"I was so sure I was ace," Parker said. "I mean, it was such a relief knowing that! Do you have any idea how complicated life can be with sex in the equation? It can get really complicated."

I nodded and put on my best commiserating face.

"I'm not sure who was more surprised," Parker said, "Kyle or myself. I mean, I made the first move before I even realized I was going to make a first move. What's that all about?"

Now the dog owners were chatting up another couple. We set our drinks down at the vacated table.

"It was like," Parker said, "this dormant part of me just woke up, like a Soviet sleeper agent or a mutant X-Men power. It started with this tingle. It was such a shock. Then it was out of control. The first time it happened, I felt, well, like Audrey Hepburn winning Best Actress for *Roman Holiday*. Now I know what all the hype is about. And we're still doing it. The last time we did it was over a ten-metre double scull in his yacht club boat house."

"That sounds pretty hot, Parker."

"Is it?" Parker slurped from his iced latte with whipped cream drizzled in caramel. "It started last month, right after we saw the Luminato production of *A Midsummer Night's Dream*. After Puck uses his magic love juice, everyone goes mad, pining and wooing and lusting after each other. In the end, all the couples are having sex on stage.

Leave it to the fairies! It was spectacular. It got a standing ovation." Parker rested his hands over his crotch. "I think I'm going to name him Oscar."

"You're going give it a name?"

"He's my friend now," Parker said. "Of course I have to give him a name."

"He wasn't your friend before?"

"He was always more like a polite and well-organized roommate."

Honeybees circled and buzzed in the blossoms overhead. "Did you give Kyle's penis a name?"

"Yes we did. But I can't say."

"Why not?"

"I promised not to tell anyone. But I'm going to tell you. We named him Thor."

"Really?"

"It's his Scandinavian heritage. Kyle is thirty-eighth generation Viking."

"Seriously?"

"Don't mock the Thor."

"I'm not mocking the Thor, Parker. I've seen the Thor. There's nothing to mock. I think Thor is a very good name. Well done."

"Since I've been with Kyle," Parker said, "I honestly hadn't felt there was anything missing in my life. But now that we've started to have sex, it's like a whole new dimension has opened up."

"That's exciting."

"It is. Except what if it goes away? What if Oscar lets us down one day? What if he packs up and never comes back. Then what?"

"Well." I sipped my coffee. "If that happens, then you talk about it. You work on it together."

"So, I've had a while to think about this," Parker said. "I think I'm actually demisexual. Being with Kyle has helped me realize this."

"If it works for you."

"To be perfectly honest, I think this would've happened on its own, even if Oberon hadn't deployed his magic love juice of insanity."

Under a nearby awning, baby swallows chirped in their nest. "Who's Oberon again?"

Parker stared at me. "He's, like, the King of the Fairies."

"Sorry."

"Love," Parker said, "is so irrational and unpredictable already." He splayed his fingers on the tabletop. "Look at my parents. They weren't in love when they got married. Now they have six grandchildren and they're the most romantic couple I know. Father still sends Mother a dozen roses every chance he gets. But then I think of what happened to Madame Bovary or Heathcliff or Princess Diana. I can't even begin to consider Elizabeth Taylor's track record. Everyone says I deserve to have love. All my family wants is for me to find a nice Canadian boy and settle down. I never told any of them I was ace. My aunties would always be reminding me to use protection. I'd tell them Kyle and I were doing just fine, thank you. But now I'm not so sure."

"Parker, you and Kyle can have sex and still be friends."

"Do you think so?"

"I know so."

"It's just that everything was already working so well already."

"Look, Parker. This doesn't need to be so complicated. What you're telling me is that you two are lovers now."

Parker flinched like he'd just bitten down onto a chili pepper. He muttered under his breath: "Crouch bind set. Crouch bind set."

I waited for him to finish.

The little spaniel wandered over on its long leash and sniffed my ankle. I reached down and patted its silky head. When Parker finally opened his eyes, he did seem to be breathing a little more easily. "I already call Kyle my boyfriend," he said. "I guess that doesn't change."

"No, Parker, it doesn't."

"And this does feel right. I mean, look at me. I'm finally getting in touch with my animalistic side."

"Go get 'em, tiger."

"Except Kyle says sex can also be an expression of our divinity." Parker leaned forward. "We've started to study the *Kama Sutra* together."

"That can be fun. Do you have a favourite position?"

"Oh, we haven't got to that part yet. But we will. It's all about the art of living and loving well. Sex is one way to help deepen our emotional intimacy. We're learning a lot. I feel like a Pokémon that's just evolved. This will take some getting used to. I just have to remember to breathe."

Now the dog started humping my leg. The owners had their backs turned, oblivious to this humiliation. I tried to pry it off, but it was like a hairy vibrator velcroed to my shin. "Maybe," I said, "you two could have sex on a rollercoaster."

"O.M.G." Parker wiped the whipped cream from his top lip. "You're a genius. Why didn't I think of that? Wait a second. Was that a joke?"

"Yes Parker. It was."

Finally, the couple turned to go. Their humpy dog followed after them, leaving curly hairs and a wet stain on my ankle.

"That," Parker said, "is funny. You know, I'm thinking of being a stand-up comic myself. They have an open-mic every Monday at the Comedy Club."

"You'd be great."

"That's what everyone tells me." Parker rested his hands in his lap. "I just want to tell you, being ace was real for me, for a long time. There's still lots of asexual people in the world."

"I'm sure there are." I wiped myself with a napkin, crumpled it up and gingerly set it aside.

"And they're happy," Parker said. "I was happy."

"And how are you now?"

"How am I now?" Parker's big eyes swivelled. His expression shifted through half-a-dozen emotions. Finally, he just shook his head.

"I feel magical."

That Sunday, Karen and Anne hosted a potluck, inviting Luke and Ai Chang, Nadia and Pat. David made a tiramisu soaked in espresso and rum. Luke arrived bearing an enormous dish of garlic fettuccini alfredo. There was also roast beef with veggies, three types of salad, spicy chow mein and a fridge full of beer. We moved back the furniture and spread everything out on Liz's frayed Persian carpet, beneath an ornate chandelier (missing just a few of its crystals). Everyone gathered on pillows picnic-style, plates in their laps. Frida and Kahlo took turns pouncing on Anne's feet.

Toward the end of the meal, Karen announced Liz wasn't coming back. She was moving in with her husband Richard in Provincetown.

"Wait," David said. "What does that mean?"

"It means," Karen said, pulling out a bottle of Prosecco, "we can stay here, permanently. We can move in."

"It means," Anne said, "we can redecorate." She scooped up the two cats in her arms. "And it means we get to adopt these little monsters."

"She'll be back to organize and pack a few things," Karen said, "but she's not taking much."

"Is she okay?" I asked.

"Liz?" Karen laughed. "The woman is having the time of her life." She lined up eight mismatched glasses, and popped the cork. "She's met someone and she's getting a divorce. She and Richard are going to stay roommates, at least for now. And they're going to be business partners. They have an apartment right above the ice cream parlour. They'll run the Pink Pistachio together." She handed out the glasses. "She says the people of Provincetown have always been her tribe and it feels like she's finally come home."

"Hey, um." David hesitated. "Can you still drink if you're trying to get pregnant?"

Ai Chang squinted. "I'm okay, David, with one drink."

Luke reached out and tousled his hair. "Relax, kiddo."

"This," I said, looking from Karen to Anne, "is great news."

We raised our glasses. "To Elizabeth McLaren and all the lemon sorbet she can eat!"

"She's giving you her car," Karen said.

"What?"

"If you can afford the insurance, it's yours."

"It's a piece of junk," I said.

"No shit," David exclaimed. "We'll take it!"

"Alright, compadres." Pat cleared his throat. "Since we're celebrating ..." Nadia held up a CD. "Hot off the press."

It was Three Dog Run's newest EP: *Tree House*. Then everyone started shouting and talking over each other. Yes, Nadia had co-written half the songs. Yes, there was going to be an official launch. Yes, we'd be able to download it off iTunes. It took five minutes before Pat could quiet everyone down.

"Here's to the band, and especially this un-freakin'-believable gal. These last six months have been a trip." He raised his glass. "And there's something else. We're releasing a single and a music video to go with it!"

Moments later, we were all lying on our backs in the dark, head-to-head in a pinwheel formation. Pat pressed play on his portable projector. The ceiling above us seemed to flicker and come to life.

I reached out and held David's hand.

The chandelier sparkled. The video began with the band playing live on the NXNE Festival Stage. Soon it was intercut with shaky video selfies by all the flash mobsters. That event had made Citytv news. The banjo phrasings and buzzsaw guitar riffs shouldn't have worked, but they did. By the final chorus, animated stars and planets were flying past, and you wanted to hug your neighbour and wave your lighter in the air. I could have stayed on that floor forever.

David and I turned our heads and gazed at each other, nose to nose. Then I wondered if, when we were old men, we might still lie together the way we did now. I imagined David's clear gaze unchanged, blue-grey and bright as the sea. And when I kissed him, would his breath smell like Jägermeister and cinnamon chewing gum? And would his hand in my own be just as reassuring, and feel just as right? And would we still be surrounded by family and friends? David's eyes crinkled and he mouthed the words: "I love you." Then he sneezed in my face (since he was allergic to cats and had forgotten to take his medication even after I'd reminded him twice that afternoon). When Luke called out "play it again!" Pat obligingly did just that.

Later, as I was stepping out of the washroom I heard a strange man's voice. Karen was at the front door talking to a uniformed officer. The group was silent, tensely observing.

I overheard "rooftop party" and the word "assault." I froze. Before I could decide what to do next, the officer spotted me.

"Sir," he called out, "are you Daniel Garneau?"

Anne got up. "No, he's not."

"May I come in?"

"Yeah, sure, officer." Karen glared at Anne. "Come on in."

'What the fuck?" Anne exclaimed. "Karen, you know he has to show you a warrant, right?"

The officer beckoned me over. "Sir, are you Daniel Garneau who lives across the hall?"

"Yes. That's me."

"I have a few questions for you, Mr. Garneau."

Karen folded her arms. "It's doctor."

"I beg your pardon?"

Her eyes met mine. "It's Doctor Garneau."

"Dr. Garneau," the officer said. "We have a report that you assaulted someone on the afternoon of Saturday June 28."

"Whoa, wait a second," Anne said. "That other guy was a total douchebag and he made the first move."

"Then you were defending yourself?"

"Um." I cleared my throat. "I was defending my fiancé."

"Was she being assaulted?"

Anne threw up her hands. "He's engaged to a man, dumbass."

"Holy shit, Anne," I said. "Just stop."

The officer didn't blink. "Your boyfriend was being assaulted?"

"My fiancé. That's him right there." David waved. "And yes, someone pushed him. I threw one punch. That's all I did. I didn't hurt the guy."

"You," David said, "knocked him on his ass."

"I think you broke his nose," Karen said.

"He was bleeding everywhere." Anne smacked a fist into her palm. "He's lucky you didn't chuck him off the roof."

I shouted: "Guys!"

The police officer took out a note pad and pen. "So then, you are admitting, sir, that you assaulted someone."

Now Anne was standing on the couch. "He's not admitting anything," she yelled, "until he talks to a lawyer!"

"I understand, Dr. Garneau, you start your residency tomorrow?"

"How do you know that?"

"That's not important. What is important is that there are consequences to our actions. Sir, do you understand?"

I opened and closed my mouth. I raised my hands and dropped them again. "No, I don't understand." Jesus fucking Christ. "Please explain."

The police officer studied me narrowly. He put away his notepad, reached down and unbuckled his belt.

What the fuck.

In one motion, he tore off his pants. Karen hit the stereo, and "Bad Case of Loving You" by Robert Palmer blasted on the speakers.

By the end of the song, Officer Give-Me-A-Panic-Attack was wearing only a purple polka-dotted G-string, his police boots and service cap. He was sweaty and just a little bit breathless. He read from a piece of paper: "Daniel, wishing you the best on this next chapter of your life. May you seize each day and make this world a better place. Your ex-neighbour but loving friend always, Liz McLaren." He clapped me on the back. "You sir are now free to go."

The guy picked up his pants and unhooked his shirt from the chandelier. As Karen saw him out, I turned to the others. "You were all in on this?"

Ai Chang, Luke, Nadia and Pat shook their heads. "We didn't know, honest."

"You knew!" I pointed at Anne.

Clutching her side, Anne was still laughing. "You should've seen your face."

"David, did you know?"

He grinned. "Maybe?"

"Okay. Alright. Okay. You were good. That was a good one."

"That," Pat said, "was brilliant."

"I," Nadia said, "am not that flexible."

"I think that little number," Ai Chang said, "just made my egg drop."

David straightened. "It did?"

"Are you sure?" Luke jumped to his feet.

"Because," David said, grabbing his crotch, "you know. I can do my thing, like, anytime you want."

"Yes, he can," Luke said.

"David. Luke." Ai Chang raised her hands. "I was just joking. Seriously. I'll tell you when."

"'Do your thing'?" I asked David.

"Do his thang!" Pat exclaimed. "Rub one out, beat his meat, spank the monkey, strangle the cyclops, shake hands with Dr. Winky."

After that, we opened another bottle of Prosecco and everyone had a second helping of tiramisu.

At the end of the evening, we all left holding generous portions of leftovers packed in Tupperware. Back in our loft, David and I decided we'd take a shower together. Beneath the hot spray, I happily got down on one knee. "Dr. Winky," David said, "meet Dr. Garneau ..." While I blew him, I fingered him with body wash. Then he had me stand and we reversed roles. After a moment, he turned me around and spread my cheeks. I bit my lip, trying not to gasp, leaning into the tiles. My hips arched. When he put in two fingers, I widened my stance. David reached past the shower curtain into the medicine cabinet where we a kept a bottle of lube. "Can I?" he asked, stroking me from behind.

"Yeah," I said.

"That guy, Daniel, was super hot."

"Yeah, he was."

"It's too bad I can't blow you and fuck you at the same time," David said. "That would be awesome." I felt the slick tip of him push up against me. I bent just a fraction to offer the best angle. Then he slipped inside. A momentary ring of pain. I reached back and gripped his hip. "Go slow."

"I know," he said.

David did know. We'd been lovers five years. We weren't new at this. We knew each other's bodies like they were our own. "You're really tight," he said, his teeth against my neck. I concentrated on my breathing. I was always tight at the beginning. This part always took time.

Soon we found a steady rhythm, and I sank into the fullness of him. David took me in his fist and in the end we came together. "You're so beautiful," he whispered in my ear.

I let the pounding water stream over us both. Tomorrow was the first day of the rest of my life. And life was beautiful. We had everything to look forward to. Nothing had been easy. But we'd arrived at this moment through our own determination and with the help of others. And because each of us had a vision of who we might be. For once in my life, I was holding hands with the universe and everything seemed right.

Just before bed, my phone rang. At this late hour, I wondered if Karen was calling to say good night.

But it was Liam.

Grandpa was in the hospital. He'd had a stroke.

CHAPTER FIFTEEN

Walls Come Down

Grandpa was home in mid-July and by the end of the month he was walking with a cane. My residency program at St. Michael's Hospital had granted me a temporary leave. But I had a decision to make that would impact the course of my career.

I sat on the back deck of our family home in Sudbury, watching Liam pile fresh lumber under our maple tree. Just this morning, the two of us had taken down what remained of the old pirate ship treehouse.

Now Liam was preparing to build a new one.

Joan was pregnant.

Betty brought out a tray of lemonade and set it on the table. It was sweltering hot and both Liam and I had our shirts off. A heat wave was moving through Ontario. Wildfires were burning in the north country. Today, Betty was wearing a low-cut paisley top and a silk skirt. Sunspots freckled her tanned shoulders and ample bosom. "I've packed a crate of cucumbers and tomatoes for you to take home tomorrow, Daniel," she said.

"Thanks, Betty."

She rested a hand on my shoulder. "We're grateful you've been able to stay as long as you have. He wants to talk to you, by the way. After you're done here."

"Okay."

I gulped down a glass of lemonade and brought one over to Liam. "Hey, you're bleeding."

"Am I?" Liam observed a scratch on his leg.

I retrieved a first-aid kit from the garage. Liam patiently stood under the tree as I carefully removed a thick splinter, cleaned and bandaged the wound. Sunlight glinted and flashed through the broad green leaves. The buzzing drone of cicadas lay heavily over the afternoon. Jackson lazed under the deck, his tongue lolling.

Sixteen summers ago, our parents had gotten married under this tree. I could still hear Pat picking out the melody to "Suzanne" on his ukulele as Mom walked barefoot across the lawn. I had presented the gold rings, while Liam scattered white flower petals from above. I remembered Dad looking down at me and tousling my hair, his face crinkled and bright. I don't think I'd ever felt happier in my life than I did in that moment.

One week later, our parents were dead.

Life was a rainbow of chaos.

Inside the house, I threw on a T-shirt and checked my phone. I fetched a cold beer from the fridge, and found Grandpa in the upstairs washroom putting away his tools. The toilet had given us trouble for years and he'd finally replaced the entire tank. "Grandpa, how's it going?"

Stiffly, he rose, leaning on the new bathtub grab bar for support. His undershirt was sweat-stained, his overalls covered in old paint. I handed him the beer. He drank and gestured at the toilet. "Now finally you can take a shit on the second floor. Should've done this years ago."

"You've been busy."

He wiped his chin on his wrist. "I've neglected this house."

"You've spent fifty years building houses, Grandpa. Look what you did with the Good Medicine Cabin."

Before Dad was born, Grandpa had built our family cottage from the ground up. In recent years, he'd winterized it, put in a septic tank, and an entire A-frame addition with a second-floor bunkroom.

"Well." Grandpa flushed the toilet. "We raised your father in this house. It was condemned when we bought it." He observed the swirling water. "I was so excited to fix it up. Your Grandma and me, we always wanted a big family. But she couldn't have no more."

"How come?"

"Not after the third miscarriage. Doctors told us it wasn't safe."

"I never knew that."

"Well, it's not something you talk to your grandkids about, is it?" Grandpa closed the lid on his toolbox. "But you're not kids anymore."

A green and gold dragonfly landed on the windowsill, its iridescent wings quivering.

"By the way, Pat just texted," I said. "He says his lady friend's driving him up from Toronto. They should be here in time for dinner."

"Then we'll set two more plates. It's lasagna tonight." Grandpa wiped his hands on a rag. "Your father, he rattled around in this big ol' house like a pinball. He was whipsmart and a hellraiser. But he had heart."

"Yes, he did."

"I remember," Grandpa said, "when he got kicked off the school bus, I made him walk ninety minutes to his first class every morning. Once I drove past him on my way to a job. You know what he was doing? He was smoking one of my cigarettes and singing at the top of his lungs. I think he couldn't decide whether he wanted to be Elvis Presley or James Dean. Now, your brother Patrick is a lot like your father."

"I know."

"Liam, well. He's got your mother's touch. She grew up in that trailer park out past Highway 144. She was like this wild spirit who followed your father home one day, and never left."

"She'd have the deer," I said, "eating right out of her hands."

"A whole herd of 'em come out of the woods when we was cutting down our Christmas tree one year."

This was a familiar story, one that Dad always loved to tell. "I wish," I said, "we had a picture of that."

"Oh, you don't need no photographs." Grandpa rapped his temple. "You just have to remember. Story stays alive in here. Christmas ain't the same without kids around. When your mother had the three of you, well, that just made up for everything."

"Except she almost died having us."

"Maggie, yes she did. Lost an awful lot of blood. But the doctors saved her. She fought her way back to life. You know what the first thing was she asked for after she woke up?"

I shook my head.

"Pizza. She was so hungry. And she wanted beef jerky. So your father went and got her pizza and beef jerky. After that she asked to see the three of you. She could be a queer one. A lightning storm rolls into town, she's up on the rooftop soaked to the skin, just sitting and watching. You boys might be crying in your cribs but that's where I'd find her. Sometimes, when I look at Liam, I see your mother looking right back at me."

Suddenly, I felt ten years old again. "And what about me, Grandpa?"

"What about you? Daniel. You were the best of us. You were one of a kind. I suppose you always reminded me of your mémère."

"You've never said that before."

"Well. You always were her favourite. She was the most beautiful human being I've ever known." Grandpa straightened. "After the Crash, you took care of your brothers. I know that. Don't think I didn't notice. I'm just sorry I couldn't raise you boys better."

"You did good, Grandpa. I think we turned out pretty well."

"Doctor Daniel Garneau, living proof."

"The one and only."

"Daniel." Now Grandpa set aside his beer. "I've been meaning to ask, when are you planning to start work?"

"I've been thinking." I leaned against the door frame. "I might take some time off. Take a gap year."

Grandpa studied me, open-mouthed. He scratched his thick, grizzled stubble. "Not on my account."

"No. Not because of you."

"That's a big decision."

"Yes sir, it is."

"Give me a hand here."

I hauled the old toilet tank outside and set it down by the garbage heap behind the toolshed. An enormous raven perched on the handle of a broken lawn mower, observing me with one bright eye. A second raven flapped overheard.

Grandpa emerged from the house with the tank lid and pointed with his cane. "Hugin and Munin," he said.

"What?"

"Thought and Memory. Odin's ravens." Grandpa squinted. "To the Anishinaabe, they're tricksters." He tossed the lid onto the pile of rotted wood, old tires and debris. "They're also symbols of creation, change, knowledge. Betty's got a raven tattoo." He tapped the inside of his hip. "Ici."

"What does it mean to her?"

"Oh, a lot of things. She got it done right after her divorce."

Betty was raised Jehovah's Witness but had been excommunicated years ago for leaving her abusive husband. Now, no one in her family or community-of-origin spoke to her. Grandpa was a lot older than Betty but the two always seemed like a perfect match. Betty, like Grandma, loved to laugh. At the nursing home, Betty took care of Grandma in the last years of her life.

"You should take the Winnebago." Grandpa lowered himself onto the stoop. Giant sunflowers nodded above him. "We made it as far as Trois-Rivières. You and David could explore the Cabot Trail."

"I thought you were going to sell the RV."

"Well, we just bought the damn thing. Spent a bundle fixin' it up. You two boys should go have some fun."

"What about Liam?"

"Liam starts teaching full-time this fall." Grandpa took out a handkerchief and mopped his brow. "And those two have a lot to plan for."

"You ready to be a great-grandpa, Grandpa?"

"You bet your ass. By the way, we're thinking your bedroom's going to be the new baby's room."

"Don't I get a say in that?"

"Nope."

"When's Joan supposed to move in?"

"Soon as she can pack her things up and sell that shack she calls a house. I recommended her a good realtor."

"I think, Grandpa, you're all going to get along just fine."

"Oh, I know we will."

Betty leaned out the second-floor bathroom window. "What's this?" she called down, holding up the beer bottle. "Thomas Garneau, you know you shouldn't be drinking."

Grandpa jerked a thumb at me. "Blame it on the doctor."

"It's just one beer," I said. "He'll be okay."

Betty took a swig and winked. In her bright lipstick and strawberry bouffant, she looked like she might run a Wild West saloon. From this angle, it was also mighty obvious she wasn't wearing a bra.

"Two more months," Grandpa muttered under his breath, waving up at her, "before I can take the Viagra again?"

"Yeah, Grandpa. We just want to make sure we get your blood pressure under control."

Now we could all hear the whine of a skill saw from out back. Liam wasn't one to waste time when he put his mind to something.

We both regarded Grandpa's battered pick-up and the Winnebago parked beside the garage. "You promise," I said, "you're not going to drive, right? Not until Dr. Barr says you can."

Grandpa only grunted. "This new Dr. Barr, he's a lot like his father. Y'know, he's even got the same bald spot? I remember seeing his baby pictures. Now he's getting ready to be a father himself."

"Is that so?"

"Baby's due Thanksgiving Day."

"He told you that?"

"I like to get to know someone first," Grandpa said, "before they start poking around my prostate. He says good luck, by the way. He can still remember his residency."

"Grandpa." I picked at the flaking paint on the porch. "I've been thinking." A monarch butterfly landed on the railing. "This fall I might volunteer with MSF Canada. I have a meeting lined up with a recruitment officer. I could be overseas in three months."

"Médecins Sans Frontières?"

"I need to travel. I need to see the world."

"When did you decide this?"

"Just these past few weeks. I've been thinking a lot." I kicked a pine cone across the gravel drive. "Grandpa, you've sailed all over the Atlantic. Liam's driven to the west coast and back. Pat backpacked across Europe right out of high school. I need to do this. Life's too short, right?"

"And David?"

"He says he'll wait for me."

"You two boys alright?"

"We're good. We're still going to get married. I'm wearing his ring. He'll be okay."

"How long do you plan to be gone?"

"Depends on the assignment." I rested one foot on the scarred bumper of Liam's Jeep. "Nine, maybe twelve months."

"You're really excited about this."

"Yes, sir. I am."

"This isn't like you at all, Daniel."

"No, Grandpa." I observed the monarch flexing its wings and drew a deep breath. I'd never felt more sure of myself in my life. "No, it's not."

⌒ When Grandpa had his stroke, it was my worst night-mare come true. It's funny how you can rise above a storm of fear and panic with just the right focus. I took the earliest flight I could out of Billy Bishop Airport to Montreal. It was my first time on a plane, a 76-seat Bombardier 1400 turboprop, turbulence all the way. My whole life, the idea of flying had terrified me. But that hardly seemed relevant anymore. I barely remembered disembarking, or catching a taxi from the airport to the hospital downtown.

When Betty met me in the lobby, she told me it was a lacunar infarct, and not as catastrophic as I'd feared. When I opened the door to Grandpa's room, disheveled and unshaven, he was sitting up and chatting with Mr. and Mrs. Milton. They all assured me the doctors said he had a good chance at making a full recovery.

After the first week, Grandpa insisted the Miltons continue on their journey to the east coast. He wouldn't have it otherwise. After two weeks, Betty and I drove us back home.

It was seven hours between Montreal and Sudbury. Grandpa wanted to visit the National War Memorial in Ottawa along the way. I only agreed to it after he promised to stay in his wheelchair. We enjoyed lunch in an ivy-covered courtyard near Sussex Drive. Double-decker tour buses roamed between the historic landmarks. Pleasure boats navigated the locks on the Rideau Canal. Over ice cream, Betty suggested we visit the National Gallery, which was just a few blocks away. Grandpa thought that was a terrific idea. It was a perfect summer's day in the capital. Why the hell not?

From inside its gleaming Great Hall, we looked out over the Parliament Buildings, the Ottawa River and the Gatineau Hills. A 3,000-square metre exhibition space was dedicated to its contemporary arts collection alone. Betty pushed Grandpa across granite floors through cool and spacious chambers, while I strolled behind.

I heard it before I saw it.

The lapping of a canoe paddle, the echo of steamship whistles, the muted radio speeches of politicians and railroad magnates.

When I turned a corner, there it was.

I'd completely forgotten that *Bodies of Lovers: Canadian Hydrologies* was still on exhibit in Ottawa.

The museum labels included expositions in English, French and Ojibwe. The immersive experience of this large-scale projection installation by Marcus Wittenbrink Jr. had captured the Canadian imagination. As I gazed upon the two rows of six-metre-high images, it occurred to me that, at least in this case, size did matter. An excerpt from the *Ottawa Citizen* extolled the work as "a monumental excavation of the political economy of sex and love." CBC Arts described it as a "triumphant deconstruction of the dialectics of desire." An article in *Maclean's* was simply titled "Decolonizing the Corporeal."

Rumors swirled that some of the nudes in the Wittenbrink exhibit were celebrities themselves: Kent Monkman, Rex Harrington, and more than one cast member from *Queer as Folk*. No one corroborated or denied this gossip (which I'm sure Marcus found utterly delightful).

Inevitably, the moment came when Betty and Grandpa stood silhouetted before the immense, glowing satellite image of the French River estuary.

As I observed their reaction from across the darkened room, a tall man in a shirt and tie paused next to them. After a moment, arms crossed, he leaned over and made a comment.

Only one month ago, at our rooftop Pride party, Marcus had left a gift for David and me: a glass-framed, matted print of *Daniel/Canadian Shield*. David took it upon himself to mount it over our clawfoot tub.

It felt like I had little say in things, these days.

I turned and walked away.

I was just finishing in the restroom when the door opened. Tall Man approached and stood at the urinal next to me, a tiny Canadian flag pinned to his lapel. For one heartbeat, I thought it was my old hockey coach Stephan Tondeur. But this man's dark chestnut hair was too thick and unruly. Still, I tried not to stare as I washed my hands. Out of the corner of my eye, the resemblance was uncanny.

I caught up with Betty and Grandpa in the Upper

Rotunda. "Didn't that Andy Warhol fellow," Betty was saying, "used to call his nudes 'landscapes'? I remember he photographed all sorts of young men." Her face lit up. "Daniel! We were just wondering where you'd gone." Peering past me, she bent and waved. When I looked over my shoulder, Tall Man waved back, departing down the corridor.

"If that man wins Papineau this fall," Grandpa said, gazing after him, "he'll be following in his father's footsteps."

"Can you imagine," Betty said, "if he became Prime Minister one day?"

Grandpa chuckled. "We could use someone in charge who knows how to throw a punch."

Betty winked. "I'd rather see him do a striptease."

"Of course you would." Grandpa rolled his eyes. "Why don't we just dress him up like a pirate or a musketeer, while we're at it?"

"Daniel, what did you think," Betty asked, "of that last exhibit?"

The two regarded me expectantly.

I raised a questioning finger, looking behind me. But Tall Man was gone. I could've said anything and got on with the day. I could've been nonchalant or flippant or dismissive. But what did I truly, honestly think of Marcus' work? I'd spent the last five years putting him down, diminishing him. I'd told Marwa I wasn't afraid of him. But that had been a lie. I'd been afraid of people like Marcus my whole adult life.

In the hospital at Grandpa's side, I'd held his hand while he slept, large and rough between my own. It was late, just the two of us. He breathed so easily. He looked so peaceful. Then I imagined what it would be like if he was dead. At my graduation he'd reminded me one day he would be. Why would anyone ever say something like that?

People don't expect change, but change was the one universal constant. It was what people needed. The only question was: what kind of change did I want to see in my life?

Crouch, bind, set. I remembered to breathe.

"I used to date the artist," I finally said. "He's actually a friend of mine. I think it's spectacular."

On my last day in Sudbury, Pat arrived from Toronto with his lady friend Sara-Lee. She drove up early in the evening in a pink, vintage Mustang convertible, spraying gravel as she rounded the bend. Then the driver's door opened and one long leg emerged, then another. Sara-Lee was what some might call a bombshell blonde. She was also probably twice Pat's age (not that I asked). Later, we all learned she had started a Three Dog Run Facebook Fan Page six months ago.

Sara-Lee was the ultimate Puppy Lover.

She was also just dying to meet Liam and me, and Grandpa and Betty. She'd heard so much about us. She brought gifts: a magnum of sparkling wine (a Henry of Pelham Cuvée Catherine) and a 20" × 24" stained-glass mosaic of our Garneau family maple tree. "It's magnificent," Betty said, holding it up to the sun. It even depicted the tree house among the low branches. As it turned out, Sara-Lee was a freelance artist, with mixed-media works

in galleries across Ontario and Quebec. When I thanked
her for the corsages and boutonnières she'd hand-made
for my graduation, Sara-Lee took off her over-sized tor-
toiseshell sunglasses and asked if she could give me a hug.
Then Betty invited her inside to help prepare cold drinks
for everyone. Just at that moment, Liam emerged from
around back, dripping in sweat and covered in sawdust
and dirt, pushing a wheelbarrow full of old bricks. When
Liam shook her hand, Sara-Lee reached out reverently
and touched his bare chest. "And this," she said, "is your
Grandma Josette." After that, Pat pulled off his own
damp T-shirt to display the same tattoo on his back and
at his insistence I rolled up my sleeve. "It was Betty's
idea," Grandpa said, "the three boys getting those done."
Then Sara-Lee asked Betty if she was also a Scorpio
which she was.

Grandpa, Liam, Pat and I watched as the two women
disappeared inside, arm-in-arm, discussing piña colada
and Mai Tai recipes.

We stared at Sara-Lee's car.

Her license plate read: MNTNLION.

"She's got some years on you there, Patrick," Grandpa
finally said.

"She's a mature woman, Grandpa."

Two ravens flew overhead, cawing harshly at each
other.

"I suppose a woman like that," Grandpa said, "could
probably teach a man a thing or two."

Pat blushed. "You suppose right, Grandpa."

I'd never seen Pat blush in my entire life. Of course,
we all knew that Grandpa was only just nineteen when
he married his former high school English teacher.

But this was something else.

"Well, you boys better wash up. Dinner's in half an hour."

"I hope she likes lasagna," I said.

"Sara-Lee," Pat said, "will eat anything."

Grandpa's lasagna was just as I remembered it. Betty had made a Caesar salad with extra creamy homemade dressing. Everyone had second helpings. The empty wine bottles piled up on the dinner table. Liam, Pat and I did the dishes. Afterwards, we all sat on the back porch with Creamsicles. It was a lot cooler at twilight and the black flies weren't so bad this time of the year. Grandpa's mosquito lamps offered a miniature light show. Pat put on the Hip's sixth album. High above us, the constellations revealed themselves one star at a time.

Liam hauled kindling from the woodshed and started a fire. After that, Betty spent half an hour teaching us all how to yodel like a loon. I can't remember whose idea it was to try out the old jukebox. We trooped around the house, wine glasses in hand, careful not to stumble in the dark. Betty and I stuck close to Grandpa's side. A mother raccoon ambled across our path with three babies in tow. Moths danced about the garage light.

The Wurlitzer was covered in a heavy tarp, buried beneath packages of fiberglass under a layer of cobwebs and dust.

Its hand-crafted, polished wood cabinet was spotless and all its glass and chrome gleamed.

When Pat plugged it in, the thing lit up like the first of July and everyone cheered. Twenty-four selections were available in its record stack. A noisy debate ensued over which song we'd play first. Eventually, everyone agreed we'd all write down our picks and throw them into an old hunting cap.

Just as we made our draw, headlights lanced across the tall cedar stands. A Land Rover, splattered in mud, pulled into the drive. Joan stepped out, still in her constable's uniform. Just coming off duty, she'd brought her overnight bag. Her backseat was jam-packed with boxes and fishing rods. "Now what's all this ruckus," she asked, "and what's the fancy occasion?"

By way of a reply, Grandpa held up a scrap of paper: "Heart of Gold!"

Ceremoniously, Sara-Lee inserted a quarter into the coin slot. As she pressed the selection button, Betty turned off the garage lights.

We all stood back, bathed in the Wurlitzer's baby blue, pink and amber glow. The beautiful machine whirred and clicked. A carrier arm swung out, the spinning turntable rose, and the vinyl record magically lifted from its tray up to the waiting needle.

At the opening guitar chords, we all fell silent. The rustling harmonica followed, a golden thread.

In this moment, in our cluttered family garage, I ached for David to be at my side. If salmon or geese or butterflies could find their way home across vast distances in space and time, then surely our human electrons could cross the four hundred kilometres between Sudbury and Toronto. All they needed was oxygen and all I needed to do was breathe. I inhaled and when I exhaled I whispered his name.

Joan started to sing.

Her voice was surprisingly pure and clear. She had one arm around Liam's waist, her other hand on the holster of her gun. She sang quietly, in harmony to Neil Young's quavering tenor. Later, she confessed she was a late-night karaoke regular at the Trevi Bar & Grill out on Lasalle Boulevard. Some nights she would even host.

Leave it to Detective Joan.

One after another, we all joined in.

Shooting stars flared across the sky.

Of course, we ended up listening to all twenty-four tracks. Here was a collection curated by Pierre son of Thomas Garneau. How could any of us not know these songs? How often had Mom and Dad slow-danced in this garage? How often had any of us on this earth held in our arms the person we loved and who loved us in return? After eighteen weeks, the baby growing inside Joan's womb would begin to hear the world outside and Joan would sing to it at all hours of the day and night. And after nine months, my brother Liam would witness the miracle of its birth into a world through which he moved like an ancient stag, sacred and majestic, full of power and light. Pat and I would become uncles. And Thomas Garneau would become a great-grandfather for the first time in his long and checkered life.

And a brand new tree house would be waiting for all of us, above the leaves of grass, behind the family home.

∿ Our parents were buried outside Sudbury at Maplecrest Cemetery off Simmons Road. I'd grown up on backcountry roads and this stretch near Onaping Falls seemed as good as any. The cemetery itself wasn't particularly large or distinctive but it was spacious and well-kept. It was late in the season and the rhododendrons were shedding their petals. Already this morning, a hazy shimmer hung over the asphalt. Cotton ball clouds drifted in lazy succession across the empty sky.

An arch of black iron framed the main gateway. We passed underneath and parked the Jeep.

Liam, Pat and I walked the short distance to the gravestone. Liam cleared some weeds. Pat set down a bouquet of dahlias we'd cut from Grandma's flowerbeds.

Mom always loved her dahlias.

Cemeteries always seemed so peaceful to me. When you were dead, nothing mattered anymore. There was nothing to be afraid of. Nothing left to fight for. One day I'd also be dead and gone. I imagined David and myself buried side by side in our final resting place. Would our children visit us like we did today? Then I wondered who between three brothers born minutes apart would die first, and who might survive the other two.

"I almost died in Mexico," Pat said.

"Excuse me?"

"After Burning Man, two summers ago." He shaded his eyes. "Remember how I rescued this kid from a five-foot diamondback?"

"Yeah."

"Well, what I didn't tell you," Pat said, "is I got bit."

"The snake bit you?"

"Yep. I felt this jabbing pain in my ankle and blood was dripping out of two puncture wounds. But it was what they called a 'dry bite.' No venom got injected.

They say that happens only one-out-of-four times. I mean how un-fucking-believable is that? I was this close to being six feet under."

"Pat, a rattlesnake bite," Liam said, "doesn't usually kill you."

"No?" Pat looked disappointed.

"Still," I said. "Holy shit."

Pat pulled up his *Big Trouble in Little China* T-shirt to show us his snakeskin belt with a wolf's head buckle. "That's why I wear this, wherever I go. It's a reminder, man."

"That's the actual snake that bit you?"

Pat nodded. "This Apache medicine man made this for me. He said it'd give me virility. It's the enemy I vanquished protecting another."

"You saved a little girl's life," Liam said.

"How did that exactly happen, Pat?"

"Well, I told you I was at this bordello, right? But then there was all this crazy shouting, and I heard a couple gunshots go off. So I kinda freaked. I panicked and jumped out a back window. Then I'm half-climbing half-falling down into this alleyway, wearing nothing but a silk kimono. I hit the ground and scramble to my feet. That song "The Lion Sleeps Tonight" kicks in—I think someone's playing it out of their convertible somewhere. And there she is, a little girl standing in front of this gigantic snake that's getting ready to strike. I'm also totally rushing on Scooby Snax. So I figure I got way better reflexes than this evil-eyed viper, right? And I did! I was Rikki-Tikki-Tavi, I was fucking Pietro Maximoff. I snatch her out of the way. The snake lunges at me. I fall on my ass. I finally decapitate it with a hubcap. My kimono's all torn, I'm covered in snake blood. Fireworks are going off. This old lady runs up and starts to thank me. But who would've thought a severed head could still bite?"

"Pat, you're making this up."

"Honest to god, Dan, I'm not. I swear on Mom and Dad's grave, right here right now."

I sighed. "Alright." I didn't have the energy to argue with him.

"I almost died," Liam said.

"Stop." I turned to Liam. "Stop. I'm sorry." I shook my head. "Look, another time?"

Liam fell silent, unperturbed. After five minutes, he glanced at the shadows of the trees. "We'd better get going."

We drove back to the house and dropped off Pat. I had planned to take the bus to Toronto but Liam surprised me saying he could drive me home. We hugged Grandpa and Betty good-bye and Sara-Lee too. Joan whipped out a gigantic selfie-stick and the seven of us crowded together for one last family photo.

Across the road, next to the Milton property, bright waves shimmered across a golden sea of wheat.

Liam and I put on our sunglasses.

As we drove away, I glanced in the side-view mirror. Everyone was still in the drive, waving at us. I stuck my arm out the window and gave a thumbs up sign.

After that, I never did look back.

CHAPTER SIXTEEN

The Rest of My Life

We called it the Crash.

We all have these moments in our lives, events that change who we are forever, that shape how we walk through the world.

In the case of our family, there was life before and life after the Crash. There was absolutely nothing heroic or tender or meaningful about what happened. Maybe they swerved to avoid hitting a deer, or maybe they dropped a lighter or a lipstick and just careened off the road. We'll never know. Mom and Dad died drunk-driving home from a night out on the town. The car had rolled twice before exploding in flames.

It was as simple and embarrassing and as stupid as that.

We were ten years old.

In one single moment, our whole world burned down.

The accident made page two in the *Sudbury Star*. Mrs. Milton helped us pick out what to wear at the funeral. At the memorial, Mr. Milton played an Oscar Peterson tune. Tearful eulogies were made. Even Grandma stood in front of everyone and read a poem by Mary Elizabeth

Frye. When we finally went back to school, it was almost a relief.

Then inevitably, someone said something stupid enough for me to punch him as hard as I could in the face. The boy was a lot older than me too. I had him on the ground in a heartbeat. It was Karen who eventually pulled me off him. Kids could be mean.

I could be meaner.

The next day, the principal met with all three of us Garneau boys, along with the guidance counsellor and a big guy in a turtleneck. (Pat called him Darth Vader since he looked just like James Earl Jones.) Every few minutes, Grandma would touch Grandpa's arm and ask (loud enough for everyone to hear) why they were there and where Pierre and Maggie had gone. Darth Vader introduced himself as a psychiatrist named Luis. He looked more like a linebacker, but what did I know?

We spent a lot of time with Luis that fall. He'd meet with Grandpa and the three of us. (The Miltons would have Grandma over for gardening or tea on these occasions.) Sometimes he'd meet with us one-on-one. He didn't ask a lot of questions but he did seem genuinely interested in what we had to say. He kept a basket of fidget toys and some art supplies by his desk. Sometimes he'd have us draw pictures of what we were talking about.

I spotted him once in the parking lot talking to a man with silver in his beard. They exchanged a peck on the lips, the way any couple might. As far as I figured, Luis was the first gay guy I'd ever met in my life. When I asked him about it, he said his partner Kevin worked at city hall, and that they'd been together a long time. I was super impressed. I liked him a lot more after that for trusting a ten-year-old kid with something so real.

Just before Thanksgiving, our sessions with Luis came to an end. He reminded us that he worked for the Rainbow District School Board and that his door was always open. As we left his office for the last time, I turned and asked if him and Kevin might join us for a turkey dinner next weekend. Luis looked surprised. Unfortunately, they had not one not two but three dinners to attend that weekend, and he let us know (leaning in conspiratorially) that Kevin was in fact vegetarian. But he patted me on the shoulder, and thanked me for the invitation.

Then Pat asked him if he ever played sports, and Luis said that he'd gone to college on a football scholarship until he hurt his knee. Then Liam pointed at a photo on the wall and asked if he'd taken it, and Luis said yes, from Silver Peak in Killarney, when he was a much younger man. In the photo it was clearly dawn and the vista glowed with a pink-golden light. The world was a forest, lakes and hills, shot through with darkness. Liam said he recognized the view. After that, Grandpa clapped his hands and exclaimed it was time to hustle if we all still wanted to make it out to Dairy Queen.

Our time with Luis didn't fix anything. It didn't bring Mom and Dad back. It didn't make the nightmares go away. But in hindsight I realized that it did put us on the right path.

The last time we saw our parents, we were eating popcorn in front of the TV. I forget what movie it was (maybe it was *The Princess Bride*). Mom kissed us on the tops of our heads, smelling like her favourite perfume, Coco by

Chanel. Dad made some joke and jangled his car keys, an unlit Dunhill dangling from the corner of his mouth.

In these last few years, I'd begun to realize no one ever really dies. A part of them stays alive, living on behind our eyes. People teach us how to see the stars, or read a book, or walk through a forest. Even after Superman died (or maybe because of it), planet Earth seemed to become, more than ever, a place worth saving.

Every bully, burnt-out coach or ex-lover also changes how we see the world. But we can choose what that change might be. Our lives are written and over-written, inked by saliva, sweat and semen, by tears of grief or rage or joy. But if thought and memory are tricksters, then we will always possess the alchemy to transform ourselves. We can become more kind, or calm, or courageous in the dark. Scars can become badges of honour, and a tragedy can inspire us to breathe more deeply and stand more tall. In our best moments, we can illuminate ourselves.

They say the human brain doesn't mature until your mid-twenties. But long after adolescence, it continues to grow, modifying its cells, fine-tuning its capacity for connectivity. Until then, we make the best of what we have, and with what we're given. If meaning-making is an art form, then yes—life is art. And each one of us is a creative spirit confronted by chaos.

Mom and Dad were among the top realtors in Sudbury, always on the move. Everyone in town knew and loved Margaret and Pierre Garneau. Once a year they'd host a party in June for all their clients. Dad would fire up the barbeque, Mom would buy a new summer dress. Us boys would serve up beers and cocktails and split the tip jar at the end of the day. The Garneau garden parties were famous. I think people might buy a house from our parents just so they could have a taste of Margaret's spicy devilled eggs or Pierre's grilled lamb sausage with rosemary and mint.

They'd have sex all the time.

We grew up hearing them at all hours of the night. Sometimes we'd catch them going at it when they thought they were alone. They'd do it in the car, arriving home late at night. They'd do it in the shower, while we'd be hungry for breakfast and running late for school. Nobody ever plans for triplets. Sometimes I wondered if our parents ever wanted kids. But when we did arrive, they made just enough space in their lives, and never thought to change who they were. I don't think they ever truly tried to tame us.

Every morning, Mom would wash down a handful of pills with a mug of black coffee. Sometimes it would be a glass of Chablis. Other times it was a shot of rye. Some nights, Dad would come home late with his tie undone. If he ever smelled of an unfamiliar perfume, Mom didn't seem to notice or care. She might've just sold the mayor's niece her first home, or a hockey player a six-bedroom cottage on Long Lake. There was always a reason to celebrate and raise a toast.

And if they didn't show up for a game, Grandpa would be in the bleachers cheering us on. And in those moments when Grandpa couldn't be there for us, then Liam and Pat and I had each other. And if my brothers ever let me down, I had my Karen.

It was Luis who reminded us that time spent with

loved ones and doing what we loved, was time well spent. He reminded us that family showed up in different ways. That people were imperfect and made mistakes. He reminded us that the universe disappointed and hurt us without even trying or caring, sometimes in devastating ways. But even after the whole world burns to the ground, life takes root and can grow again.

⌢ After Grandpa's stroke, I'd been away over a month, and I was looking forward to seeing David again. Of course, we'd kept in touch every day. David had offered to come up to Sudbury to help but I told him there was no need. Betty and Liam were also there and Pat would replace me before I left. As we approached Toronto, David wasn't answering my texts and I wondered if he was working a shift this afternoon.

Liam dropped me off and I climbed the steps to our loft. I had just taken out my keys when the door swung open.

"Oh." I stepped back. "Hello."

A pale woman stood stiffly in front of me. Grey streaked her temples and deep lines scored her stern face. Her eyes flickered over my dishevelled clothing and patched rucksack. "Daniel!" David waved. "This is Mrs. Cho, Ai Chang's mom."

The woman firmly shook my hand. Despite the heat wave, she wore a thin cardigan over her blouse. David handed her a neatly-folded grocery cart. "Thank you," she said, "for hospitality. I come back three days." She looked me in the eye and raised a finger. "Your grandfather, he will be fine."

She put on a pair of headphones, pressed play on her Walkman and brushed past.

David and I watched as she descended the stairs with quick, precise steps. A faint odour of mothballs and Tiger Balm lingered in her wake. "Hey," David said. "Welcome home."

I ran my hands through my hair. "Hi?"

David stepped forward into my arms. "How's your grandpa?"

"He's fine."

"Glad to hear."

"Was that," I asked, "Justin Bieber she was listening to?"

"Yeah." David stood back. "She's a big fan."

"So, um." I closed the door behind me. "What was Ai Chang's mom doing here?"

"She brought me some food?"

"David." I shook my head. "How does she even know who you are?"

"She knows I'm Luke's brother. We met once back in the spring, when she dropped in on Ai Chang. She seems to know everything. She's like a walking talking Sorting Hat. Actually, she's more like this Bene Gesserit. It's actually kinda scary."

"More like this what?"

"It doesn't matter. Look, I'm really glad to see you. I've missed you." David hugged me again.

"What do you mean she knows everything?"

David cleared two glasses from the kitchen table. "Ai Chang told her about having to terminate the pregnancy back in April. She also told her that she and Luke were trying to start a family. So since then, Mrs. Cho has been doing everything she can to help them get pregnant again."

"And, does she know they're using you as a sperm donor?"

David nodded.

"How on earth did she find that out?"

"I don't know. But listen. Ai Chang and Luke don't know that she knows. And she made me promise not to tell them she knows."

"What? Why?"

"Most traditional Chinese believe talking about sex is dirty and bad, even between married couples. Any kind of PDA or even hugging is frowned upon. It just isn't something you do. I think Mrs. Cho doesn't want to embarrass Luke. As far as she's concerned, he's her *nu xu*, her son-in-law. She's convinced he brings luck to the family. The day after they met, she won a hundred dollar Lotto Max prize. That made a big impression on her. Since then, Luke's been helping Mr. Cho with his rehabilitation and getting back in shape. He even got him to join Mrs. Cho's tai chi group. And he got Ai Chang's kid brother to help him fix the satellite dish on their roof. That woman thinks Luke's the best thing since sliced bread. And did you know, Daniel, my brother speaks Mandarin?"

"You're kidding."

"Luke lived twelve years in Vancouver. The Eastside Boxing Club where he worked was right in the heart of Chinatown. Go figure."

"Sure. He's Luke Moretti." I looked skyward. "Of course he speaks Mandarin."

"He's the Boss."

"Yes he is."

"So, Mrs. Cho knows he's trans then?"

"No!" David sat down on the couch. "That's just it. I don't think she does. She mentioned once how Luke has a lot of really hot yang energy. But apparently so does Ai Chang. Frankly, Mrs. Cho's surprised they both get along as well as they do. But there's yin and yang in everything, right?"

"If you say so."

"We're talking about masculine and feminine energy. Mrs. Cho says they interact to generate *qi*. She says if you're going to live a healthy life in harmony with Heaven and Earth, you need to balance the qi that's flowing through your body."

"David, how many times has Mrs. Cho come by?"

"She showed up the day you left. I opened the door and there she was, just standing there. She scared the bejesus out of me. Since then, she's been visiting two or three times a week. Once she dropped by my work. Look, Daniel, you've had your hands full, which is why I didn't mention any of this. But I'm really glad you're home."

"What," I asked, "is that smell?"

David glanced at a pot on the kitchen counter. "Um, I think that's the clam congee she brought for me."

"And why is she bringing you food?"

"Like I said, it's her way of helping out. She insists on it. She started by getting me to eat fresh ginseng and goji berries, to, well, you know, get the juices and energy flowing down there."

"Okay."

"That's how it started. Look, can we have sex? I'm super horny and I haven't masturbated in a week."

"What? Why not? What's wrong?"

"Nothing's wrong!" David jumped up. "It's just that Mrs. Cho, well, she's forbidden it. She's convinced that if we want her daughter to get pregnant, then my contribution needs to be as potent as possible. Like I said, she's scary. I can see where Ai Chang gets it from. But she didn't mention having actual sex. So you, Daniel, could make me come. Trust me, it won't take a second."

"David." I laughed. "You're getting by on a technicality. The next time she sees you, aren't you afraid she'll be able to tell that you went ahead and blew your load?"

"You're right. Shit." David paced. "She'll probably be able to sniff it out, or see it in my aura or something."

"Oh my god, I was joking."

"Fuck it." David thrust his hand into his crotch and smelled his fingers. "It can't wait. She says congratulations, by the way, on our engagement."

"She knows we're a couple?"

"Yes." David unbuckled his belt and threw aside his shorts. "She says the Rabbit God will watch over us."

"Wonderful."

David pulled down his underwear. "Please, can we do this now?"

I stared at David. "I'm glad I'm home too."

Later, after sex and then dinner (and a second round of sex), I crossed the hall to visit with Karen. She and Anne had redecorated the entire loft. All that was left of Liz was the chandelier and a bougainvillea in a gigantic pot. Frida and Kahlo lounged in bean bag chairs, licking their paws. Anne's drafting table filled up one corner. Framed prints by Norval Morrisseau decorated the kitchen. Karen made us gin and tonics in two keg-sized bubba mugs, which we took topside. She wore a tank-top with "A Tribe Called Red" emblazoned across the front. We kicked off our sandals and reclined in duct-taped lounge chairs beneath beach umbrellas propped up by cinderblocks. The sun was just touching down on the horizon. We'd left the disco ball up from our June Pride party and a hundred points of light danced across the rooftop.

"She's feeding David caterpillar fungus?" Karen said.

"You can take it as a powder." I sipped my drink. "That and horny goat weed."

"Horny goat weed?"

"It comes in a tonic or a pill form. Oh, and also sea cucumber and geoduck."

"Sea cucumber sounds healthy." Karen crunched on an ice cube. "What's 'gooey duck'? Is that like Peking duck? Peking duck is delicious."

I pulled up an image on my phone and held it out.

"Oh my god." Karen peered over her sunglasses. "What is that?"

"That," I said, "is a geoduck. Apparently, it's a really popular aphrodisiac in China."

"I can't imagine why. Well. If that doesn't get all the cylinders firing, I don't know what will." Karen handed back my phone. "And who's this Rabbit God again?"

"Tu'er Shen, the Chinese god of homosexuality. For such a traditional society, they have a lot of queer culture and history."

"Meaning?"

"Just that there's all sorts of myths and folklore about same-sex relations and gender-swapping, including humans getting it on with demons and animal spirits and dragons."

"Are you sure you're not talking about one of your D&D adventures?"

"Look, I'm just telling you what David told me. Mrs. Cho is a big believer in traditional Chinese medicine and stuff."

"I'm starting to get that impression."

"She's special."

"Aren't we all." Karen turned to face me. "Listen, Daniel, I have to tell you something. Anne goes by 'they and them' pronouns now. They're identifying as non-binary, and they think they might be Two Spirit. I recommended an Elder for them to talk to about that."

"Why am I not surprised?"

"And they might change their name. They're not sure yet."

"How do you feel about this?"

"Anne's discovering who they are." Karen shrugged. "I just have to get used to calling them my 'sibling' instead of my sister now. And if Anne changes their name, well, I'll just have to get used to that too."

"Where is Anne tonight, anyway?"

"They're over at Ai Chang's getting some help with their cosplay outfit."

"For Fan Expo? Are we still doing that?"

"Absolutely yes."

"Is Ai Chang making our costumes for us?"

"Absolutely not! She's happy to consult. But we're making our own costumes." Karen turned to me. "Wait a second, do you even know who you're going to be?"

"Not yet. I told David I'd be whoever he wants me to be. I really don't know much about comics or anime or whatever."

"Well, Anne and Rick are going as the Elric brothers."
I shrugged. "Like I said."

"Okay. So I'm going as Wonder Woman. Have you heard of her?"

I sighed. "I know she grew up on an island where they didn't have or need any men."

Karen was silent for half-a-minute. "You know, Daniel," she finally said, "I love all the men who are in my life."

"I know you do. I'm sorry. It's been a long four weeks."

"You've been through a lot. I look forward to seeing your grandpa this Thanksgiving. How was your ride down with Liam?"

"Good. He's driving to Prince Edward County to help with a missing person case." Liam was officially a civilian recruit on the Sudbury Police payroll but he consulted across the province. "Karen, did you know Liam almost died last summer? The RCMP flew him up to Timmins to help track an escaped convict. The guy took a shot at him with a hunting rifle, at close range. The bullet grazed his neck and he had to get stitches. How fucked up is that? But he's got a baby coming now and he says he won't be taking those kinds of risks anymore."

"What happened to the convict?"

"Liam took him out with a chokehold. These things don't get into the news."

Now the sky blazed as if it were on fire. A pageantry of clouds drifted overhead.

"It's funny." Karen drew a big breath. "I used to worry about him all the time."

"And now?"

"Liam's an adult. He can take care of himself. And he's got Joan."

"I think they're going to make good parents."

"They will."

"And how are you, Karen?"

She stretched and lay back. "It's strange. The truth is, I feel so much lighter these days. It's like I've finally got some balance in my life now, you know? I thought being single would be scary. But I feel great."

"Congrats again on your new job."

"Thank you." We bumped mugs. "I guess I won't be bartending or waiting tables after all." Karen had accepted a full-year teaching contract with the First Nations School starting in September. I was so proud of her.

I sat up. "I have something for you."

"Ooh, is it something from Montreal?"

"No."

"Ottawa?" I shook my head. "Well, I already have shot glasses from Montreal and Ottawa. What is it?"

"I've been thinking a lot about us. About all of us." I observed the twilight panorama: the graffiti and crumbling brickwork, rusted satellite dishes and hydro poles. As I watched, street lamps and neon signage flickered on. I could feel the city's vibration all around us. I could feel it moving through me, and inside me. The world was a shining metropolis, shot through with darkness, liminality and wonder. "You and me. Anne, Pat and Liam. David. All of our friends. You know how I'm planning to volunteer overseas, right? I won't be leaving for a few more months. But when I do, it'll be a long time before I see everyone again."

A cool breeze unfurled. The heatwave had broken.

"I was going to save this for a special occasion. But I think this is it. Here. Karen, I want you to have this."

I held out a gold ring.

By now the flaming sky has settled to a numinous glow. A single point of light appeared before us, glinting in the west. "It's the ring …"

"I know what it is," Karen said.

Of course, she did. She had helped me pick it out. The city bowed down and enthroned us. The Evening Star shone. Inscribed inside the band were the words: *forever my love.*

"I mean it," I said.

Karen examined the ring, her dark bangs falling over her brow. In the end, she held it over her heart in her clenched hand. "I'm going to miss you, Daniel Garneau."

"I'm not saying goodbye. Think of this as a hello."

"Well, then." She looked up at me. "Hello."

⌒ That August on National Creamsicle Day, Three Dog Run played Sneaky Dee's Wavelength Music series. Band stickers, decals and event posters plastered the walls. Air ducts and lighting trusses crowded the low ceiling. Pat wore a Fraggle Rock T-shirt, Nadia a black crop top with a diamond in her navel. Bobby sported a Jays jersey, while Rod pogoed with his bass guitar in his signature plaid shorts. The Egster hunched behind a stripped-down drum kit, shirtless and drenched in sweat. Keith Haring-inspired figures gamboled across the projection screen.

"Heeeeey puppy lovers!" Pat shouted at the top of his lungs, his hair plastered to his cheeks. The air smelled of spilt beer and overheated bodies. People were packed shoulder-to-shoulder, pierced and tatted, in toques and tank-tops and tie-dyed tees. On the dance floor, we pushed forward and backward, buoyed by the rush and the kick of the beat, jumping and diving through waves of music crashing over us and lifting us up. And after each song, people were high-fiving and whistling, their arms in the air. And if someone slipped and fell on the slick floor, a multitude of hands would reach out to lift them back to their feet. We were slam-dancing and relentless and joyful and alive. And in this moment everything was forgotten, the past and the future, but each face was breathless, boundless and beautiful, and we were shining and where we belonged, young and old and young again, lost together, spiraling forward in an endless ocean wave of humanity.

I was going to China.

I didn't qualify for Médecins Sans Frontières, despite my fluency in French. But the recruitment officer seemed impressed by my attitude and reviewed with me a list of other global volunteer opportunities. I informed St. Michael's Hospital that I was withdrawing from their residency program. I could tell they weren't happy with this news. But they asked me to reapply next year and I thanked them for their understanding. In the end, an international NPO holding special consultative status with the United Nations assigned me to Suzhou in the province of Jiangsu on the Yangtze River. My flight out of Toronto was on December 31.

On Thanksgiving, we gathered for our traditional turkey dinner at the Miltons. As always, there was buttered green beans, corn-on-the-cob, mashed potatoes and gravy, stuffing and Grandpa's famous tourtières. David made candied yams and Joan a succulent venison roast with cranberry sauce (she'd shot and field-dressed the deer herself), while Sara-Lee gifted the Miltons with an extravagant wreath.

This year, it was Betty who had us all hold hands and led us in a gratitude prayer. We named the loved ones in our lives, present and past. Mom, Dad and Grandma. And old Dr. Barr. After that, Mr. Milton toasted Bo Diddley who had also recently passed. Then I toasted Estelle Getty, my favourite Golden Girl. Liam had survived cancer, Grandpa a stroke. Anne announced they were now going by Jaydee (Mrs. Milton had helped them pick out the name). Over sugar pie and pumpkin pie, we shared photos from Fan Expo. In the Masters of Cosplay Grand Prix, Jaydee and Rick had come in third place as the brothers from *Fullmetal Alchemist*. To my utter shock, David and I won the favourite Fan Vote as Wiccan and Hulking. Karen herself had met no less than seven other Diana Princes, and joined a Wonder Woman Facebook group. It had been epic.

While we loaded the dishwasher, David reminded me that Heath Ledger had also died earlier that year. Pat came by with a tray of sambuca shots and clapped me on the back. He was thrilled that I was heading abroad. "As they say in China," he exclaimed, "gan bai, bitch!" Later that evening, he asked: "So, Dan, you were holding your dick in your hand when Justin Trudeau walked in on you?"

"Yes, Pat. I suppose you could put it that way."

"I heard," he stage-whispered, "that Justin's like kinda your wet dream jerk-off fantasy."

Across the room, Sara-Lee pursed her lips, raised her glass and winked in approval. Karen threw up her palms: It wasn't me!

Then it was David who I put in a headlock.

〜 In December, I arrived at Nathan Phillips Square in front of Toronto City Hall. The snow was gently falling and the Cavalcade of Lights in full glory. This year, the white spruce Christmas tree was almost twenty metres tall, presiding over a dazzling wonderland of ice sculptures and sparkling wreaths. Half-a-million LED lights illuminated the plaza with changing hues. People ate hot fries out of paper cartons with wooden forks. I caught the delicious aromas of maple syrup and hot chocolate. As I approached the skating rink, Charles and Megan shouted and waved from the ice, promptly falling over each other in a tangle of red mittens and scarves. I settled on a bench, and sipped from my thermos. Nearby, a woman in a hijab was helping two children lace up their skates. Luke in his bomber jacket glided past with Ai Chang, now three months pregnant. Across the rink, I spotted Parker performing a two-foot spin before kicking into an arabesque. When Kyle patted his shoulder and pointed my way, I raised my arm and waved back at them. Pat came to a hockey stop in a spray of ice. "Bro, you made it!" Nadia and Karen sat down on either side of me.

"Did you get it?" Karen asked. I'd just come from the Chinese Embassy. When I pulled out my new travel visa, everyone cheered. Both women kissed me on the cheeks and jumped back onto the ice. Tonight, a DJ was hosting a free skating party and the music was thumping. Sleigh bells rang out. By the bandstand, I spotted Marwa enjoying her cigarette, laughing as Ghazwan petted the enormous ushanka on her head. Marcus would be in Berlin by now. Who knew when he might return? Jaydee and their art school friends were lined up by the rental booth. With rosy cheeks, David stepped up off the rink. He gave me a hug, rummaged in a hockey bag and handed me my skates.

"Don't wait for me," I said. "I'll catch up."

The clock tower of Old City Hall chimed. I laced up carefully, taking my time. It'd been eight years since I'd put on skates. Lucky number.

I finally stood, walked forward and paused at the edge of the rink. There was still so much to do and so little time.

"Hey." David skated up to me. "You good?"

"Yeah."

"C'mon." He reached out, smiling. "Everything's going to be okay."

"I know," I said.

I stepped down onto the ice, and took his hand.

AUTHOR'S REMARKS

The B-Side of Daniel Garneau (2023) concludes the Boy at the Edge Trilogy that began with *A Boy at the Edge of the World* (2018) and *Tales from the Bottom of My Sole* (2020). This closes one chapter of Daniel's life. Of course, as in real life, there are no tidy endings to anyone's story. But I invite you to imagine the best for Daniel and David, their family and friends on their continuing adventures. Rest assured, there will be setbacks and losses. But no matter how many times Daniel may stumble or fall, he will always brush himself off and stand up again. That is the least and the most we can ever ask of ourselves. For young queer and trans people, it is all we need. Let us all seize the day.

ACKNOWLEDGEMENTS

This book was written on the traditional lands of the Haudenosaunee, the Anishinaabe, and the Huron-Wendat, and on the treaty territory of the Mississaugas of the Credit.

I'd like to acknowledge use of the following Canadian songs as chapter titles: "Baby Have Some Faith" by 54-40; "Born to be Wild" by Steppenwolf; "The Kid is Hot To-night" by Loverboy; "Fight the Good Fight" by Triumph; "The First Day of Spring" by The Gandharvas; "As Make-shift As We Are" by The Tragically Hip; "When We Stand Together" by Nickelback; "Raise a Little Hell" by Trooper; "Waiting for the Miracle" by Leonard Cohen; "Heart in Two" by Reuben and the Dark; "La Fin Du Monde" by Robert Charlebois; "In Praise of the Vulnerable Man" by Alanis Morissette; "Very Good Bad Thing" by Mother Mother; "Unholy, Dirt and Beautiful" by David Usher; "Walls Come Down" by Meghan Patrick; and "The Rest of My Life" by Sloan.

I'd also like to acknowledge the liberties I have taken in this work of fiction to respectfully represent actual persons: Igby Lizzard, Justin Trudeau, Mandy Goodhandy and Sunny Leone.

Lastly, I'd like to express my heartfelt thanks to Michael Mirolla and all the dedicated staff at Guernica Editions for their support, and for their hope that the books they publish will make this world a better place in which to live and love.

ABOUT THE AUTHOR

David Kingston Yeh has worked twenty years as a counsellor and educator in Toronto's LGBTQ+ community.
He holds his MA in sociology from Queen's University,
is an alumnus of George Brown Theatre School, and attended Graduate Studies in Expressive Arts in Saas Fee,
Switzerland. David lives in downtown Toronto up the
street from a circus academy, with his husband and a
family of raccoons. His short fiction has appeared in
numerous magazines. He has published three novels.

Follow David's blog on Instagram at *davidkingstonyeh*.

Printed by Imprimerie Gauvin
Gatineau, Québec